FORESIGHT

FIRST PHASE

Foresight
First Phase

by R. Gregory Lande

Dedication

To my wife Brenda and our son Galen.

Brenda's assistance, patience, and encouragement are found on every page of this book
and Galen is the creative genius that inspires me.

Table of Contents

Chapter One – Letter	1
Chapter Two – Conflict	53
Chapter Three – Escalation	110
Chapter Four – Treachery	163
Chapter Five – Research	220
Chapter Six– Jeopardy	277
Chapter Seven – Foresight	335

Chapter One – Letter

Nadene was anxious. As she strolled the short distance from the mailbox back home, she turned the large brown envelope slowly from front to back carefully inspecting the official document with a mixture of curiosity tinged with concern. Printed conspicuously above her address was a warning not to discard the hand-delivered envelope along with an admonition to open the letter upon receipt. A large, luminescent, metallic intaglio occupied the area below the return address and glittered under the bright morning sky; a brilliance that could not dispel the darkness that clouded her mind as she minutely examined the radiant engraving. Nadene ran her fingers along the edges of the embossed engraving and then across the three-dimensional landscape. It was an impressive relief of a human brain with two raised somewhat, semicircular central arcs, standing like mountain ridges in the middle of the engraving. As expected, there was no postage stamp with that space instead occupied by the Central Government's imprimatur.

The door creaked as Nadene entered her small apartment. She had meant to get that annoying squeak fixed but asking her young, local landlord to intervene was a lost cause. At most he would smile, promise to fix it, and then promptly forget the request. Nadene laid the letter on a small table adjacent to her tiny kitchen, this time frowning as the worn piece of furniture wobbled as she brushed by.

It was teatime and the young woman relished the moment. She gingerly reached into a cabinet perched precariously above her tiny cooktop and withdrew a small box of English tea. Setting it aside, she filled her lone teapot with water, ignited the gas range, and placed the vessel squarely over the flame. By all measures, it was a puny blaze, and she knew from long experience that it would take upwards of 20 minutes to boil.

With a quiet sigh, Nadene returned to the small table, sat down, pushed the letter to the side, and thoughtfully surveyed her room. Across the 900 square foot expanse resided her worldly possessions. It was a roughly rectangular space with three small rooms and one bathroom. In the bedroom, two large handles on the wall near the bathroom hinted at the bed built into the wall; a space-saving design during the day but at night when fully deployed it stretched across a third of the room. Like everything else in the apartment, it wore its age without grace and sagged pitifully in protest to the years of use.

To the far side of the bathroom were twin bassinets; the two sleeping occupants oblivious to their mother's looming decision. Alexander lay contentedly on his back while Clio seemed restless and about to awaken. Both were ten months old and in another two months, their parents would decide their lifelong fate.

The missing member of the household was Nadene's husband who was an officer in the Central Government's Home Guard. Lloyd was an imposing figure, not by stature, but through a forceful nature that resolutely commanded respect. As a behavioral trait, it served the man well, and in tandem, with an uncompromising competence, it had propelled him to the upper echelons of the Home Guard.

Although she never openly admitted it, Nadene knew that her husband's strength of character was a central attraction that cemented their relationship. A youthful picture of the pair on the wall amplified her wistful reverie with memories of their meeting; animating a smile followed by soft laughter.

Nadene met Lloyd at the insistence of her friends who arranged the blind date. She reflected on that twelve-year-old encounter and remembered the trepidation that preceded their first meeting. As might be expected, she recalled the possibilities with an anxious expectation but most gravitated towards a doubtful outcome. Nadene vividly recalled her first impression of the man, and while expecting a dour, dumpy figure, she was pleasantly surprised with his lean athleticism. That first get-together was awkward since Nadene was naturally shy and she sensed the same in her date. Their conversation was polite, apolitical, and uninformative but Nadene left that encounter both surprised and relieved and agreed to another date.

A whistling teapot jolted the woman back to reality. She walked to the range and lifting the lid examined the boiling water as if to verify the noisy salute's message. Soon afterward a teabag was submerged in a cup of hot water and after a few minutes unceremoniously dropped into a garbage can. A generous portion of skim milk and artificial sweetener completed the task. Nadene wrapped both hands around the hot cup, luxuriating in the warmth that dispelled some of the room's coldness.

It was a blustery day outside and the cold seemed to seep in through every crack in the apartment. Nadene looked at the thermostat and frowned at the mandated 60-degree temperature before taking a sip of the hot tea. Tea always lifted her spirits and while clutching the cup she resumed her reminiscences.

Gazing contentedly at a picture of her husband and herself on their wedding day brought a glow that even more than the tea warmed her soul. When they first met both were students at different colleges. Nadene was finishing her degree in education and Lloyd was a senior at a prestigious military academy. Glancing towards her hand, a small diamond ring remained as tangible evidence of that summer day when Lloyd proposed and she readily accepted.

It all seemed so long ago. Looking back in time-compressed momentous events, stripping their significance in a world now so utterly changed from those blissful days. Despondency and an ill-defined dread now dominated her daily discourse; an emotional state relieved by her husband, children, and artistic creativity.

The sun was beginning to set and shadows darkened the room when the door opened and Lloyd wearily came in; placing his briefcase on the floor and taking a seat next to Nadene. Her face brightened but sensing his fatigue she prepared another cup of tea, this one extra strong and not diluted by any adulterants.

A few months earlier, the Home Guard honored Lloyd with a promotion. As a Colonel, his responsibilities now were administrative but a dense overgrowth of even more senior members encumbered even the simplest decisions. Unclear missions and mandates subtracted greatly from any job satisfaction but the monthly credits paid the bills.

Lloyd rarely talked about his work. Rehashing the day's frustrations only increased his tension and so husband and wife sat quietly together. In the beginning, her husband's silence was annoying, leading the woman to conjure all sorts of reasons for the stillness; none of which were flattering.

It was dark now and Lloyd reached for the light switch which did little to illuminate the room but it did awaken their two children who began restlessly moving about. Even with the dim light the forgotten letter cast-off sparkles as if enjoining someone to notice. Lloyd reached for the letter and upon closer inspection immediately recognized its importance.

Turning towards Nadene, Lloyd wondered "when did the letter arrive?" Nadene sheepishly replied, "it came late this afternoon. I know we were expecting it but I couldn't bring myself to open it until you came home." Lloyd shrugged his shoulders with indifference but the slightest furrowing of his brow suggested unspoken displeasure with Nadene's disregard for the letter's contents. After a moment's pause, Lloyd was about to open the letter when baby Clio started crying.

Nadene was the nurturer and her baby's crying was the signal for motherly intervention. It soon became apparent that Clio needed dry clothing but after taking care of that baby chore Alexander started screaming for attention. With Clio now quiet Nadene reached into the bassinet and scooped up the noisy troublemaker and walking around the tiny apartment sought to soothe his ruffled feathers. After a few minutes, all was quiet.

Opening the letter would have to wait until after dinner. Clio and Alexander took their customary seats in highchairs and Lloyd helped set the small table with flatware and napkins. The night's meal was a simple but hearty menu of freshly baked bread, a thick mushroom soup, small triangular pieces of cheese, and rosy, red apple wedges. A large pitcher of iced tea completed the adult's meal. At the same time, Nadene patiently fed her two children; taking great care to bite-size the cheese and bread, puree the apple, and make sure the soup was not too hot.

After the dishes were cleared away Clio and Alexander returned to their cribs and Lloyd turned his attention to the letter. Nadene was not particularly interested in reading the letter so close to bedtime, but her husband lived by the maxim of not putting off to tomorrow what can be done today. And so it was that the letter retrieved much earlier in the day and set aside as the daily duties took priority would now be opened.

Lloyd took a small penknife from his pocket and carefully cut a slit across the envelope's top margin; taking great care not to disturb the contents. It only took a moment more for Lloyd to effortlessly remove the letter. The letter was from Foresight, an agency in the Central Government, and just like the envelope, it sported the same embossed insignia. With an air of formality, the letter invited Colonel and Mrs. Lane to register for the Foresight Education Symposium. Lloyd read the letter aloud:

Colonel and Mrs. Lane

Records maintained by the Central Government indicate that you have two children that are ten months old. As you know, all parents or guardians are required to register and attend a regularly scheduled Foresight Education Symposium. The sessions are comprehensive, didactic, and interactive. You will join with others in small groups to further process the information. Your Central Government sponsors this education to guide you in making this most important decision for your child's future. After the Symposium you will make your binding decision. Please remember – your final decision is irreversible.

Upon receipt of this letter go to your nearest Home Guard precinct and register for the Foresight Education Symposium. Clerks will assign you to a Symposium that will ensure completion in a timely manner that will allow you to make your decision, as required, on or about your child's first annual birthday.

Attendance and attention must assume priority and employment and other non-essential activities must be suspended. Your Central Government will arrange childcare during your daily attendance. All educational materials and meals will be provided. Employers are required to continue your pay during this Symposium.

In closing, your Central Government stresses once again that attendance at the Foresight Education Symposium is mandatory and failure to follow through will be reported to the Central Government's Home Guard for analysis and appropriate action. Waivers voiding attendance must be submitted through official channels.

Your support is critical for our social welfare.

With regards,
The Foresight Education Committee

Lloyd laid the letter down and waited for a response from Nadene. The normally talkative woman sat motionless with a pensive expression. She knew what was coming and did not feel it necessary to prod the response. Her husband waited for a few minutes, an unusually long time for him, before he bluntly asked, "Nadene, when can you make the arrangements?"

"Lloyd," using her affectionate, usually disarming tone, "I would prefer if we went together, after all, I think that is what the Central Government expects."

Her husband bristled imperceptibly but his icy response left little doubt where this conversation was going, "I think I know more about what the Central Government expects, you seem to forget that I work at the Home Guard."

Nadene's face flushed with the backhanded criticism; an observation her husband immediately recognized and attempted to mollify, "I'm sorry. That was over the top. What I should have said is that it is more than awkward for me, as a senior officer in the Home Guard, to accompany you to a local precinct. It is more than likely that I might run into a friend, a neighbor, or even some well-known individual that could come under my professional purview. I am concerned that such an encounter could turn divisive or even violent. As you know I am eligible for a waiver from attendance given my position."

"You're right," Nadene admitted, "but you know I do not look forward to this. I'm too much of a free spirit to be ordered about by anyone." Lloyd agreed with his wife's self-characterization but his lifelong career grounded in obeisance did not countenance disobedience. If there was a habitual sticking point in their marriage it relentlessly revolved around the pair's basic natures. While their respective personalities created friction at times it was also an essential ingredient in their marriage; his strength, drive, and resolve complemented by her empathy, innate intelligence, and flexibility.

"Lloyd, it is late and if you don't get to bed now, you'll be so grumpy tomorrow. I'll join you as soon as I check on the twins." It was an invitation Lloyd willingly followed and after a few minutes brushing his teeth and changing clothes he pulled the hidden bed down. In response, it squeaked and groaned with its nightly protest. The bed sagged noticeably but not to the point where Lloyd or Nadene wanted a replacement. Beds were costly and Lloyd figured that it still had a few more serviceable years left, despite the aching back that followed his night's sleep.

Lloyd awakened at his customary time; just minutes before an alarm clock announced it was 5 am. Over the years the alarm clock assumed a decorative role since the man always awakened before the clock ever had a chance to awaken him. Nadene always lingered in bed a few minutes after her husband showered but well before he was dressed, she was busily preparing the morning's breakfast.

Breakfast was a chaotic time. First, Nadene slipped into comfortable but attractive black culottes with a black and white striped cotton top which were the utilitarian options while tending to the twins and her husband's breakfast. Alexander and Clio, her drowsy duo, grew more animated at the prospect of the morning's meal. Nadene counted herself fortunate that both were not picky eaters and usually consumed their nutritious meals without fuss.

Her husband was a different story. His tastes gravitated towards more mundane fare and long experience had taught Nadine that more creative, elaborate entrees while reaping obligatory praise, were less welcome than plain food. A few weeks past she had made a morning souffle that her husband greeted with disappointment but quietly consumed without a murmur of protest. It was another painful culinary lesson but this morning's repast would not suffer the same response.

Lloyd always ate his breakfast after showering, shaving, and donning his Home Guard uniform. He was always impeccably attired in a spotless white shirt, red tie, blue trousers with a two-inch-wide black strip running vertically from top to bottom. His shoulders wore the rank of Colonel; symbolized by four silver triangles. A jacket neatly hung by the door had the same rank on twin epaulets and was further ornamented with four rows of colorful ribbons.

Nadene joined her husband for breakfast. A hot, steaming cup of black coffee sat next to a bowl of grits and dry toast. Lloyd ground a liberal portion of pepper into the grits and scooped out a generous portion of butter and stirred the concoction together. His toast served as a spoon and also obviated the need of buttering the toast which in his mind served two purposes; saving money and calories. Nadene preferred the more mellow taste of tea to the bitterness of coffee and she liked her grits seasoned with brown sugar.

Lloyd liked to have an hour after breakfast as a sort of buffer between leaving his apartment and reporting to the Home Guard. That time always passed too quickly; at least in Nadene's mind. Her husband signaled his imminent departure by donning the uniform's jacket.

"Have a good day at work. Do you have your lunch?" Lloyd always had lunch in his office except when travel or meetings intervened. "Yes, I have about half a jar of peanuts and several cans of tomato juice." Like breakfast, it was a monotonous meal but one that the man never ceased to enjoy.

As he stood near the door Lloyd asked, "What time do you plan on going to the Home Guard precinct to register for the Foresight Symposium?" Nadene had not forgotten even though she would have liked to. With some irritation, she replied, "I need to arrange for a babysitter. I will try to register this afternoon if that works out." Lloyd would have preferred a more definite plan but pushing the matter further would only cause an argument. "Well, do what you can. I should be back at the normal time tonight. Call me if you need anything."

It was too early to arrange for the babysitter. In the meantime, Alexander and Clio both needed a bath. While bathing her children she absent-mindedly considered the change in her life brought about by the birth of the twins.

Nadene was a librarian and her first employment in that field consisted of stacking books in the college library while a student pursuing a degree in library science and information technology. The pay was minimal, but it was a welcome supplement to her husband's military scholarship.

After graduating, Nadene and her husband spent their first three years together; Lloyd teaching at the military school and Nadene accepting a position as an assistant librarian at the college library. As she mused about those early years and compared them to her present circumstances it was obvious that much had changed; mostly for the worse except for her two children who lightened what had become a darker existence. It was only natural that such pessimism would inevitably refocus her attention on the urgent matters of the day.

Alexander and Clio were playing on the floor in constant sight of their attentive mother. With a sigh, Nadene walked over to the phone hanging on the wall and dialed the number for the local childcare center. Mobile phones were in short supply and only government officials or those deemed in vital need could have one.

Of course, Lloyd had one, but its use was strictly monitored for government business.

As she expected the phone rang and rang for nearly a minute before the recoded message intervened and urged the caller to try again later. Nadene knew that meant hours later and even then, the likelihood of getting a same-day babysitter was doubtful. That would upset Lloyd but there was no alternative.

It was nearing lunchtime and Nadene was preparing her children's meals when the doorbell chimed. She walked to the door and peered through the peephole and recognized Mona; one of her fellow apartment dwellers. Nadene unlocked the door and removed the security chain while welcoming her neighbor inside.

Mona was a slim, attractive woman who just celebrated her 34th birthday. She was not a particularly close friend or confidante, but the two women were the same age and also shared the joys and burdens of raising young children. As Mona entered, Nadene wondered what motivated her unannounced caller's visit.

Nadene only had the scantiest knowledge about her visitor. She knew that Mona's husband was a physician who worked at the nearby Central Government Infirmary and before the birth of her child Mona had worked at the same facility as a nurse. The two women shared another similarity in their children's ages. Like Nadene, Mona's young boy was ten months old.

It was obvious to Nadene that Mona was nervous and, in an effort, to relax her visitor she suggested a cup of tea. Mona readily accepted the offer and Nadene began preparing the beverage. The slow boiling water provided the opportunity for casual conversation and Nadene innocently inquired, "Mona, it's good to see you. I hope you don't mind that I prepare the twins their lunch while I make our tea."

Mona was fidgeting less but her timorous response still betrayed her unease, "I hope I am not upsetting your schedule. I know my coming over is a surprise, but I just needed to talk to someone and I know you have two children the same age as my boy."

"Yes," Nadene conceded, "and they are such a joy but at times I get so frustrated! Just today I tried to get a babysitter, but I could not get through to the child care center." Mona nodded her head in agreement, "I know exactly what you mean. I feel the same way."

Mona and Nadene continued their polite conversation, but an invisible wall still loomed between them and it took the hot tea to breach the barrier. "How do you like your tea?" Nadene asked as she placed both milk and sweetener on the table. Mona reached for both and sheepishly admitted, "I like my tea sweet. My husband says I drink sugar diluted with a bit of tea."

They both laughed at her husband's description and with that bit of levity, Mona was now fully at ease and took the opportunity to broach the reason for her impromptu visit. "I just received a letter from Foresight. It seemed impersonal for such a momentous decision. It ruined my morning. Anyway, I remembered that you had twins and they look to be about the same age as Jonathan, my boy."

Nadene sensed her neighbor's anxiety but while trying to reassure Mona she also betrayed her concerns. "Our twins are ten months old and that triggered the sclerotic Central Government. We received a similar form letter which just like yours rather dispassionately ordered us to comply with the mandatory educational seminars."

Nadene's response hinted at displeasure with the Central Government that extended beyond the letter from Foresight but Mona's discomfort came from a different source. With her guard completely lowered Mona shocked Nadene by revealing an intimate detail of her marriage. "What makes it so difficult for me is that Curt, my husband, is completely indifferent. I think he made his decision even before Jonathan was born. Curt won't do anything that might jeopardize his ambitions. I am undecided."

Foresight required both parents agree but if irreconcilable differences remained after completing the Foresight Symposium then the Central Government referred the matter to the Foresight Judicial Forum. It was here that the interests of the government took priority but in a spirit of equanimity, the disputing parents could argue their respective positions. A magistrate would hear arguments from the parents along with the Central Government's position and render the final opinion; a judgment that precluded any appeal.

Disagreements between parents that were settled by judicial inquiry carried another risk. It was common public knowledge that divorce was another outcome of a Foresight decision sidestepped by parents and settled by the courts. These acrimonious separations almost always favored the parent that supported the Central Government's position with primary custody of children and alimony awarded to that individual.

The Central Government's subtle but discernable influence promoted a dynamic exploited by aggrieved partners. Disaffected parents could, and did, take advantage of the Central Government's bias by overtly or covertly manipulating their partner through crude extortion campaigns; hoping to bend or break their adversary by reminding them of the consequences of disagreement.

Mona alluded to this threat when she tensely remarked, "Curt and I don't see eye to eye on this. More than anything I'm worried that even after attending the Foresight Symposium we still won't agree." Nadene thoughtfully probed her guest, "So…what are your feeling about this?"

Before answering, Mona took a deep breath and tried to measure Nadene's position but throwing caution to the wind she finally admitted that "I want Jonathan to experience life to its fullest, with all the pain and joy that rewards our brief existence." Nadene was not surprised at the response, but a subliminal dysphoric note struck a discordant tone that worried the woman.

The telephone brusquely rang and resonated throughout the small apartment startling both women. Nadene lifted the receiver off its cradle and greeted the caller, "The Lane home."

A familiar voice quickly responded to the woman's announcement. It was her husband calling from work during his lunchtime which reminded Nadene how the morning had slipped by.

"Nadene," her husband began, "I just wanted to call and let you know that I may be about an hour late tonight. I had to send a team out to round up two naysayers and I do not expect them back before early this evening."

"Thank you for letting me know," Nadene glibly responded, "I will start dinner a little later. By the way, I called the childcare center and could not get through. I will try again this afternoon, but I may have another option."

Nadene did not elaborate but her husband's curiosity could not be satisfied without more details, "What other options are there?"

"Do you remember meeting Mona and her husband Curt a few months ago?" Lloyd thought for a moment and replied, "Is he the physician who works at the nearby infirmary?"

Nadene confirmed her husband's answer and went on, "Mona is with me right now. We have been talking for a little while. She just received a letter from Foresight and we were figuring out how we could swap childcare for a few hours and register for the Symposium."

The subject of coordinating childcare with Mona never came up between the two but Nadene felt it prudent not to mention her visitor's qualms about Foresight. Part of Nadene's hesitation was motivated by her husband's responsibility for apprehending naysayers. Mona seemed to be teetering on the edge of desertion, joining the ranks of the naysayers, but Nadene was not certain and with an abundance of doubt she squelched her suspicions. The Central Government levied steep fines and punishment for deserters and any collaborators who aided their escape; the latter an insinuation that would imperil both Nadene and her husband.

"Nadene, are you there?" her husband wondered at the prolonged silence. "Yes, I just asked Mona to stay a few minutes more so we could work out the cross coverage. It looks like Mona can take care of the twins tomorrow morning. The Foresight Registration Center opens at 9 am which will give me plenty of time to feed, bathe, and dress the twins before Mona comes over. I can then return the favor the following day."

Her husband breathed an audible sigh of relief, "Thank you Nadene, that sounds like a great plan. Maybe we should invite Mona and Curt over for dinner after this is all arranged." Nadene liked the idea and before hanging up assured her husband that she would invite Mona.

While Nadene and her husband spoke, Mona sat quietly but she understood the gist of the one-sided conversation that involved swapping childcare so they both could register for the Symposium. After hanging up Nadene turned to Mona and broached the subject. "I guess you heard what I said. Are you OK with taking care of Clio and Alexander tomorrow? I will have them both ready around 8 am."

Based on the telephone call Mona anticipated the request and placidly agreed. "I will come over around 8 am and bring Jonathan with me. From what I have heard it generally takes about two hours to complete the registration." Nadene agreed and thanked Mona for her flexibility.

A cloud seemed to pass across Mona's face after agreeing to the childcare arrangements as she blurted, "I can't possibly take care of your children during the symposium!"

"No problem," Nadene glibly responded, "I am sure we can arrange suitable coverage."

After Mona left, Nadene thoughtfully rehashed the encounter; principally motivated by trying to understand a sadness that seemed to permeate the morning meeting and then lingered like stale perfume. When Mona first arrived, she was anxious but at the same time seemed eager to talk. With a bit of coaxing and hot tea Mona shared her worries about Foresight. That seemed reasonable to Nadene since she had her worries, but the conversation took a decidedly negative turn when Mona timorously and obliquely brought up festering tensions in her marriage. It was that disclosure that weighed on Nadene's mind and left her wondering if Mona would become a naysayer.

Mid-afternoon was approaching and Nadene reckoned that a call to the Foresight Registration Center was in order. She reluctantly picked up the telephone and dialed the number. Surprisingly, the call connected with an automated message and assured the listener that a representative would be available shortly.

Despite the message's optimistic recording, Nadene figured she would have a long wait and so she pressed the speaker button; freeing her hands to attend to other activities. A piece of monotonous music flowed from the telephone and was punctuated every few minutes with Central Government public service messages.

With the phone in her pants pocket, Nadene washed a small pile of dishes and then took both twins out of their cribs. Both were walking with an unsteady gait and giggled when they fell.

Nadene could not see the pleasure in falling but it amused her children and likewise buoyed their mother's mood.

Nearly an hour passed and still, nothing emanated from the telephone except the music and prerecorded messages. The prolonged wait was draining the telephone's battery and Nadene was on the verge of returning the device to its charging cradle when a voice interrupted the music. "Good afternoon, I am your Foresight Registration Clerk number 2020. Can I have your name?"

Nadene quickly retrieved the phone from her pocket and almost dropped it in her haste to answer. Any significant delay ran the risk of the Registration Clerk hanging up; an outcome that would penalize Nadene with another round of music.

"My name is Nadene Lane and I am calling to register for the Foresight Symposium." The phone crackled in response and then the Clerk replied, "I need the registration number you received in the letter from the Foresight Committee." Nadene walked over to the table and picking the letter up responded, "The registration number is 19535485."

A lengthy pause followed and Nadene again worried that the clerk's call was disconnected. "That number is associated with Lloyd Lane and Nadene Lane, is that correct?" the clerk queried.

"Yes, that is correct." a slightly bemused Nadene responded. "Can you tell me when is the earliest we can join a Foresight Symposium?"

"That will be decided at your in-person registration," the clerk brusquely replied. "We open at 9 am. Come to the registration office, sign in, and take a number. Remember to bring your invitation letter, marriage certificate, and birth certificate for your children. You might want to bring something to occupy your time because the waitlist can be very long. Have you arranged childcare?"

Nadene squelched her irritation at the bureaucrat's condescending and impersonal attitude and muffled her response with a short, polite answer, "Thank you for the information and the reminder about the childcare. I will have everything arranged and look forward to registering tomorrow."

The registration clerk accepted Naden's humility but that did little to improve his attitude. "Remember to bring the aforementioned items. If these documents are not presented to your registration clerk, you will not be allowed to schedule a Foresight Symposium." A loud click terminated the discussion signaling the clerk's summary dismissal of the caller.

Nadene expected poor customer service from a Central Government agency, but that awareness did little to mitigate her annoyance at the Foresight clerk's rude behavior. She wondered how any representative of the Foresight Committee, charged with administering one of the most sensitive social programs, could be so callous. A flash of anger set her imagination ablaze and with a smile, she considered reporting the clerk to the Foresight Committee's Parent Protection Program. Her smile slowly faded as reality replaced reverie with the certain knowledge that a complaint would prove useless and possibly even dangerous.

Alexander was getting cranky, and Clio was drooping which the attentive mother interpreted as nap time. She tenderly scooped them up in turn and placed the tired children in their cribs. Both were soon sleeping soundly which presented Nadene her first opportunity to gather the required documents for the registration meeting.

Lloyd had a filing cabinet in one of the small rooms in the apartment, designated as the office, which contained the family's important letters, financial data, employment records, and personal documents. It was always locked and Nadene retrieved the key buried in a deep recess in her dresser drawer. She unlocked the file cabinet and leafed through the contents until she spied the personal document folder. After removing the folder from the cabinet Nadene took the marriage certificate out but the children's birth certificates were missing.

Now alarmed and anxious, Nadene examined every folder in the file cabinet but the missing documents eluded her search. She briefly considered calling Lloyd but prudently decided to await his arrival. To allay her anxiety, she turned her attention to preparing the night's dinner but the distraction was not entirely successful in quelling her worries. Her mind relentlessly returned to the registration clerk's ominous closing comments, "if these documents are not presented to your registration clerk you will not be allowed to schedule a Foresight Symposium."

Dinner would be a simple affair for everyone. Nadene reached into the pantry and removed several containers of prepared food for her twins; something she generally avoided but it was getting late in the day and cooking more nourishing and wholesome fare was not possible. She knew her husband would be disappointed with a sandwich, cup of hot soup, and potato chips but he would understand after she explained her afternoon meeting with Mona and the subsequent call to the Foresight Registration Office. She was also concerned about the whereabouts of the missing documents and still smoldering from the registration clerk's offensiveness; both events sapping her energy.

Nadene glanced at the clock and at the same time heard rumblings from the cribs. Clio and Alexander were up and about; earnestly looking at Nadene with imploring eyes that suggested their hope to escape the crib's confines. Nadene figured Lloyd would be home in about an hour, and since dinner was essentially done, she took both children from their cribs and began playing with them on the carpeted floor.

Loose threads in the carpet were another annoyance and reminder of the apartment's overall poor condition. These negative thoughts were beginning to pile up and in response, Nadene shook her head as if to cast off the creeping dysphoria. Focusing on the children was difficult but when Clio fell and started crying her mother's attention instantly returned as she comforted the little girl.

The front door opened with protest as a series of creaks and squeaks announced Lloyd's arrival. His haggard appearance worried Nadene as waves of guilt simultaneously swept over the woman as she thought about the pitiful dinner. Setting her concerns aside, Nadene took her husband's jacket and followed him into the bedroom where Lloyd lazily donned more comfortable clothes.

Lloyd liked to spend some time unwinding before dinner. Sometimes he played with the children, listened to the radio, or read a few pages in a book or magazine. Tonight, he simply slouched on the couch; doing his best to avoid the sagging sections. Nadene joined him and after a few minutes gingerly asked, "How was your day?"

Of course, she knew the answer but hoped her gentle entreaty would entice Lloyd to share his thoughts. He obliged by soberly noting, "We had to arrest two naysayers today. Normally that doesn't bother me - I mean that is a primary function of my position – but these two young women threatened to kill their children. Both had been in court pleading their case and as expected they lost. The magistrate awarded primary custody of the children to the fathers and an instant later both mothers seized their children and ran from the courtroom. A vehicle was waiting outside and the naysayers sped away. It took hours to finally catch up with them. My boss was livid and blamed me and my staff for not anticipating the naysayer's actions."

Nadene struck a sympathetic note hoping to lighten her husband's despondency, "I'm sure General Roderick was just upset. He probably got an angry call from some senior authority in the Central Government and was still fuming from that when he spoke with you. General Roderick knows you too well. After all, the two of you were battle buddies in some of the worst conflicts."

Lloyd always appreciated his wife's level-headed thoughts by voicing that feeling, "You're probably right. I certainly get my share of criticism from the news media and politicians. Maybe I should call General Roderick later or stop by his office tomorrow and we can chat about this."

"I think that is a great idea Lloyd, but it might be better to wait until tomorrow and give General Roderick some time to relax and recalibrate. And talking about relaxing, would you like dinner now? It's not much tonight. Between Mona coming over and my later hassles with the Foresight Registration I just didn't have the time or energy."

"Sure," Lloyd said, "and let me help with Alexander and Clio."

Nadene was waiting for the best opportunity to discuss the missing documents and after dinner with a cup of hot tea seemed the best time. The dishes were swiftly cleaned and Lloyd sat on the floor between Alexander and Clio. Nadene joined her husband on the floor and began reviewing her day, "Mona agreed to watch Alexander and Clio tomorrow. I need to be at the Foresight Registration office at 9 am, sign in, take a number, and wait. The clerk suggested that it could be a long wait, so I am taking some reading materials and my crossword puzzles."

"I can only imagine how inefficient they are;" coming from a man who owed his allegiance to the same authorities but in private conversations shared his contempt for the legions of mindless government drones.

Nadene nodded her head in agreement, "the registration clerk was incredibly rude but even more galling was his lack of empathy. The Foresight employees are entirely devoid of emotions."

It was Lloyd's turn to nod his acquiescence; an agreement that included an even more pointed criticism, "Customer service training would be useless and the Foresight Committee knows this. The typical employee could not retain the information and would need to rely on a checklist to guide their behavior. Even with that, it would come across as robotic."

Nadene knew that she had to mention the missing documents and now, diving in, she nervously noted, "The registration clerk made it clear that I had to bring the Foresight Invitation Letter, our marriage certificate, and the children's birth certificates. I found our marriage certificate, but I looked everywhere for Alexander's and Clio's birth certificates and couldn't find them. We can't register for a Foresight Symposium without those documents."

Lloyd could scarcely contain the smile that spread across his face; an animation that provoked Nadene, "You seem to think that is funny. I spent all afternoon searching for those certificates and when I couldn't find them, I was so upset and worried. This just seems to be one of those days where everything goes wrong."

"I was not laughing at you," Lloyd apologized, "but I know where those certificates are. The Foresight Symposium requires parents to obtain identity cards for each child and I know the department leader of that section so I called her up and asked if she could do that for me. I must admit though, I was surprised when she said she did not remember meeting me but she would have the identity cards made as a courtesy based on my position."

"So, you took the certificates yesterday," Nadene surmised.

"Yes, I plead guilty," Lloyd admitted and with a dramatic flourish flashed the documents carefully concealed in a pocket. "I hope you won't punish me too harshly," he playfully suggested.

They both laughed and with that exchange, the tension from the day's frustrations ebbed away. In the meantime, darkness heralded the late hour and with it the fatigue that beckoned sleep. The twins were also slowing down and Nadene placed both sleepy children in their respective cribs. As a matter of bedtime routine, Lloyd assembled a clean uniform to expedite his morning activities, and with that chore completed the married couple settled in for a night's sleep.

Nadene and Lloyd awakened refreshed and ready to tackle a new day. Nothing momentous interfered with the morning's humdrum missions and Lloyd left for work; leaving Nadene to cope with the Foresight Registration. She knew that he was only a phone call away if the need arose and that was sufficient support for her to independently complete the Foresight Registration.

Alexander and Clio must have sensed the nature of the day's activity and were unusually active. Perhaps, Nadene wondered, the twins somehow sensed the nature of the day's activity and were apprehensive in consequence; a thought she assuaged by calculating that her children were far too young to experience such emotions.

Just before retiring the previous night Nadene had collected the required documents and placed them in a folder. She now awaited the arrival of Mona but was becoming increasingly anxious as the minutes sped by. It was half-past eight o'clock and Nadene figured it would take roughly 15 minutes travel time to arrive at the Foresight Registration facility and be in line by nine o'clock. That left only 15 minutes of leeway.

Nadene did not want to be late since that would prolong the agony of waiting to register for the Foresight Symposium, but she was at the mercy of a nervous neighbor. Her thoughts gravitated to the worst penalty of a tardy arrival which might include the possibility of being denied registration as a result.

During their meeting Nadene and Mona had casually exchanged contact information; an afterthought suggested by Nadene and now rewarded as a means to address the looming crisis. With mounting concern, Nadene reached for the telephone and slowly dialed the number. Her efforts were thwarted when the phone rang a lonely tune that went unnoticed by any recipient.

It was now nine o'clock and Nadene's anxiety was turning towards despair as the reality of registering was slowly slipping away. She was on the verge of calling Lloyd with the bad news when a knock at the door startled her. Nadene hoped it was her belated neighbor and with a renewed sense of optimism opened the door.

Mona awkwardly entered and quietly acknowledged, "I know I'm late. I'm so sorry. Curt was upset that I had agreed to come over and has been sulking after I told him."

Nadene sympathetically responded," I'm sorry that I caused you so much trouble. Would you prefer not to stay now?"

Curt had angrily demanded Mona do just that but to her credit, Mona resisted and now reassured Nadene, "If you don't think it's too late to register then please let me watch your children while you are gone."

"Thank you, Mona," Nadene replied, "I have everything ready so I think it best to go. The wait may be a bit longer, but I would prefer that to the risk of not getting to register in a timely fashion."

Mona's son Jonathan was squirming in her arms and wanted to roam around. Mona obliged and at the same time, with Nadene watching, took Alexander and Clio out of their cribs. Without a moment's hesitation, the three children started exploring their environment together; with squeals and giggles echoing in the small apartment. Nadene was relieved, and now in a hurry, rushed out the door.

Running out of the apartment complex occasioned stares from passersby but Nadene was intent on getting a ride and was fortunate in flagging down a cruising taxi. She quickly jumped inside and instructed the driver to make haste to the local Foresight office. The driver was nonplussed by Nadene's behavior and similarly unmotivated to exceed the speed limit. With each stop sign, Nadene's anxiety grew as it seemed like the driver was purposely thwarting her plans.

Finally, after what seemed an interminable trip the taxi driver pulled into a parking lot adjacent to the Foresight office, and turning around to face Nadene he said, "This is a free parking area.

I am not allowed to get any closer so you will have to walk from here. Your fare is listed on the meter."

Nadene reached into her purse and withdrew crisp new bills and paid the driver. The taxi sped away and Nadene sprinted across the street in a determined effort to traverse the quarter-mile in record time. What time she saved was dissipated as Nadene stood just outside the building's entrance, breathless from the exertion. During her recovery Nadene winced when two other women entered the Foresight office; a motivating observation that resulted in a herculean effort as Nadene stifled her gasping and followed them in.

For a Central Government building, the Foresight office was remarkably spacious, warm, and inviting. A low counter greeted each visitor, behind which were arrayed a dozen clerks faultlessly adorned in their impressive, white uniforms. Overhead a monotonous recorded message instructed the newly arrived to take a number and then wait in the adjoining room.

Nadene walked over to the ticket machine, pulled the handle, and retrieved her number. Her penalty for arriving nearly an hour after the office opened was revealed when she examined the number 165 and from the overhead announcer learned that the clerks were now calling for number 28.

With a quiet sigh, Nadene settled into one of the uncommonly plush but firm chairs; resigned to a long wait. She set her reading materials on the ground and looked around the room. The waiting room could seat 250 people and the steady flow of people was already filling every vacancy. A few people were standing which Nadene considered a foolish choice.

There were no tables in the room and the space between chairs was uncomfortably close. A man and woman sat next to Nadene, muttered an acknowledgment, and then whispered to each other; totally ignoring their neighbor. Nadene was not inclined to be sociable being preoccupied with what was to come and she welcomed their reclusive behavior.

Scanning the interior left Nadene once again impressed with the near opulence of the office. Dominating the room was a large sign with an illuminated relief of a human brain with two raised interlocking central arcs; just like the emblem on the envelope, she received days earlier. Pastel shades emanating from blue and pink lights decorated the sign; unavoidably riveting the viewer's gaze on the symbol. Nadene correctly assumed that the Foresight Committee chose those specific colors to subliminally characterize boys and girls. All things considered; the trademark symbol was visually quite fetching Nadene admitted to herself but an involuntary shudder betrayed her subconscious skepticism.

Male and female employees standing behind the imposing counter wore unisex clothing with a white shirt, light brown pants, brown belt, and black side cap. The Foresight Committee replicated the emblem on the employee's uniforms with a small circular badge above the right shirt pocket and with an enameled pin on the cap. Each clerk had a single chevron on the shirt's left sleeve although Nadene noticed that other employees not assigned to the front desk had more chevrons.

A slow but steady stream of registrants approaching the front desk and then disappearing into a maze of office cubicles encouraged Nadene that perhaps her wait might be less than she expected. With the passage of an hour, the overhead announcer once again interrupted the incessant buzz from the waiting room's roughly 200 people and droned, "Number 65 report to station 12."

Nadene did the mental math and calculated that the clerks processed 37 individuals in the last hour based on number 28 being called when she arrived and number 65 now. If the clerks continued that pace Nadene figured her wait time would be about three hours. Unfortunately, she did not anticipate that each clerk received a lunch break; a staggered event that decreased the number of employees from 11 am to 1 pm.

Nadene loved a mystery and reaching into her bag she retrieved a hard-bound copy of a Sherlock Holmes book. This book was "The Adventure of the Second Stain," which was one of the author's short stories and seemed about the right length for Nadene to finish while waiting for the registration clerk. Lunchtime was fast approaching or so it seemed as her stomach grumbled with impatience and once again reaching into her bag Nadene withdrew two plastic bags. One bag contained a generous portion of bright orange baby carrots and the other a smaller sample of seedless green grapes. Still left in her bag for want of space in her lap was a plastic bottle filled with freshly made black tea.

Nadene contentedly munched on her carrots and while absorbed in the Holmes story was oblivious to the irritated glances cast her way by those within earshot of the cracking and crunching as she consumed her lunch. Until now the people sitting next to Nadene had carefully avoided any interactions, but the man's wife was fit to be tied by the carrot cacophony and reaching across her husband tapped her neighbor on the shoulder. Nadene was momentarily startled by the touch, and looking at the source's angry manner, quickly interpreted the behavior and with an uncaring shrug returned to reading Sherlock Holmes and eating the remaining carrots.

A few empty chairs some distance from Nadene offered the promise of relief for her disgruntled neighbors who gathered up their belongings and with a series of gesticulations and audible utterances hoped to provoke a response. It failed and further infuriated the pair as Nadene took no notice of their shenanigans although both were convinced that a smile flitted across her face.

Nadene took advantage of the empty chairs and placed her bag and drink in the nearest one. Glancing at her watch suggested maybe another two hours but the pace of registrant numbers had slowed. "Maybe," she thought, "I will be called around 3 pm which still leaves time before the office closes for the day." Discreetly place signs warned newcomers that the office closed promptly at 5 pm and no one would be called after that time. Those left behind had no choice but to return the next day.

Setting her book aside to rest her eyes let her mind drift to thoughts about Mona and the children. Mona was torn between supporting her husband and keeping her childcare commitment; an outcome that both favored and relieved Nadene but did not quell a nagging suspicion that Mona's decision contrary to her husband would reap bitter fruit. With a tinge of remorse, Nadene imagined that the children were probably taking their afternoon naps.

Lunch was over and Nadene put the empty plastic bags in a nearby waste can and returning to her seat resumed reading her book. Now and then she would take a sip of her tea but soon it too was empty. Even though she enjoyed the book Nadene was getting restive as the hours piled up and bore down on the woman with their heaviness. She stood up as if that act would somehow magically speed the course of events and she stared with a penetrating gaze at the Foresight clerks.

From overhead, the announcer droned, "number 155 proceed to registration desk 6." Nadene's gloom dissipated with that announcement as she thought; "It is 2:30 and only ten numbers to go. Even with the lunch slowdown maybe I will get to register in the next hour."

With a lighter heart, Nadene sat back down but left the book in her bag because she expected to be called soon and did not want her reading interrupted. Looking about the room Nadene spied her recently departed neighbors who looked glum and worried. They caught her eye and frowned.

"Those two don't seem very happy," Nadene reflected, "They must have a high number and won't be seen today. Serves them right for being mean." Nadene relished her moment of private retribution but on further deliberation, she understood their apparent anguish, and in a sympathetic reconsideration, absolved their pettiness.

Nadene's reverie was interrupted when the overhead announcer directed "Number 165 to registration clerk 7." The long-awaited announcement startled the woman who nervously gathered her belongings and approached the registration clerk.

Clerk 7 was a young man crisply attired in the Foresight uniform. His impassive features and cold eyes unnerved Nadene but by drawing on her inner resolve she displayed a calm exterior. She placed her bag on the floor and faced the clerk who shoved a paper in her direction.

"Read the document and then sign it," he peremptorily demanded. Nadene carefully studied the document beginning with the bold title, "Rules, Penalties, and Obligations of Foresight Registrants and Symposium Attendees."

Each section of the document sets forth legalities and punishments. The Rules section discussed document delivery, attendance, homework, and small group assignments. The Penalties section set forth the consequences for tardiness, absences, inattention, procrastination, and contentious behavior. In the final section on Obligations, the document required that registrants and attendees maintain respectful attitudes, accept the leader's authority, and acknowledge that disobedience could result in rejection from the Symposium. The document's last sentence was set apart from the rest and italicized "All Symposium graduates must submit a final decision within seven days."

Nadene was taking too long, and the clerk intervened, "You need to sign the document in two places. The first signature is for the Rules, Penalties, and Obligations and the second signature represents your compliance with the seven-day decision mandate."

The signing was obligatory and despite her reservations, Nadene knew there was no alternative. The clerk handed Nadene an ink pen and without a word, she signed the document. "You can now proceed to cubicle 23," the clerk intoned and turning his back on the woman brought forth another document for the next registrant.

Cubicle 23 bore none of the rich trappings of the lobby and was instead a space just large enough for a desk and two chairs. Nadene approached the desk and the solitary occupant gestured with a wide sweep of her arm for Nadene to sit in the vacant chair. Doing as instructed, Nadene sat down and placed her bag just outside the cubicle which immediately prompted a scowl from the Foresight registration clerk and a rebuke. "Do not place your bag in the aisle, keep it in your lap."

It was a rough start, but Nadene hoped the process would get smoother, but here she was mistaken. The registration clerk was a young woman, neatly clad in the Foresight uniform, with her attention directed to a folder with Nadene's registration number inscribed on the front. A small nameplate sitting askew on the tiny desk identified the woman as Natalie.

In a friendly gesture, Nadene asked Natalie, "how are you doing today. It certainly looks quite busy."

Natalie responded with a vacant stare, ignored the speaker's pleasantries, and opened the registration folder. "According to the Foresight Records you are currently married, have two children, and you are a professional librarian. Your husband is a senior officer in the Central Government's Home Guard and a decorated veteran of the Cataclysmic Conflict. You and your husband live in the administrative district of Siloportem. Is this all correct?"

"Yes," Nadene said, "everything you stated is correct."

"You have two months to complete the Foresight Symposium and submit your decision. Are you ready to pick a date and begin the commitment?" the Registration clerk asked while simultaneously reaching for the appointment book.

Nadene answered affirmatively and then queried the clerk, "What are the earliest available dates, and how much time do I have to coordinate this with my husband?"

A seemingly harmless question but Natalie's response suggested otherwise, "most people have already discussed their availability before this meeting and come prepared with several potential dates. Since you have not done that the Foresight Committee's rules require you to accept one of two dates that I will provide you. Call me tomorrow with your choice."

Up to this point, Nadene had tolerated the day's travails with resignation but this person's imperious behavior conquered her composure and, like a dam bursting with floodwaters, she let loose a torrential tirade. "I think you are most unhelpful. As you know from our records, Colonel Lane is with the Central Government's Home Guard and his duties take priority. His schedule is unpredictable and any time off must be cleared by General Roderick. It is my understanding that senior officers have greater latitude when scheduling the Foresight Symposium and if you check with a supervisor you will see your error."

Nadene knew that her anger would not affect the clerk who, as predicted, simply stared impassively before responding, "I forgot that rule. You are correct. I will give you a copy of the open dates over the next month. Fill out this Exception Form with your chosen dates and return it within three days."

Natalie looked past Nadene to the next person waiting outside her cubicle and stated, "You can leave now." At this point, Nadene was beyond being further irritated as her thoughts mellowed in anticipation of returning home.

A line of taxis greeted Nadene as she hurriedly left the Foresight building and without a moment's pause, she entered the nearest and was soon speeding back home. Time flew by and in what seemed like mere seconds Nadene was opening the door to her small abode. Alexander and Clio squealed with peals of joy when they sighted their mother and even Jonathan joined the chorus.

Mona was more reserved. "How did it go?" the woman inquired. "I was expecting you around 6 pm."

"For the most part it was boring and uneventful," Nadene conceded, "but the registration clerk was obnoxious. Some of these government officials are entirely devoid of any social graces. It just seems to me that the Foresight Committee should have more empathic employees, even if they need to teach them. I mean, seriously, they could teach them a script."

Mona nodded her head in agreement but said little. She seemed distracted and Nadene wondered if the worried expression on her face foreshadowed some brewing battle. With that in mind, Nadene broached the silence, "You look tired and maybe a bit worried. I hope Alexander and Clio did not cause any trouble."

"Oh, no," Mona protested, "Your kids were almost angels." A faint smile lit her face but almost instantly vanished as she continued, "Curt came by when you were gone. He only stayed for a moment at the door but he was so mad. I told him you would be back around 6 pm and then he left in a huff. So, I can look forward to another night at the fights."

Nadene always felt guilty after talking with Mona and this brief exchange was no different. "Would it help if I went back with you now? It's only 5 pm and I could use the visit to familiarize myself with your apartment when I come over tomorrow to watch Jonathan."

Nadene was caught off guard by Mona's response. "I was hoping I could bring Jonathan over to your apartment tomorrow. I'm sure Curt would not approve of two more children coming over to where we live – not even for a few hours."

Such frank disclosures were unsettling and Nadene's discomfort was growing. "Please bring Jonathan over here tomorrow." And with an abruptness that seemed appropriate Nadene added," Thank you again for your help today and since I got back early you should be home well before 6 pm."

"That may soften my reception," Mona wistfully added, and without further delay, she was gone.

Chapter Two – Conflict

A bullet whizzed by barely missing Major Lane's head. In a war, without boundaries, Lloyd had come to expect the unexpected but his brush with death was still unnerving. As he slumped to the ground Colonel Roderick rushed to his aid, unaware of the circumstances precipitating Lloyd's dramatic descent. Deep furrows darkened Roderick's brow in a visible and almost palpable demonstration of his anxiety, "What happened Lloyd? Are you injured?"

The prostrate man turned towards the speaker and with a vacant stare whispered, "I came so near to death. A stray bullet grazed my helmet…only an inch in any direction and I would be dead." With that admission, Lloyd reached to his left and picked up the helmet which the bullet had hurled from his head. He slowly moved his fingers across the helmet's scar; shuddering as a morbid memory magnified the wound.

For as long as he could remember a persistent, repetitious dream had invaded his sleep; yet it was not the redundancy that seared his memory. It was instead a vivid, ominous realism; almost as if fate had provided a glimpse of his future destiny.

The same dream had preceded Lloyd's close encounter on the battlefield by only a few weeks. Now dazed and stuporous, Lloyd's mind drifted and shifted between the dream and the acute trauma. In the dream, Lloyd was chasing a vehicle speeding down a dark, lonely road. A sense of urgency and fear propelled the dreamer but aside from this emotional propulsion, there was no explanation for the pursuit. This incongruity along with his fleet locomotion was never questioned.

Lloyd's dream always ended badly. As he came within striking distance of the vehicle a shadowy figure appeared in the rear window and at what seemed like point-blank range fired a weapon. There was a brilliant orange flash and a numbing sense of impact. Lloyd always awakened at this point with a sense of relief, sometimes disbelief, that he somehow survived the assault.

Try as he might, Lloyd could never forget the dream and over time simply accepted the disturbing vision as a clairvoyant insight. His more rational side dismissed the dream as wholly improbable setting the stage for a life-long tug of war that pitted his emotions versus reason.

Colonel Roderick knew nothing of Lloyd's internal strife as he helped the man regain his feet and composure. "Can you walk? Let me help you over to the forward field hospital."

The field hospital was only a few hundred meters distant, but their slow pace ensured a lengthy travail. Roderick was a tall, athletic man but the effort was quite taxing and when he came within shouting distance of the hospital he cried for help. Two nurses responded by sprinting across the barren ground and quickly relieved Roderick's burden.

Lloyd was gingerly placed in a bed in the field hospital and a doctor minutely examined the patient. By now, the fog had cleared, and Lloyd's famous impatience returned. It was a reassuring emergence greeted with relief by Roderick.

A crowd of well-wishers surrounded Lloyd as he struggled to a sitting position in his bed. As he scanned the group Lloyd recognized most but not all of the dozen or so people loosely clumped in a quiet, somewhat somber semicircle. "Come now," Lloyd demanded, "don't look so glum. I wasn't even injured. I was just a bit shell-shocked when a stray bullet hit my helmet and rang my proverbial bell."

Murmurs of mirth followed the patient's short monologue; mostly from a sense of relief that the man was on the mend. In a further attempt at reassurance, Lloyd swung his legs over the side of the bed and slowly assumed his six-foot posture. He swayed momentarily eliciting a gasp from a nurse who quickly rushed to his side and steadied his gait. Lloyd was visibly annoyed by the intrusion and claimed a chair near the bed while exclaiming, "Let me thank all of you for your show of concern and support but I am fine and we have patients here that need your attention. I will join you for some bedside visits after I have my morning coffee."

The crowd disassembled with a chuckle following Lloyd's polite but pointed reminder of their duties. Most would have preferred to linger rather than face the wards full of ill and injured service members, but they collectively understood the necessity to move on and in doing so left Lloyd alone.

A few minutes later Colonel Roderick, bearing two hot steaming cups of black coffee, took a seat near Lloyd and hesitantly inquired, "Are you feeling well enough to go over a few items? If not, I can come back later."

Lloyd took a sip of the hot beverage and for an instant reveled in the liquid's warm sensation, but he knew Roderick too well to dismiss the man's entreaties. "David," Lloyd began by using his boss' first name, "I am fine. I appreciate all of the attention, but it is rather embarrassing. It was just a minor blackout for a few seconds after a bullet hit my helmet."

Roderick accepted the explanation being eager to resume important business but privately retained some doubt about Lloyd's quick recovery. In any event, the present exigencies required the two men to compare notes and set the day's agenda. "We have no empty beds," Roderick began, "and more casualties are expected later today."

Aside from placing cots in the hallways, the only other option involved the grim task of triaging. "We can place 50 of our folding cots in the hallways," Lloyd offered, and anticipating Roderick's thinking he added, "and probably avoid any triaging."

Originally triaging was a pedantic procedure matching the level of care with treatment urgency as dictated by the seriousness of the patient's condition and prognosis. That changed as the sheer volume of sick and wounded service members swamped increasing strained medical resources. Triaging then morphed into a euphemism for euthanasia.

Thankfully it seemed that triaging was not needed as Lloyd and Roderick huddled in conversation. After a few minutes, more discussion Roderick reached over to his bedridden partner and helped him to his feet. With a supporting arm, Roderick helped Lloyd walk to the nearby canteen, and together they enjoyed a light dinner.

The night was fast approaching and, with the earlier repast rejuvenating the previously depleted pair, both went their separate ways. Lloyd returned to his quarters, threw himself on the bed, and before falling asleep long-forgotten memories invaded his mind.

With a faint smile, Lloyd recalled his graduation from a prestigious private military academy with honors. His academic interests centered on history and his research in that field focused on the social and humanitarian aspects of America's many wars. Of course, all cadets received instruction in military science and the school required their participation in the arts and sports. The young cadet fulfilled the arts obligation somewhat tangentially through creative writing and his athletic requirement as an adept center fielder on the school's baseball team.

Life at the military academy was difficult and, in the years, succeeding graduation Lloyd's thoughts often turned to how and why he survived the ordeal; privately conceding that his youth and naiveté buffered the experience. In weighing the pros and cons, Lloyd's mind inevitably drifted towards the negative experiences; a mental affliction that tinted distant memories with dysphoric shades.

Lloyd rationally acknowledged moments of pride, exultation, and accomplishment and could consciously enumerate many such examples. Perhaps foremost among the list was his academic prowess. Lloyd was smart and some would say even brilliant. Of course, the man himself credited this success to hard work which in his calculation was a substitute for a supposed innate intelligence possessed by others.

He invented a fairly unique system of study, and it was to this that Lloyd attributed his success. It began with taking copious notes during classroom lectures which became his trademark. Other cadets eschewed the practice or relied on notes generated from a roster of students in one of the many groups devoted to that task. The appeal to that practice was visible; the latter was on display as bored, disinterested cadets populated the classroom.

Lloyd consumed reams of paper. During his first year at the school, Lloyd joined one of the note-taking groups but found the results uneven with important material often neglected. Consequently, he took the almost heretical step of abandoning the group effort and striking out on his own. His pencil swiftly transferring the speaker's words to paper reinforced his learning and became the foundation for the next step in his learning system. It also attracted a mixture of curiosity, jealousy, and derision from the other cadets.

After dinner, Lloyd returned to his small room and began the next phase of the study. He placed the day's notes on his desk, carefully reviewed each, and then, on separate sheets of paper, set about designing questions based on the material. Hours would swiftly fly by as Lloyd created the questions followed by a review of the previous days' questions and answers. It was tedious but the activity focused his attention in an almost hypnotic fashion that drowned out extraneous thoughts and sounds.

The success of his approach was endlessly rewarded when the school's instructors publicly posted the cadets' scores. Lloyd was always among the top three in the highly competitive and at times contentious class of cadets. These memories carried with them a rosy glow; an affirmation of the man's competitive spirit and pleasure in winning.

Cadet Lloyd's time was nearly totally encumbered by his studies and when not in his room he could reliably be found at the school's library. He would select a cubicle far removed from the noisier patrons, and then with papers and books neatly placed for easy reference, settle in for long hours of study. As a consequence of the rigorous regimen Lloyd made few friends and to the extent possible avoided social get-togethers. This, when combined with his stellar academic record, earned the enmity of a rowdy clique.

Whenever his mind returned to those days at the military school one particularly noxious memory forced its way into Lloyd's consciousness as a most unwanted visitor. Unfortunately, this visitor could never be evicted, cleverly hiding in the deeper recesses of his mind and only surfacing in parallel with memories of those early school days. When it made its presence known the emotions and facts, tempered by the passage of many years, allowed the man to dispassionately analyze and rationalize the memory.

As Lloyd recalled, the events unfolded over a weekend and culminated late on Sunday. It all began innocently enough when loud music began pouring from a nearby room. Lloyd ignored the cacophony and as in the past expected the disruption to eventually fade away but this time was different. Incensed by his indifference, the musical cadets increased the decibels to an earsplitting level. Lloyd was agitated and walking briskly across the hall confronted the revelers; reminding them of the rules that forbid such loud noises. His intervention seemed effective and with the volume reduced to a manageable level Lloyd returned to his studies.

Sunday brought retribution. Like the day before, music blared from the room across the hall, and with a resolve buoyed by yesterday's success, Lloyd again requested their silence. The three offending cadets glared at Lloyd with the nearest angrily proclaiming, "you aren't in charge here and I am tired of your whining."

Lloyd quickly and correctly noted his antagonist's virulence but his emotions trampled his common sense, "if you don't turn the music down, I will report you to the section leader." He then started down the hallway and disappeared around the corner. Lloyd had no intention of reporting the cadets but wanted to leave his tormentors with that impression. In retrospect, it was a mistake since Lloyd did not anticipate the cadets' response.

It was later that day when Lloyd experienced the cadet's response. At the moment the insurrection broke, Lloyd was laying in the lower bunkbed lazily reading a book. A loud grating, scratching sound forced his attention to a commotion in the hallway. With a sense of bewilderment, Lloyd watched as two cadets rolled a large waste barrel to his room's threshold and then tilted the container: flooding the room with a torrent of water.

Several inches of water sloshed about the room but the cadets were not through. Striking an angry attitude, both advanced menacingly through the water-logged room, and with fists clenched they seemed determined to assault their foe. Lloyd retreated the few inches his position in the bed permitted and dared the pair to hit him.

News of the malicious prank spread quickly, and a senior cadet soon arrived on the scene and ordered the offending cadets to vacate the premises. They meekly did so, no doubt sensing the gravity of the looming disciplinary action. Lloyd took their departure as an opportunity to scoop up a few books and after wading through the water he directed his steps towards the library.

When Lloyd returned to his room later that evening the floor was dry and his tormentors' room was empty. As he later learned, both cadets were summarily suspended and after their disciplinary hearings, they were dismissed from the military school.

Lloyd's school reminiscences terminated with a fitful night's sleep. Reality abruptly returned when an overhead announcement signaled ward rounds. It was a traditional clinical practice with doctors, nurses, and aides meeting with every patient; an efficient method of monitoring their progress and adjusting as needed. Lloyd was an administrator but his presence at the clinical activity was appreciated by staff and patients alike.

Lloyd joined every group's ward rounding by rotating his attendance and through the course of a week managed to see every patient. The exercise was both rewarding and emotionally draining but it provided Lloyd firsthand knowledge of the organization's needs and armed with this information he spent the remainder of many days seeking supplies and other support.

When time permitted, Lloyd updated a personal journal that documented salient events. He intended to use the journal to write a comprehensive first-person account of the war but the bulging folder served as a depressing testimonial to what seemed to be an intractable conflict. Lloyd would never countenance calling the journal a diary but its recorded moments of emotional and personal revelations fit that definition as well as being secretly stowed in a dresser drawer.

There were times when Lloyd would thumb through the journal; reminiscing and even marveling at past entries often separated by a few paragraphs alternately describing the horrific, humorous, and humdrum events. The journal's contents encompassed personal observations, opinions, and origins of the great conflict all of which he figured was necessary for future readers curious about the cataclysmic conflict.

As with most wars, it started from an insignificant spark that ignited long-smoldering passions. It pitted east versus west in ways reminiscent of America's Civil War which forced painful personal reassessments and realignments as the conflict tested individual and family loyalties. Over the preceding decades, westward-oriented mass migration and an eastern importation of western values increasingly stressed the bilateral relationship.

In the beginning, politicians from both sides extolled the virtues of the cultural, economic, and educational exchanges. From a macroeconomic perspective, the western countries benefitted from an endless supply of inexpensive material goods while the eastern countries built enormous factories that reduced unemployment and increased their monetary reserves. Trade deficits surged in western countries and the hollowed-out manufacturing base was partially offset by technological innovations.

Flush with money, the eastern economies turned their attention to increasing their military dominance; regional at first but inescapably aimed at broader horizons. Western governments observed the trend but were collectively wary of upsetting supply chains that could cripple their economies. As might be imagined, eastern leaders exploited the passivity and aggressively challenged treaties and territories.

A creeping sense of inequity and exploitation slowly developed with both sides calculating the rising cost of the mutual exchanges in terms of a rising tide of nationalism. Politicians and military authorities rode the crest but like any popular wave, it was destined to crest and crash.

A coordinated series of terrorist attacks destabilized the uneasy status quo. Oil fields, pipelines, and storage containers were set ablaze in the middle-east and North America. Emergency crews toiled tirelessly to contain the damage but the terrorist's hit and run tactics foiled their efforts. Rumors ran rife blaming the attacks on environmental activists or secret agents from the eastern or western aligned countries.

The terrorists were disciplined, organized, and essentially invisible which strengthened suspicions of government collusion. Of course, both sides denied complicity but the attacks not only continued but grew more daring when offshore drilling rigs and heavy oil-laden container ships were attacked. With each ship damaged and drilling platform destroyed millions of gallons of oil eventually washed ashore; not only starving the world's hunger for the precious commodity but inflicting incalculable environmental damage.

As the oil supply dwindled the economic harm took a serious turn with factories idled, generating plants sidelined, and entire chemical industries decimated. Authorities mandated gasoline rationing in a desperate bid to support essential services but in doing so swaths of the service sector, such as discretionary travel and tourism, collapsed; leaving millions of people destitute.

Governments responded to the crisis with a mixture of restrictions such as rationing and costly social support programs. In both the east and west corruption eroded the public's trust and confidence when it became increasingly evident that a slim sliver of the privileged elite escaped the misery they imposed on the populace. These individuals always had a paycheck, accessible healthcare, fully stocked pantries, and absolute dominion. No one dared question the privileged few and when mentioned in the media they always received respectful attention.

Societies started fraying and buckling under the weight of denial, deprivation, and disobedience. At its height, in what seemed like a collective decision surreptitiously made by the western and eastern politicians, the governments rallied and united their citizens by blaming each other for their perilous predicament. Demonization inexorably led to military mobilization resulting in the Cataclysmic Conflict.

Patriotism was rediscovered in western nations with the news media taking the lead in promoting a newfound nationalism. Politicians sensed the advantages and hungry as ever for power joined the crusade from their offices. Social media increasingly censored dissenting opinions and calls for calmness.

Long lines became the norm at military recruitment centers as volunteers eagerly flocked to join one of the armed forces. While waiting their turn, the prospective recruits could hardly escape the posters adorning the walls; some excoriating the enemy while others praised the selfless and valorous recruits ready to defend western values.

It was a carefully orchestrated symphony of social propaganda that inextricably seduced men and women to forsake families, careers, and aspirations in exchange for a military uniform. At the time, no one seemed to notice or care about a developing schism in the demographics. By and large, the recruits hailed from rural communities with lesser numbers from the suburbs and densely populated cities. Men still accounted for the greater proportion of recruits; a group further defined by those with less than a college education.

Public educators tacitly supported the new nationalism but few among their ranks joined the armed forces. Only a trickle of recruits came from the colleges and universities. Military schools slowly increased their class sizes, but they too were cautious. When pressed, the schools of higher learning collectively responded with a belief that any conflict would be short and intense, with their heroes ultimately triumphant.

As a consequence, their support extended no further than partisan speeches, rallies, and endless exhortations advising the public to sacrifice evermore at the altar of western interests. An elite cadre of educators, politicians, professionals, and celebrities coalesced and alternatively persuaded and admonished others to enlist in the military. As a group, they took pride in seeing the long lines of young men and women waiting patiently at recruitment centers.

Of course, the enemy was aware of the growing threat as the western nations mobilized and assumed a more aggressive posture. Both sides relentlessly and resolutely became more strident with diplomacy the first casualty of the looming conflict. It was a dangerous time in human history awaiting a spark that would ignite a global war.

Leaves were just beginning to make their earthly descent in Missouri heralding the onset of autumn and cooler weather. Bright yellow, orange, and crimson leaves blanketed lawns in a beautiful patchwork quilt knitted by nature. The air was crisp and clean with cloudless blue skies. Autumn also signaled the advent of a cornucopia of festivals and holidays with their customs, crafts, and cuisines. Even the noises of war seemed to take notice and adopt almost reverential respect.

Fall's metamorphosis from a lush verdure to a kaleidoscopic collage warmed hearts despite the cooling temperatures. Even Lloyd, who prized pragmatism over passion, had a bounce in his step. He was now a senior cadet and with a bit, more leisure time could afford a glance at the color palette adorning the landscape.

Lloyd was reserved, not shy; a quiet behavior most often interpreted as strong-willed, tenacious, and sometimes as inflexible. Truth be told though; Lloyd had a bohemian streak which he consciously acknowledged and usually suppressed. When vented it released a charming and creative artistic air but at the same time wafted an iconoclastic breeze. It was his fierce individualism that kept him distant from most social milieus;

gatherings that Lloyd detested for their mindless conformity. Lloyd tacitly understood his personality and in idle moments sometimes wondered at his success in an organization that demanded unswerving fealty.

The Senior Military Ball was the social event of the year and all cadets attended the lavish and strictly formal affair. Lloyd liked the pageantry but silently abhorred the regimentation that was an emotional straight jacket. Lloyd also dreaded the prospect of inviting a woman to the Military Ball and was tortured by many sleepless nights obsessing about his timidity.

Serendipity rescued the man. One of Lloyd's friends was similarly afflicted but somehow managed to snag a date with a girl from a nearby college but it came with a hitch. She had a girlfriend who also wanted to go to the Military Ball and Alfred, Lloyd's benefactor, quickly seized the opportunity to arrange a blind date. Lloyd was relieved and his acceptance quelled the lingering anxiety and with that matter resolved he turned his attention back towards more mundane issues.

Nadene Homes eagerly anticipated the Military Ball but a deep skepticism about her escort gnawed away at her exuberance. She preferred the term escort as opposed to a date since the latter conferred an intimacy that she was mentally unwilling to accept given the almost business-like arrangement.

Nadene came from a military family and from watching her mother prepare for a formal event was thoroughly familiar with the pomp and circumstance. Even so, she felt it necessary to consult a book on military etiquette to reduce the risk of a possible faux pas. Nadene learned little from the reference which bolstered her confidence and with that, she went shopping for the perfect outfit.

Nadene principally relied on her family experiences and common sense to guide her shopping choices. First and foremost, Nadene implicitly understood her role was to honor the traditions and heritage of the military. This was not a high school prom where girls vied with each other in selecting a wardrobe. A formal Military Ball required a sophisticated, timeless, and classic look. According to Nadene's informed vision, decorum typically demanded floor-length ball gowns that were modest, relatively free-flowing, and certainly not form-hugging habitats. Neutral colors and minimal patterning added to the classic appeal. Military protocol demanded certain compliance and restraint but it still offered enough latitude that Nadene knew she could safely add some flair and fashion without being ostentatious.

Nadene and Natalie, the winsome pair planning their Military Ball ensembles, traveled to a nearby upscale shopping complex that offered a wide range of designer threads to choose from. They both shared similar sensitivities in making decisions about their wardrobe for the event which preempted haggling and rivalry. Neither were affluent and cost restraints fenced their enthusiasm within tight budget boundaries.

Several boutique shops catered to formal events and the women perused their line of apparel first. It soon became apparent that none offered the pizzaz desired and the price tags were simply prohibitive. With a sense of despair, Nadene and Natalie decided to take a break for lunch and reassess their plans.

A delicatessen offered a seemingly endless array of sandwiches and offered outdoor seating in the crisp autumn air; an invitation they enjoyed by themselves as other diners elected the warmer tables indoors. Their small table soon boasted two platters with large sandwiches, heaping portions of house-made potato chips, and two teapots. Nadene placed a sachet filled with Lapsang Souchong in the teapot and quietly enjoyed the smoky incense that curled forth.

After a few minutes, Nadene poured a cup of tea, added skim milk, and an artificial sweetener. She clasped the cup firmly and both her hands and mood warmed in response. Nadene took a sip of the hot beverage and simultaneously savored the flavor and aroma.

The sandwich almost seemed an afterthought but the once warm chips now cooled by the slight breeze were still crunchy and tasty. Their stationary outdoor posture soon caught up with both women who shivered ever so lightly and hurried their meal. Natalie picked up the paper bill and with a gesture to her friend hurried inside to warm up.

After lunch, Nadene suggested visiting the department stores; a mundane retreat from the costly designer shops but a more reasonable choice she reasoned. The first store was a disappointment and both women turned their steps towards a more upscale experience.

Passing quickly through the maze of cosmetic stalls and proceeding upstairs brought Nadene and Natalie to a large selection of women's clothing. Nadene's eye caught sight of a manikin regally adorned in a classic white gown, and she excitedly strode in that direction. Racks of multicolored dresses greeted her gaze as Nadene exclaimed to her friend, "Natalie, surely we can find something here!"

Nadene rifled through the racks and in short order amassed a collection of six dresses. With the garments in hand and a wave to Natalie, she entered a small dressing room. Two of the dresses were simply too small as she struggled with the zippers. Another two were too long and dragged on the floor. That left two competitors.

A floor-length light rose-colored gown with a snug lace bodice was the first contender. It fit well and tiny, discrete sequins added to the garment's flair. Even so, the remaining dress beckoned to Nadene; an ankle-length lime-colored gown with a vintage floral lace adorning an empire waist.

Nadene slowly oscillated in front of the mirror while examining the gown's flow, drape, and overall fit. The mirror in turn reflected a 21-year-old woman crowned by long chestnut brown hair with evanescent hints of crimson glinting under the lights, medium height, and just a few unwanted pounds. Modest make-up accented her dark green eyes which Nadene considered her most attractive feature.

Natalie was satisfied with her dress; a long sleeve and gradient-blue gown of shimmering satin and was looking forward to completing her wardrobe. "Nadene, are you happy with anything you tried on?" she inquired while standing outside.

"Yes," Nadene pertly replied, "I like the green gown. I will be out in just a minute."

The next few hours passed quickly as difficult decisions were made about shoes, jewelry, and perfume. It was getting dark when Nadene and Natalie happily concluded their shopping. Both were burdened by boxes and bags but a short stroll brought relief when the day's treasures were carefully deposited in Nadene's car.

Nadene and Natalie shared a small apartment within walking distance of the nearby state university. A short walk up one flight of stairs brought both women to their front door. With a grunt, Nadene dropped her packages to the floor and reaching into her purse withdrew the key and opened the door. Once inside, they separated and deposited their purchases in their respective bedrooms and soon were fast asleep as exhaustion from the day took its toll.

Lloyd always kept his uniforms in crisp condition, ready for an unannounced inspection, and the same applied to his dress blues. He had just bought a set of new gold epaulets bearing his rank as cadet captain. For the military ball, rules authorized the wearing of the red braid from the right shoulder signifying his elite status as an honor roll scholar. Since his uniform and accouterments were always pressed and clean the only task remaining was adding a high gloss to his dress shoes.

One of the first things any cadet learned was how to shine shoes. Sitting at his desk, Lloyd placed the black shoe polish and lighter in easy reach while he balanced a shoe on his left hand. A thick coat of polish was followed by the lighter warming and ever so slightly melting the wax. Lloyd then dipped a cloth in cold water and promptly proceeded to polish the wax. His efforts were rewarded by a high gloss. The full process was repeated multiple times until Lloyd was satisfied that he had a scuff-proof finish.

Lloyd's preparations for the military ball were now complete and he set the shoes aside. In a final step, he mentally ran through a checklist: the uniform was good to go and he had an escort.

Alfred sauntered into Lloyd's room and noticed the unmistakably pungent odor of melted wax and correctly guessed that his friend was getting ready for the military ball. Lloyd was known for his unerring planning and Alfred's offhand comment was intended as nothing more than a bit of prattle, but the response surprised him. "What sort of corsage did you get?" Lloyd visibly blushed at the question and stammered, "I, I guess I forgot that. I hope I can still get one." And with that, he rushed from the room and ran to the florist's shop.

Breathless from sprinting, Lloyd swung the store's door open, alarming the young woman inside. "For the military ball, are there any corsages left?" The florist immediately understood Lloyd's concern and calmly replied, "yes, we always keep an ample supply. Can I show you some examples?"

"Please do," the relieved cadet politely responded.

The florist disappeared for a few moments and returned with an assortment of corsages. It was a dizzying collection and Lloyd had no idea what to do. "How well do you know your date for the military ball?" the florist asked recognizing the man's blankness.

"Not at all," the embarrassed cadet admitted.

"In that case, I would suggest a wrist corsage. This one with ivory rose, white ribbon and greenery presents a classic look and should complement any gown."

Lloyd accepted the recommendation, paid the florist, and left with a profound sense of relief. He carefully placed the corsage in the small refrigerator in his room. Finally, everything was done.

Lloyd called Nadene the next day and after a few pleasantries innocently inquired, "Are you somewhat familiar with a military ball?"

Nadene correctly interpreted the apprehension, "yes, I am from a military family. I also attended last year's ball. I look forward to this one!"

Lloyd was glad and with a rare bit of exuberance exclaimed "That's great! I look forward to meeting you. Can I pick you up at 6 pm tomorrow?" Nadene agreed and both awaited their in-person introductions.

Lloyd's military school did not permit cadets to own vehicles so taking a taxi was his main mode of transportation. Cadets also received a discount which made the ride even more palatable.

Nadene's apartment was only a few miles distant from the military school but traffic was heavy so Lloyd settled into the worn backseat for the ride. Looking out the window he mused about what Nadene might look like and while not expecting much he was grateful she agreed to accompany him. Thirty minutes later he arrived and carefully picked up the corsage, paid the taxi driver, and made his way upstairs.

After verifying the apartment number Lloyd tapped briskly on the door and awaited a response. He listened intently and, in a few moments, heard a rushed rustle approaching, no doubt the woman's gown he concluded, and then the door opened.

Lloyd caught his breath as Nadene stood before him. Her dark eyes met his gaze and she softly responded, "You must be Lloyd."

Nadene's attractiveness had caught him off guard and for what seemed like forever he fumbled for a reply before regaining his composure. "I am indeed Lloyd and it is my honor to escort you to the military ball and I also hope that this wrist corsage will compliment your beautiful gown."

It was now Nadene's turn to be embarrassed by her date's tribute. She held out her left hand and Lloyd deftly placed the corsage around her wrist. With sly glances, Nadene had to admit that Lloyd was extraordinarily handsome and recognizing the accouterments was additionally impressed by his scholarship and cadet rank.

Fortunately, the apartment complex had an elevator; avoiding what would have been an ungainly traverse down the stairs. Lloyd quickly flagged a taxi and soon both were on their way to the military ball. For a moment he regretted not hiring a limousine but taxis were acceptable as evidenced by vehicles waiting in line to deposit couples at the auditorium where the military ball was held.

During the 45-minute journey, Nadene and Lloyd exchanged personal information. She described her interest in library science; centered around two seemingly incongruous areas of information technology and children's literature. She also worked at the circulation desk at the university's main campus library.

Lloyd discussed his interests in military science, healthcare, and history. He particularly enjoyed reading about the more human aspects of military history as opposed to the various tactics and strategies involved in the various campaigns.

Nadene and Lloyd completely lost track of time and were startled when the taxi driver turned towards the back seat and testily asked, "Are you two getting out?"

"Yes, sorry," the sheepish cadet responded and after paying the driver quickly jumped out and gallantly opened Nadene's door.

A short walk brought the pair to the military ball's festive entryway, and they took their place in the receiving line.

As he approached the military ball's adjutant Lloyd stated, "I have the honor to introduce myself cadet Captain Lloyd Lane and Nadene Homes." The adjutant passed their names to the next person in the receiving line and Nadene and Lloyd made their way slowly along. At the end of the receiving line Lloyd shook hands with the school's commandant and along with Nadene was escorted to their table.

Rank and class year determined the seating. Lloyd and Nadene were seated at the front-most table directly within sight of the commandant and his staff. All-in-all it was a gracious event with good but not extraordinary food and non-alcoholic drinks. Nadene was comfortable throughout and clearly understood the protocol. Lloyd was entranced by her charming composure and easy social graces which complemented his military bearing.

With his closing salutations, the commandant thanked everyone for attending and the gathering slowly departed the auditorium. Lloyd joined the queue for a taxi and after a short interval, Nadene joined him in the drive back to her apartment.

Nadene thanked Lloyd for a lovely night and the journey was otherwise marked by idle chit-chat. Lloyd walked Nadene to her apartment door and before departing asked the young woman if she would like to meet again. Nadene could scarcely contain her eagerness, "I would love to. Maybe next Saturday?"

"That is perfect. Let's make a day of it. I will come by at 9 am," Lloyd suggested.

Nadene quickly accepted the proposal and their first date was set.

It was dark in her apartment which told Nadene that her roommate had not yet returned from the military ball. Even though it was late, the woman was still glowing from the night's social event and was far too energized to contemplate sleep. She decided to make a pot of tea, watch a game show on the television, and wait to hear about Natalie's night.

Nadene was sipping her tea when a rattle at the door hinted at her roommate's arrival. She turned towards the door in anticipation and watched as Natalie exuberantly sashayed in. The television was now a distraction and Nadene turned it off fully expecting Natalie's review of the military ball to fill the void.

"I had a wonderful night," Natalie breathlessly admitted. "The pageantry, music, and even the food were so delicious."

Nadene could not help but notice the omission. "How was your date?"

"He seemed more interested in himself than me. I couldn't count the number of times he left me alone to hobnob with another cadet or the cadre."

Nadene thought for a moment before replying. "Well, I guess that is a disappointment, but I am used to that growing up in a military family. These social events are first and foremost for the cadets to honor military traditions but even so, it sounds like your date could have been a bit more attentive."

"Oh, well," Natalie complained with a sigh, "there will be other balls and other cadets but how was your date?"

"I was pleasantly surprised," the woman exclaimed. "We even made another date."

"Lucky you," conceded her roommate.

"Yes, I guess I am, but I must admit that I am tired now," Nadene said as she began preparing for a night's slumber.

Just before turning the lights off Nadene turned the television back on waiting for her roommate to also be ready for bed. As the screen flickered to life a somber announcer intoned, "An explosion at the airport killed at least 20 people but many more were seriously injured. No one has claimed responsibility. Law enforcement is on the scene and we hope to have more information soon."

Both women awakened the next day refreshed and while munching on toasted bagels washed down with hot tea listened to the news. Although it seemed odd and premature the chief law enforcement investigator assured the audience that the explosion was not a terrorist attack but was a kitchen gas leak ignited by a careless worker. Following that brief report, the subsequent news cycles made no mention of the explosion.

The week passed quickly; accelerated by Nadene's eagerness about her date with Lloyd on Saturday. She had no idea what the day would offer but she had a quiet conviction that it would be a pleasant affair.

Lloyd arrived on time and after greeting, Nadene tantalized her. "I have a taxi waiting to take us for a short drive."

"Where are we going?" Nadene naturally inquired.

"That is a surprise. I just hope you are not afraid of heights!" Lloyd answered, which only added to the mystery.

The taxi swiftly navigated through the dense traffic and in doing so invited a constant blare of horns from irritated drivers and moments of panic from the occupants. With palpable relief, the taxis pulled to a sudden stop just outside a low building with a faded sign marked, Fixed Base Operator. Nadene was puzzled but a sense of mystery and excitement encouraged her quick exit from the taxi.

Lloyd retrieved his small rectangular bag which up to this point had attracted no attention and removed some papers while entering the building. He approached the counter and after a brief discussion with the attendant invited Nadene to accompany him on a short stroll.

At this point, Nadene correctly surmised that her surprise had something to with airplanes. Lloyd entered a hangar and after matching his documents with the numerous airplanes opened the door of a small two-seat, fixed-wing aircraft. "Are you ready for an excursion?" he asked.

Nadene softly gasped, "Are you a pilot?"

"I am and I just filed a flight plan for a trip over the ocean."

"Oh, my," Nadene responded, "I did not know you were a pilot. This looks like an adventure."

"I hope you like it," Lloyd sincerely added, "and once we are out of the traffic control area and our altitude is around 5,000 feet, I will let you take the controls."

Both were now seated in the aircraft, with barely a foot between them, as Lloyd went through a pre-flight check in preparation for the day's journey. Everything checked out and after contacting the control tower, he began taxiing to the runway. After holding short of the runway for a few minutes, the control tower permitted the little aircraft to take off.

Lloyd advanced the throttle and the spritely machine responded with vigor, accelerating rapidly down the runway. After a few moments, Lloyd gently pulled the control wheel back and Nadene watched as the aircraft left the ground. It took a while for the plane to reach the desired altitude but when it did the ocean was clearly in view.

Above the cabin's noise, Lloyd loudly inquired, "Are you ready to take over?"

Nadene eagerly and a bit anxiously replied, "Yes, as long as you help me. I don't want to crash."

Lloyd chuckled and after a minor trim adjustment asked Nadene to slowly turn the control wheel to the left. She did so while at the same time Lloyd actuated the rudder pedals. The aircraft moved in a lazy arc before Lloyd returned the aircraft to a straight and level course. Over the next half hour, Lloyd demonstrated the basic aircraft controls. Nadene was a quick learner and at the end of the instruction, she thoroughly impressed her teacher with her new skills.

They were about twenty minutes from the airport and Lloyd figured it was time to return, promising Nadene that on a future trip they would land on a deserted stretch of beach. When he was about ten minutes away Lloyd contacted the control tower for landing instructions. Remarkably, there was little traffic, and the control tower permitted the little plane to land immediately.

After returning the aircraft to its hangar Lloyd asked, "are you hungry? I thought we could get a pizza."

Nadene was famished after the exhilarating flight, "That would be great. And maybe a salad too!"

Lloyd was looking forward to graduation. He was tired of classes and ready to exchange academic routines for military service. Being at the top of his year group conferred advantages one of which ensured his choice of assignment. Long ago he had decided that the medical service corps was his first choice followed by air defense artillery. He liked the humanity of the first and the precision of the latter. Lloyd also harbored dreams of pursuing medical school, but the current regulations forbid graduate studies until the completion of a utilization tour.

Roughly three months before graduation was when cadets expected their branch and location assignments. With the winter now blanketing the campus with ice and snow, Lloyd had another few months of anxious expectation before learning his fate. The time went quickly and weekends with Nadene seemed to compress the trajectory.

To his fellow cadets, the infatuation with Nadene provoked good-natured banter in as much as they correctly concluded that Lloyd was thoroughly captivated by the young woman. Their relationship had entered a comfortable phase where awkward posturing gave way to a quiet, open acceptance. As their relationship matured Lloyd was impressed with Nadene's sagacity; not yet quite realizing that her unassuming nature and common sense was an antidote to his occasional temerarious eruptions.

Cold weather seemed to linger that year even though the calendar announced the arrival of spring. Early spring flowers rebuked the temperatures with snowdrops, daffodils, and even some brave tulips reaching for the sun. Among the trees, the large white magnolia blooms glowed against the blue sky and tabebuia trees sported yellow trumpet flowers.

Lloyd and Nadene loved the changing of the season with colorful flowers and fragrant scents filling the air. A walk through the nearby botanical garden was an especially enjoyable pastime and perhaps it was the enchantment with nature's rebirth that persuaded Lloyd to act.

They had just finished dinner at a Mexican restaurant and were waiting for the check. In what seemed impetuous, Lloyd leaned slightly across the table and announced, "We should get married."

It was delivered by the man, and received by Nadene, as a proclamation and not a question. Where other women might have been offended, Nadene had long ago reached the same conclusion and without a moment's hesitation simply replied, "yes."

Lloyd had meager finances but managed to save enough money to buy Nadene a promise ring. It was a small diamond set in a sterling silver mount with a glitter entirely eclipsed by the sparkle in Nadene's eyes as she proudly accepted the ring.

Natalie was simultaneously happy, sad, and even a bit jealous of her roommate's engagement. Her sadness and jealousy were two-pronged; triggered by the looming loss of her roommate and the realization that romance had so far alluded her. In any event, the emotional twinges were fleeting and Natalie quickly reestablished her ebullient equilibrium and looked forward to helping Nadene with the marriage's details.

Nadene's parents were not surprised. Her open and honest lines of communication with her family left little doubt in their minds as to the eventual outcome. A local newspaper in Nadene's hometown reported the engagement and the summer wedding.

Perhaps surprisingly, Lloyd had little interest in a formal military wedding although he never mentioned this to his betrothed. Nadene preferred a simple wedding, but not knowing her fiancé's wishes, cautiously suggested the wedding ceremony take place in one of their families' homes. Much to her relief Lloyd agreed, leaving the pair to navigate the location with their respective parents.

Lloyd's parents were tactful and circumspect in discussing the matter although a subterranean current seemed to pull the deliberations towards a military affair. Their son resisted the congenial drift as the conversation ebbed and flowed from formal to informal before finally cresting and culminating in a decision for an outdoor wedding at Nadene's home.

Nadene was a mid-west girl raised in a small town in southern Missouri. Family and religion were traditions strongly supported in the community and the decision to host a wedding, even though not a traditional church ceremony, was greeted with approval from Nadene's immediate and extended family.

Finishing military school left the soon-to-be-married cadet little time to assist in the ceremony's preparations. Nadene kept him up to date on the progression which Lloyd in turn passed along to his family.

A series of events unfolded together in late spring. Lloyd scraped together a sizeable sum of money through personal budget tightening and a gift from his parents which permitted the man to purchase a more suitable engagement ring. It too was a diamond but much bigger and was set in a classy white gold solitaire setting.

Fortunately, Lloyd had enough money left over so the pair could shop for their wedding rings. Nadene wanted a distinctive look, eschewing the banality of a gold ring. A patient jeweler presented a dozen choices none of which struck her fancy. She was on the verge of quitting when a stray glance landed on a green gemstone.

Nadene pointed to the gemstone and asked, "what is that ring?"

The jeweler retrieved the case containing the ring, "Do you mean this one?" he said while at the same time explaining, "this is a custom-made jade ring."

Nadene thought for a moment and quizzed Lloyd, "What do you think? I like it. It is unique and you know jade is supposed to bring good luck."

Lloyd was more invested in pleasing the woman than deciding on a specific stone and with a lighthearted note responded, "I think it will match my green uniform!"

The jeweler took the brief exchange as an agreement. "It will take about a week to cut the jade and set the stone in a gold band. The first step is to carefully measure your fingers."

After leaving a deposit, Lloyd and Nadene celebrated their decision with a quick lunch. They parted company for the balance of the week as other realities intruded. Final exams awaited Nadene and she wanted to maintain her high scholastic standing. Lloyd faced a similar situation and could not afford any distraction that might imperil his class standing.

Graduating military cadets anxiously awaited their career assignments. Over the years, the school had vacillated between publicly posting the results en masse or privately with a career counselor. The former method had detractors complaining that the group release was insensitive since cadets were naturally competitive. Those ranked at the bottom of the list and assigned less desirable assignments faced overt or, perhaps even worse, covert ridicule.

For the past few years, the military school opted for private revelations. Lloyd received his notice to meet with a career counselor in May; a pending appointment filled with anxiety and hopeful expectations. He passed the news along to Nadene who confidently predicted his first choices.

Captain Alexander was a young army officer newly assigned to the school. In addition to his counseling role, Alexander taught military history and was familiar with Lloyd's avid interest in the subject. The two met on a Friday afternoon and after exchanging pleasantries the senior officer began, "Let us move to the purpose for this meeting. As you know, the

Commandant just released the graduating cadet's assignments, and I can now discuss that with you."

"Please do so," was Lloyd's muted reply. "I must admit I am a bit nervous."

"Based on your proclivities I think you will be pleased," Alexander suggested while at the same time noticing the cadet relax. "You will be assigned to the medical service corps and serve your first tour of duty at the military hospital in Georgia. The hospital commander is Lieutenant Colonel David Roderick. You will report directly to him in your capacity as commander of the hospital's medical management unit."

"That sounds wonderful," the ecstatic cadet exclaimed. "I have heard good things about Lieutenant Colonel Roderick, and I look forward to working with him."

Lloyd left the meeting with Captain Alexander eager to share the good news with Nadene. With his opening line, he teased the woman, "how would you like to live in Georgia?"

"Now you are teasing me!" she admitted. "Now please tell me the rest."

"I will be a medical service corps officer in charge of the medical management unit at Lieutenant Colonel Roderick's hospital in Georgia," Lloyd proudly relayed.

Nadene could scarcely contain her excitement. "Oh! I knew you would get a great assignment," and, "yes," she coyly added, "I would love to go to Georgia with you."

Following a moment's reflection, she wondered aloud, "what is a medical management unit?"

Lloyd took the entreaty as an opportunity to expound on his upcoming assignment. "A medical management unit or medical holding company is where soldiers awaiting the results of a fitness for duty determination live. Most of these soldiers have been hospitalized for medical or emotional conditions and their treatment teams have submitted their cases to a physical evaluation board. That board will review their medical records and decide whether or not to place the soldier on retired disability status. It generally takes several months and during that time the soldier is attached to the medical management unit."

Nadene listened attentively to Lloyd's narrative and correctly guessed, "it sounds like an assignment where you can learn about medical practice and maybe figure out whether you want to pursue a medical degree."

"Yes," Lloyd agreed, "and at the same time hone my skills as a leader."

The next few months were a whirlwind of activity as marriage, school graduation for Nadene and Lloyd, and moving to Georgia dominated their every free moment. Neither one sacrificed their studies in a determined effort to maintain their academic standings. As a consequence, planning for the marriage was relegated to a second-tier status but their families help fill the void. Arranging the move was the least stressful activity since Nadene and Lloyd jointly had but the barest material possessions.

Nadene proposed and Lloyd agreed that their marriage should take place a few days after graduation. The military authorized sixty days between graduation and reporting to an assignment so this consideration provided a valuable buffer during which marriage, honeymoon, and the final coordination of the trip to Georgia could be realized.

Time slipped by quickly. Fortunately, Nadene's graduation preceded Lloyd's graduation by three days which allowed their respective parents to attend both while staying at a local hotel in the interim. For a moment, Nadene thought about skipping her graduation but Lloyd counseled otherwise suggesting that her parents would be disappointed. She reconsidered her initial opposition after mulling over Lloyd's sage advice and her beaming countenance as she strode across the stage receiving her diploma was savored by all in attendance.

Lloyd's graduation was an elaborate event filled with military tradition and stirring patriotic speeches. The Commandant conferred special honors on selected cadets, Lloyd included, recognizing their academic and leadership prowess and at the same time officially announced their forthcoming military assignments.

After the ceremonies, Nadene and Lloyd along with their parents celebrated at a local restaurant. Before parting company, each graduate received a bevy of useful gifts. They would all be reunited in one short week at Nadene's home for the marriage ceremony.

After their graduations, Nadene and Lloyd traveled to their respective homes. It was a painful parting but a reunion in one week softened the separation. Lloyd arrived home after taking a short airplane trip and immediately phoned Nadene. She too was at home and they spent several minutes discussing the details of their marriage ceremony and honeymoon.

Nadene's vision for the honeymoon was a luxury ocean cruise. Lloyd preferred a more adventurous destination and suggested a trip to Switzerland. Once there they could ski the tallest mountains during the day and enjoy fine dining at night. Lloyd had researched the various ski resorts and was convinced that several offered the ideal mix of luxurious accommodations and top-notch skiing. Package rates include the ski equipment, lift tickets, room, and all meals.

Nadene countered his proposal, "I like the idea of some activity. If we take the cruise, we could go scuba diving from any of the islands. It's not very expensive and one island, in particular, has shipwrecks in fairly shallow water that would make a super interesting dive. We're both trained in shipwreck diving so it would be an opportunity to sharpen our skills. For whatever reason, cruising is not very popular, and we can get some really good last-minute deals."

An awkward moment's silence followed Nadene's expostulation, finally relieved when Lloyd remarked, "Well, as much as I would like the ski trip, I think we would probably have the best luck getting a good deal on a cruise so let's do that."

Lloyd spent the next day searching seven-day cruises and settled on two before calling Nadene. Towards that evening he revealed the choices, "I found two cruises that are reasonably priced. One travels in the Caribbean and the other goes to the Yucatan and has several shore excursions to Mayan ruins. They both have scuba diving."

"Do you have a preference," Nadene queried and without waiting for a reply, "I like the Yucatan trip. We can explore the local history and go scuba diving. I also like Mexican food!"

"That was my first choice too," Lloyd admitted. "I will make the reservation tomorrow. They still have nice cabins with ocean view verandahs, and I thought we could splurge on one of those."

Nadene agreed and after some updates on the marriage, Nadene wondered, "who is your best man?"

"I asked Anthony Lukin. We were good friends at school. He agreed so that is all set. He plans to arrive a day before the ceremony."

"Where is his assignment?" she asked.

"He will be joining an infantry unit as a platoon leader overseas." Lloyd said and further noted, "He plans to leave shortly after we return from our honeymoon. I invited him to stop by in Georgia before he leaves which worked out well. He can catch a military transport from there."

With only three days remaining before the marriage, Lloyd and his parents began the trek to Nadene's home. They decided on a leisurely two-day drive as a more economical choice; even though Lloyd quietly hoped they would not be delayed. Fortunately, traffic was fairly light, and the traveling party arrived a day before the ceremony.

Worries about the weather dampening the outdoor ceremony faded in the bright, warm light. Not a cloud was in sight; taken by Nadene as a sunny forecast of a blissful future. The simple ceremony and reception occupied the midmorning and at its conclusion, the newly married couple took a taxi to the airport. After a three-hour flight, they began their weeklong honeymoon.

When making the cruise reservation the clerk asked if this was a special occasion. Lloyd had no desire to draw attention to their status and declined the opportunity to promote their honeymoon. As it later became known, however, both of their parents secretively conspired to alert the cruise staff and at the same time add amenities such as generous shipboard credit and an upgraded cabin.

Warm breezes wafted across the verandah as the newly married couple enjoyed the blue-green water with small whitecaps cresting in the distance. Fluffy clouds dotted the horizon with gray bottoms heralding stormy weather. Nadene lazily looked at her watch and then with an exclamation, "Lloyd, if we don't hurry down to the buffet we will miss out on lunch."

After closing the balcony door, they both hurried to the Lido deck, grabbed a plate, and sped down the buffet line. It was a delectable meal and after a cup of tea, they decided to take a stroll on the outside decks.

Opening a door to the outside passageway proved to be a herculean task with a strong wind impeding Lloyd's effort. Once outside, rain splattered across the desk and Nadene huddled closer to Lloyd but neither retreated inside. The ship rolled in the turbulent sea and Nadene and Lloyd prudently steered clear of the railing even as they were getting drenched. Curious eyes from onlookers inside the ship peeked at the couple; some nodding their disapproval at the pair's antics.

The ship's stern offered some protection from the inclement weather and a relatively dry perch from which to observe the frothy wake. Even so, Nadene was soaked and shivering; the signal to return inside. They noisily sloshed to their cabin and once again suffered unwelcome attention. After a quick, hot shower and dry clothes, they headed to the Tip-Top lounge for some hot tea and cookies.

Their port of call was Progresso; reached after two ocean days. Insufferably hot winds swept across the gangway as Nadene, and Lloyd joined a small excursion to the Mayan ruins at Chichen Itza. Despite the soaring temperatures and oppressive humidity Nadene and Lloyd explored every nook and cranny.

On the way back to the ship Nadene remembered, "Tomorrow we go diving in a cenote. I'm glad you contacted the company when you booked the cruise. It's so busy here we might have missed out."

"The tour operator is supposed to meet us just outside the gangway. I guess they will have a sign with our name to identify them." Lloyd added.

Once back on board the ship, Nadene and Lloyd dressed for dinner. Tonight, they would sample the main dining room, having opted previously for the informality of the evening buffets. The service was impeccable and the meal acceptable, but both agreed that the three-hour dining experience was too long.

Nearly everyone attended the cabaret show in the theater following their dinner but Nadene and Lloyd skipped the noisy venue preferring a quiet walk on the outside deck instead. Moonlight rippled across the gentle waves and a distant ship cast an eerie glow on the coming fog. A few trips around the ship and they retired to the secluded sanctuary of their cabin.

Now mid-way through their cruise, Nadene and Lloyd once again descended the ship's stairs and briskly walked across the gangway eagerly searching for the scuba operator. A bright yellow placard, with their names misspelled, was setting on the hood of a small, rather battered cargo van.

Nadene had wondered just how safe this scuba operator was and the dilapidated vehicle was not reassuring. Their tour operator greeted them enthusiastically, and perhaps sensing their trepidations, pointed to his scuba certification pasted on the windshield as Nadene and Lloyd took a seat.

After a bumpy 30-minute ride the van came to a stop outside a ramshackle building littered with scuba tanks and regulators. Their host beckoned them inside where they were greeted by a dark-haired, athletic woman. "Welcome to Scuba Pro. Before we travel to one of the larger cenotes in the area, we need to get you fitted with your tank, regulator, buoyancy compensator, 5mm wetsuit, and weights. Did you bring your mask and snorkel?"

Lloyd spoke up, "Yes, I have them both in our scuba bag."

"That's good," the woman said.

Nadene was impressed with the quality of the equipment. It was modern and well maintained. As she later learned, the older gear was left outside and sold to the locals.

The tour staff loaded the equipment into the van and Nadene and Lloyd resumed their uncomfortable seats. They soon arrived at their destination, donned their gear, and after a briefing by the scuba guide, entered the crystal-clear cenote.

The cave structures were softly illuminated from above and the light danced over the rock formations in a mesmerizing display. Their cave guide kept a close watch on Nadene and Lloyd and would periodically point out interesting sights. Thirty minutes later the guide gestured for both to surface.

A box lunch filled both the divers and the time required to traverse the road to the second and final dive site. It was equally spectacular, and it was not until they surfaced that Nadene noticed how fatigued she was. Even the worn, rough seats were a welcome relief as they journeyed back to the ship.

Fortunately, they arrived in time for dinner. Both were famished and filled their plates with generous helpings of the fare.

Desserts were a specialty of the cruise line and did not disappoint the diners.

The remainder of the cruise was at sea; a relaxing time after the strenuous shore activities. Disembarkation was uneventful and the newlyweds made their way to the local airport for the short flight to their new home in Georgia.

Lloyd had the choice of a house on the army post or, with a waiver, a rental in the nearby city. Nadene did not want to live on post and Lloyd agreed. With that decision, their military sponsor had suggested some local housing options. Nadene opted for a three-bedroom townhouse in a tony neighborhood, and it was to that location that they spent their first night in Georgia.

Lloyd was sound asleep when the telephone rudely awakened him. Fumbling in the dark, he reached for the telephone and with a touch of irritation, "hello, who is calling?"

"I am Anthony Lukin's father. I am so sorry to call you, but I have some really sad news."

Chapter Three – Escalation

Dazed and momentarily disoriented, Lloyd simultaneously glanced at the clock reading 2 am and reached for the phone on his bedside table. Nadene stirred but did not awaken as her husband talked on the phone. "You said you were Anthony's father, right?"

"Yes," came the subdued reply, "First let me thank you for asking Anthony to be your best man. It meant a lot to him."

There was something in the man's tone that alarmed Lloyd, "You said something about the sad news."

An audible sigh followed Lloyd's prompting, "Anthony is dead," the man choked.

The response startled and numbed Lloyd and for what seemed an eternity he struggled for the right response before simply asking, "What happened?"

Emotional, Anthony's father reported, "He was spending some time with us at home before returning. He left last night on a flight to Florida and the plane blew up shortly after takeoff. We were notified several hours later."

Nadene was now awake and from her husband's voice sensed something was wrong. She gently nudged the man to get his attention. "Who are you talking to?"

Lloyd turned towards his wife and somberly said, "Anthony Lunkin's father. He just learned that Anthony was killed when his airplane blew up."

With a profound sense of sorrow, Nadene suddenly seized the phone from her husband, "Mr. Lukin, I am so sorry to hear this dreadful news. Anthony was such a wonderful person. Is there anything we can do?"

"No but thank you for your kindness," he said, and as an afterthought added, "We will let you know about the funeral."

For the remainder of the night, neither Nadene nor Lloyd could go back to sleep. They talked for a few minutes but concluded that the subject was just too painful to dwell on. Nadene busied herself with making Lloyd's breakfast after which they both silently consumed the light meal. Later that morning, they both watched the televised coverage of the airliner's explosion.

A solemn reporter summarized what was known, "Law enforcement is investigating the scene of the crash. Debris is scattered across a large area and drenching rain is hampering their efforts. We have unconfirmed reports that an eastern nation is claiming credit for the attack in response to crippling sanctions levied by the US Government. They promise more attacks if the sanctions are not immediately lifted. We hope to learn more as the investigations unfold."

Lloyd was tired and still reeling from the news of his friend's death when Nadene exclaimed, "Lloyd, do you see what time it is? You need to meet with Colonel Roderick in an hour."

In a few frantic minutes, Lloyd donned his camouflage jacket and rushed outside. As he settled into his car, Lloyd was thankful that he had previously taken a test drive to the hospital; fearing that the new geography might contribute to an unwelcome delay. The prior practice drive reduced his anxiety and he uneventfully arrived at the hospital with fifteen minutes to spare.

Lloyd entered the hospital, announced his presence and purpose at the welcome desk, and waited while an enlisted soldier called Colonel Roderick. While consciously controlling his posture to avoid any semblance of anxiety ten minutes passed before Roderick appeared in person.

Roderick was an imposing man; standing a bit over six feet tall, with jet black hair, vivid blue eyes that seemed to bore through a person's soul, a fit, athletic but not overly muscular build, and an affable, disarming smile. Lloyd was instantly impressed by the man's military bearing which exuded confidence and deserved respect.

In a simple, direct, and warm tone, Roderick addressed Lloyd, "I am glad to meet you, Lieutenant Lane. Let's go to my office."

Lloyd dutifully followed the man and was soon ushered into the Commander's office; a large but unpretentious, utilitarian space. A polished wood desk, two chairs, a leather sofa, and a coffee table were the main pieces of furniture. Books filled shelves behind the desk and neatly aligned diplomas, certificates, and awards illustrated the walls.

Roderick invited Lloyd to take a seat on the sofa while he brought one of the two chairs next to the coffee table. Lloyd was nervous but betrayed no evidence of his anxiety but grew curious when his host examined the contents of a folder on the coffee table.

"Your school record is impressive," Roderick commented as he leafed through the documents. "I look forward to your leadership of the medical management unit. It can be a challenging but rewarding command."

At this point, Lloyd noticed a change in Roderick's congeniality as the man's attitude assumed a more serious, formal manner. "I assume you heard about the terrorist attack on the civilian airliner."

Up to this time, Lloyd's exclusive focus on making a good first impression had vanquished all thoughts of the attack and his friend's death. Struggling to restrain the welling emotions Lloyd's voice cracked as he responded, "Yes sir, I listened to the news coverage earlier this morning."

The astute commander instantly assessed Lloyd's discomfiture and gently probed, "You seem upset."

Like a pin pricking a balloon, Lloyd burst forth, "I first learned about this from the father of my best friend and best man at my wedding. Anthony – that was his name – was on board that flight. It's so hard to believe that just a short time ago we were together."

Roderick was quiet after this disclosure; an opportune interlude that allowed both to calibrate their next steps. For his part, Lloyd quickly reestablished his equilibrium and with an apologetic tone, "I hope I can take a day off to attend the funeral."

"That won't be a problem," Roderick acknowledged, "and in fact, I would expect your attendance."

Lloyd left the meeting with the hospital commander with mixed emotions. On the one hand, he admired Roderick's leadership style and genuine empathy but in weighing his performance he was disappointed. Lloyd worried that his emotional response to Anthony's death betrayed a weakness that Roderick would judge negatively. In the coming months as their relationship matured Lloyd would learn just the opposite.

Nadene was excited. She just learned that an eagerly anticipated job interview was scheduled for later in the week. When Lloyd returned home, she could scarcely contain her enthusiasm, "I have an interview at the college library!" she expostulated, "and there are two positions available for reference librarians, so I hope I get one of them."

"I'm sure you will," Lloyd reassuringly offered in return.

"So, how did your first day go?" Nadene pleasantly inquired.

"I met with the hospital commander, did some in-processing, met with my staff in the medical management unit, and then came home."

With a twinkle in her eye, Nadene teased, "Do you have a corner office, Lieutenant Lane?"

Lloyd accepted the challenge and responded in kind, "Yes, and it has large windows, plantation shutters, a minibar, and a kitchen."

They both laughed, after which Lloyd amended the description. "Well, in reality, it's a tiny office with no windows but I have my phone!"

Turning to a more serious comment Lloyd gratuitously offered, "The subject of the airline attack came up and I mentioned Anthony's death. Roderick also verbally approved my absence for a few days to attend the funeral."

Memories of the fateful event placed a damper on further conversation and Nadene turned her attention to making dinner. Lloyd slipped into a more casual dress and soon they were sharing a quiet dinner before retiring for the night.

Over the next several weeks Lloyd settled into a routine at work. Nadene also started her new job as a reference librarian leaving less time for domestic chores. Meals were much simpler now and Lloyd shared the load on those days when Nadene worked late. Her schedule was more unpredictable with evening hours rotating with the preferred daytime work.

Roughly a month after starting work, Lloyd sensed creeping anxiety seeping throughout the hospital. The main contributor to the growing unease was the certain conviction that another terrorist attack was inevitable. Several weeks had passed since the eastern nation demanded relief from the crippling economic sanctions imposed by western governments but the peaceful interval paradoxically heightened the concern.

Adding to the worry was an afternoon town hall meeting led by Colonel Roderick. He began the briefing by addressing the reality of another attack. "These are uncertain times that demand certain responses. We do not know if or when another terrorist attack may happen, but we must be prepared. The Department of Defense just notified all senior staff to increase the threat level. What that means in practical terms is an enhanced security posture. Entry points will be fortified with barriers and staff, along with the patients, will be subjected to additional scrutiny. All staff will receive security-specific training. Aside from that, please carry on with the usual expert, empathic care for our patients."

Roderick opened the forum for questions, but a somber group had none. After waiting a few awkward minutes, the hospital commander left the auditorium with the remainder of the meeting devoted to a security video describing approaches to identifying suspicious activities.

After the meeting, Lloyd returned to his office and hastily assembled his staff. Once gathered, it was clear that everyone was worried. Lloyd put their concern into words, "I think we all are apprehensive but as Colonel Roderick stated preparation is the best option. Going forward we must be vigilant but at the same time supportive of each other and our patients."

Lloyd hoped his brief comments would fortify his role as a leader by balancing compassion with determination. A measure of his success was an easing of tensions as the group chatted amiably together before leaving for the day.

The muted mood infected Nadene when her husband disclosed the day's announcements, "It seems like we are spiraling down into a deep, dark abyss. Every time I turn on the news it sounds so dreadful. Even after subtracting the reporter's hysterics, the future is looking gloomy. Earlier today a national network television figure suggested people start stocking up on necessities. Of course, that just heightens people's panic and quite frankly I think it is irresponsible."

Her husband agreed but borrowing the same approach used earlier with his staff conceded that, "We need to counter political uncertainty with the certainty of action. We should build an emergency supply of food and other daily necessities. I'm convinced that this wave of fear will wash grocery shelves clean."

"Maybe you're right," Nadene pensively observed. "I can start foraging tomorrow morning."

A fitful night's sleep disturbed the married couple. They both tossed and turned before finally surrendering to a shortened slumber. Awakening sore and with a headache, Lloyd quickly quaffed a lukewarm cup of coffee and two glazed doughnuts. His bleary-eyed wife kissed him, and, in a reassuring, partly playful manner said, "I will check out some stores and start building our survival larder!"

"You can drop me off at work and then take the car on your expedition," Lloyd sensibly suggested.

Before leaving, Nadene called the college library and took a day's sick leave, feigning a sudden gastric discomfort. A twinge of guilt accompanied the false confession but Nadene consciously swept that aside fearing that to do otherwise might leave their cupboards bare.

Nadene fumbled in her purse for the military identifying card while a civilian security officer waited impatiently. After scrutinizing the card, the officer raised the gate and she drove her husband to the hospital's front entrance. Lloyd kissed his wife and then disappeared inside the concrete behemoth.

Pointing the car to the exit, Nadene left the army facility and drove to a nearby big-box store. She reasoned that a general merchandise store would offer the best option to gather everything at one location. Traffic was extraordinarily heavy and numerous police suggested an accident was the culprit. Nadene turned on the radio and soon learned that the clogged traffic was the result of panicked shoppers flooding stores.

After two hours of agonizing stop-and-go traffic, Nadene finally spied her destination. Another thirty minutes passed, and she entered the parking lot and began the hunt for a spot. Rounding a corner, she slammed on the brakes to avoid hitting two cars blocking the road. Screams captured her attention and looking in that direction Nadene watched as two women left their vehicles and menacingly approached each other. Alerted by the noisy fracas, a police officer sprinted towards the combatants and ordered them off the property.

Nadene was closest to the contested parking space and under the vigilant watch of the store's security she slipped in with a sigh of relief. Nadene walked slowly to the store after taking a moment to relax from the harrowing drive. A line stretched outside the store with a noisy throng of people kept in line by armed guards.

A cool breeze made the 40-minute wait tolerable but once inside the store Nadene gasped at the melee. Security was nowhere to be seen and pandemonium reigned as shoppers darted from aisle to aisle snatching items off the shelves. Harried stockers did their best to keep the shelves filled but soon collectively gave up as shoppers emptied the boxes.

Nadene reluctantly joined the fracas and in turn, was rudely jostled as more aggressive shoppers pushed her away. Slowly and with infinite perseverance Nadene pointed her shopping cart to a checkout lane and with a profound sense of relief finally carted her purchases outside.

The waiting time for a parking space during Nadene's sojourn inside had grown considerably longer and as she attempted to back her car out two racing, kamikaze drivers were in a standoff. She was blocked until the two settled the logjam. The drivers hurled a few loud expletives from their vehicles before one finally moved enough so that Nadene could leave. Looking in her rearview mirror she noted that both cars had inched closer to the parking space but neither seemed inclined to budge.

Darkness was descending across the landscape when Nadene returned to the hospital. Parking was not a problem and she scampered inside and called her husband. In a few minutes, Lloyd appeared and the two made their way home. On the way they stopped at a fast-food restaurant; both being too tired to cook dinner.

Once home they carried Nadene's groceries inside and then settled in for the night. The takeout food was cold, but the microwave warmed the sandwiches nicely. While eating, Nadene discussed the day's trauma. "I've never seen anything like it. Traffic was horrible. People were fighting over parking spaces and scrambling for everything inside the store. I was so glad to get out of there!"

"I guess I'm not surprised," Lloyd cynically commented but more sympathetically said, "but imagine where we would be if you had not braved the crowd. You did a great job."

Over the next few weeks, the panic dissipated. Nadene and Lloyd welcomed the humdrum routine with both becoming more comfortable with their new jobs. On the weekends they enjoyed hiking in the local area.

A sense of normalcy displaced the fear of terrorist retaliation, but the calm was illusory. More sober-minded individuals harbored deep suspicions that the calm was a planning prelude for the next attack. Going to work reminded Lloyd of the existential threat and daily staff briefings helped keep everyone alert.

Even with enhanced security and periodic public announcements, the next attack exposed major vulnerabilities. Instead of isolated bombings on airplanes or large crowds, the enemy assaulted America's infrastructure. Lightning fast and breathtaking in scope the enemy targeted public water systems, electricity grids, gas pipelines, cell phone towers, server farms, and regional distribution centers. Ten large cities; three each on the coasts and four in middle America were crippled as public utilities struggled under the attacks.

It soon became clear that the enemy's strategy was less about injury and death but instead to spread suffering, fear, and confusion. Disrupted public utilities forced millions of households to cope without electricity, natural gas, and cell phone communications. The attacks buckled the internet and led to widespread outages.

Damaging the community water supply seemed to be the main target as the enemy boldly attacked water purification systems and distribution networks. Attacking regional distribution centers that supplied groceries added to the misery as potable supplies of water and food dwindled.

Local politicians urged calm and held emergency meetings to respond to the growing crisis. Service crews from neighboring areas joined in the relief effort but the extent of damage was enormous. The slow recovery sharpened calls from community leaders with a chorus of blame directed at federal authorities. In response, national guard troops helped with water and food distribution, electric generator installations, and security.

Weeks passed as communities struggled in their efforts to return to normal. Restive elements of the public vented their frustrations in public demonstrations. Rumors were rampant and quickly spread by suspicions and fear.

Nadene and Lloyd were not among those directly affected by the coordinated attacks, but both predicted that like a pebble dropped in a lake there would soon be ripples effects. "I'm certain that security will be tightened even more going forward," Lloyd mentioned with a sigh.

Nadene nodded her head but then changed the subject, "Do you think we should get a small portable generator?"

Lloyd pondered the question for a moment before answering, "I think some sort of emergency power supply is a good idea, but a gas-powered generator would be dependent on fuel supplies. Maybe a solar panel and battery would be a better option."

"That seems like a good idea," Nadene conceded, "but I wonder if they are still available. Maybe we should call some stores and find out."

Lloyd signaled his agreement by thumbing through the phone directory and passed prospective numbers to his wife. Call after call deepened their disappointment as each store perfunctorily professed their exhausted supplies and on further query expected no further shipments.

Nadene was on the verge of quitting, but Lloyd suggested a few more calls. His persistence was rewarded when an independent lawn and tractor company surprisingly acknowledged having an integrated solar panel and battery backup system for sale. It was pricey for sure, but only one remained so Lloyd paid for it, sight unseen.

A quick cross-town trip brought them to the lawn and tractor company. Nadene's heart sank when she spied the dilapidated building; privately wondering if they had been cheated. Her reservations seemed confirmed by a cardboard sign crudely lettered "closed."

Despite its unwelcoming appearance Lloyd walked to the store's entrance, turned the doorknob, and much to his surprise, the door opened. Darkness greeted the man as he peered searchingly inside for any evidence of human habitation, but finding none, was backing out of the store when a faint rustling sound caught his attention. In a moment more, the store's lights sprang to life and illuminated an elderly woman.

"I'm sorry if I startled you but the door was open," Lloyd sheepishly admitted.

Nadene joined her husband once the lights came on and together, they walked towards the vintage cash register; behind which stood the store's proprietor. "We get very little business anymore and with the cost of electricity the lights stay off until someone comes in and triggers the sensor," she good-naturedly apologized.

"You must be the people that purchased the solar battery system."

A wave of relief swept over Nadene as she gushed, "Yes, we called so many stores looking for an emergency power system. I was so happy when we discovered your store."

"I have your purchase in the back room. It's fairly heavy, Can the young man give me a hand?"

Lloyd acknowledged the request and followed the woman to another room behind the cash register. A few minutes later he emerged carrying a large box. He set it on the counter by the cash register and waited while the woman completed the sale and handed Nadene the receipt. After thanking the woman, Nadene and Lloyd returned home with their prized purchase.

While eating dinner Lloyd and Nadene typically watched the evening news; much of which focused on the recent attacks. After several days, a theme emerged among the network reporters as they collectively replicated the same talking points. They acknowledged the public's widespread anger and fear but counseled government officials to proceed with caution.

Lloyd was disgusted with the news coverage and rising from the dinner table found another television channel hosting a popular game show. "I don't understand the timid approach from the network news. The scale of destruction is breathtaking, but the news media seems more invested in placating the enemy. Our politicians parrot the same line with the President insisting that diplomacy is the only way forward."

By no means was Lloyd dismissive of the repercussions that could arise from a more resolute and robust response. Nadene favored a more measured approach and in response to her husband wondered, "What can we do? If we attack indiscriminately, it will unleash Armageddon. The enemy has no compunction about escalating the conflict and even though their targets mostly spared human casualties this time I'm not sure they would be so considerate if we respond in kind."

Years of military training schooled Lloyd's analytic response, "Our enemy would consider diplomacy at this point as a weakness and if we dither in responding militarily, they will exploit the delay to their advantage by demanding even more concessions. I think we should send a large naval task force to the area and place our strategic bombers on a higher alert. We should also posture our immediate response forces for rapid deployment. None of this involves any combat but it does position our forces in the event of an escalation, and it should send a powerful message of our capabilities."

Nadene conceded that her husband's approach avoided direct conflict and wanton destruction while not surrendering to pacifist voices, but it was the latter argument that prevailed in Washington, DC. The president organized an emergency response team populated by state department personnel and members of congress but conspicuously missing any military members.

The members of the president's emergency response team leaned on crisis management and de-escalation strategies in crafting their suggestions. Reprisal was off the table as the members struggled to develop a unified approach. They all agreed that communication with the enemy was paramount in defusing the crisis but disagreed about removing trade sanctions that constrained the enemy's aggressive capabilities. Swaying the discussion was the president's representative who casually suggested that the group should consider lifting the punishing trade barriers.

Two days after assembling the emergency response team the president announced his decisions in a nationally televised appearance before congress. As a peace gesture, the president removed the trade barriers and signaled that the enemy agreed to a high-level delegation as a first diplomatic step to resolving the tensions. Members of Congress applauded the president's restraint and predicted a speedy return to normal relations with the enemy.

Lloyd listened to the president's speech but presciently mused, "The first task of any leader during a crisis is to understand your enemy. Unilaterally surrendering to the enemy's request to relieve the trade sanctions removes the only leverage we had and will further embolden them."

Lifting the trade sanctions earned no response from the enemy and the silence puzzled pundits and politicians. The prevailing sentiment supported a positive spin and often evoked the maxim that no news is good news. Some went even further and applauded the enemy's restraint and diplomacy; seemingly forgetting the recent attacks.

A week later the enemy's leader held a press conference with eager reporters in attendance. The noisy throng awaited the leader's remarks, but he was predictably late and the room's decibels increased with time. A hush descended over the group as the leader finally made his appearance and after some social commentary directed towards those in attendance solemnly complained. "Western nations imposed inhumane sanctions on our country. We are a strong people and these terrorist actions united us. Even so, our people suffered from lack of food, our industries from lack of materials, and our hospitals from critical supplies. As our country's leader I cannot forget the consequences of this immoral and illegal attack and eliminating the trade sanctions is meaningless. Our nation has suffered immense damages directly attributable to this negligent and illegal behavior and we now demand reparations. Our economists estimate that one trillion US dollars will help restore our country and repair international relations."

If the reporters expected an opportunity to ask questions they were disappointed when the man abruptly left the podium and his entourage dutifully followed. After the leader's exit, the various news organizations quickly summarized the speech and unequivocally endorsed economic reparations as the appropriate moral course of action.

Western leaders convened a summit the following week to discuss the enemy's proposal and after a long day of meetings agreed to the demand. Representatives from both sides then met to arrange the exchange of funds; with the enemy demanding and the western nations agreeing to payment in the form of gold bullion.

One trillion US dollars in gold proved to be a difficult computation but after some additional haggling, the enemy generously settled on 250,000 tons of the precious metal. Western nations shared the burden based on their reserves, but the massive transfer took weeks to complete. Whatever concerns the western leaders quietly harbored were assuaged by the conviction that their diplomacy was a victory for peace.

As time passed, the subsequent calm silenced the small group of critics who initially had argued that ransom was a better word than reparations. The critics were castigated as cynics, warmongers, and worse by the intelligentsia who relentlessly hammered their misgivings but disturbing developments in the enemy's behavior at home reignited doubts and suspicions.

Politicians from the western countries faced no headwinds from a fawning news media who promoted a narrative extolling the adroit diplomatic maneuvering. Without missing a beat, the yoked news media giants editorialized the supposed benefits of the deal, emphasizing the enemy's moderation and genuine grievances with the western power's bullying tactics. At the same time, they legitimatized the massive transfer of wealth as a small step towards social justice. After all, the enemy was a poor country, and the monetary infusion would lift the average's person standard of living.

While western countries' politicians saturated their populations with self-congratulatory news the story was much different with the erstwhile enemy. In their inner sanctum, the leaders plotted the next move; confident that the weak western nations would avoid conflict, literally at any cost. Without mentioning the amount, the leaders officially announced an agreement with the western powers that would compensate their losses during the imposition of the illegal trade war.

Rumors soon spread across the eastern nation. From the trendy coffee houses to the shabby hovels a growing fear of war crept across the land. Perhaps crafty leaders planted those speculations in a land fertilized with paranoia with an insidious goal of cultivating western animosity. Whatever the source, the effect was galvanizing. Nationalism flourished, deprivation was virtuous, and the leadership's popularity soared.

None of this was noted in the western press which had long since moved on to more esoteric and banal reporting. Celebrity news, sports, and weather dominated a media seemingly oblivious to the sinister developments in the eastern nation.

The west's military-industrial complex welcomed the surge in orders from the eastern nation. Their diplomats assured western leaders that an enhanced military posture would stabilize a dangerous part of the world and perhaps even lead to a mutual defense alliance. Once again, skeptics with raised eyebrows were marginalized as money flowed into the coffers of western nations desperate to replenish their monetary losses.

Armaments of every description, except nuclear, filled the ports of the eastern nation. Patriotism swelled the ranks of the military and in a short year, a formidable force was taking shape. Despite their newfound wealth poverty was everywhere but government employment promised relief as the leaders steadily built a massive police state.

Western nations yawned when their erstwhile enemy attacked a neighboring island which for decades had defiantly resisted efforts at reunification. It was a dark, foggy night when the enemy launched their surprise assault. Amphibious forces, paratroopers, precision bombing, and a naval blockade crippled the island.

Panic and fear gripped the island. The enemy quickly displaced locally elected leaders with martial law and proclaimed victory. Western leaders hesitated, clearly cognizant that a defense treaty with the island mandated their response to the aggression. Diplomats appealed for calm and communication; an appeal eagerly embraced by the invaders.

Face-to-face diplomatic meetings were as pleasant as they were ineffectual. The invader endlessly asserted history and tradition as consistent with their territorial claims and cast the displaced leaders as traitors. While the discussions dragged on the invader relentlessly consolidated their control over the island.

The island's deposed leaders made an emotional appeal to their citizens to respect the new regime. They were confident that their nation's liberties would not be compromised, and the new leaders promised substantial economic assistance. Western diplomats sighed with relief; seeing the assertion of good intentions as sufficient to declare a diplomatic victory and return home.

Seemingly overlooked by the western nations was the island's strategic location straddling important shipping channels including an important transit point for global oil. Over the next few months, the invading leadership publicized their public commitment to maintaining the island's sovereignty and at the same time began investing in their infrastructure.

Soothing words and innocent actions once again convinced western diplomats of their adroit handling of the nascent crisis. With the latest fire now seemingly extinguished the diplomats and politicians resumed their banal behaviors but keen-eyed observers noted a troubling trend.

Ships clogged the island nation's ports with a long line restively waiting for entry. Satellite imagery revealed hundreds of containers partially unloaded with mechanized military vehicles, rocket launchers, missiles, and smaller crates presumably filled with individual weapons. Virtually every type of offensive and defensive system lined the harbor.

Western politicians muzzled the defense strategists and with the cooperation of the news media hid the ominous military events from the public. If nothing else, they reasoned, it would prevent panic but in their private moments admitted that it was a diplomatic disaster unfolding that threatened their careers.

When the enemy struck again it caught the public off guard. Slowly a sense of betrayal eroded trust in the government officials when their duplicity became clearer. Complicit news organizations feigned ignorance and in an attempt at credibility began an ersatz investigative campaign. With a wink and a nod, a reporter "grilled" the politicians, salting their performances with heaping doses of disingenuous discontent.

With their reputations sullied, the marriage between politicians and the news media started fraying as the full impact of the enemy's latest salvo hit home. With the curtains now drawn and their duplicity and conniving exposed, distrust in both groups hit historic lows as ordinary people turned away in disgust.

The collapse in public trust did not go unnoticed by the enemy who took the occasion to roil the troubled waters further. A long list of grievances against the western nations' tyranny surfaced again, only differing by not mentioning the previous monetary exchange.

No demands were made by the enemy. It was now obvious that territorial domination and global subjugation were their goals and with the unwitting assistance of placating, pandering politicians they had the military means.

Deprivation and pain spread throughout the western nations as the full impact of the enemy's bold behavior took hold. Collectively, the politicians were paralyzed, vacillating between further appeasement and tepid consideration of military action. While they dithered, social misery exploded exponentially as the loss of faith in government fused with the crushing hardships.

Western nations teetered on the edge of economic collapse with the enemy's seemingly impenetrable naval blockade of the world's primary oil shipping routes. Decades of profligate social spending and mountains of debt left the western nations with little economic reserve. Hollowed out militaries precluded offensive actions and encouraged the enemy's audacious behavior. With little room to maneuver, western leaders covertly capitulated.

With international shipping hobbled, not just oil, but all products transiting the narrow isthmus controlled by the enemy soon dwindled. Shortages in industrial materials gradually impacted factory productivity and led to idled plants and furloughed employees.

Adding to the cascade of misery was western outsourcing which siphoned jobs and skills to the enemy. While the practice promised inexpensive and plentiful merchandise it was socially corrosive as evidenced by urban rust belts. Generations of politicians responded with ever more elaborate and expensive government programs.

Western government leaders resorted to rationing; encouraging their citizens that ongoing negotiations with the enemy were producing promising results but month after month the malignant melancholic miasma deepened. Small bands of disgruntled citizens loudly voiced their discontent; peaceful in the beginning but believing their voices were ignored they amplified the message with riots.

News media mostly ignored the riots; presenting political pablum as a soothing prescription to spare the leaders any further criticism. Their blackout did not eliminate the suffering nor did their news embargo foster confidence.

Lloyd and Nadene adapted to the current crisis with a mixture of resolve and resignation; the former was a product of their innate resiliency and the latter an acknowledgment that bungling leaders were incapable of alleviating the situation. For them both it was particularly troublesome that the news media's mission seemed less focused on conducting critical journalistic inquiries but were instead subordinated to the government's vacuous propaganda.

The dialectical tension between the reality of everyone's daily existence and the government leader's insensibility was fertile space for breeding emotional problems. Dysphoria, anxiety, resentment, fear, and anger propagated but with medications in short supply clinicians and counselors relied on behavioral therapies, but a sizeable majority of disillusioned citizens distrusted the government's health care and turned to home remedies.

Lloyd observed this at the military hospital which still retained a reservoir of trust but even here murmurs of concern were voiced by an increasing number of patients. Hospital statistics were slowly ebbing as general medical clinic visits declined but remained robust for psychiatry and the alcohol and drug treatment programs. Despite the surge in these two areas, hospital administrators refused urgent requests to increase the support: offering no explanation to the beleaguered staff.

Lloyd learned the reason for the staffing disparities at a commander's briefing. The attendees were department leaders and in an unusual move, were required to sign non-disclosure agreements. Lloyd reluctantly signed the form recognizing that to do otherwise would be a fateful dissent fraught with risk.

Colonel Roderick collected the non-disclosure agreements and after scrutinizing each for the required signature ominously intoned, "I just received a communique from the Army Surgeon General ordering all military hospitals not to provide additional staffing to psychiatry and the alcohol and drug treatment programs. Although it was not stated in the order; my discussions with other hospital commanders lead me to believe that this is part of a coordinated plan to deny or at least minimize the public perception that psychiatric problems and substance use disorders are rapidly increasing across America. In particular, the Surgeon General, most likely at the behest of the Pentagon's brass and the President, want to reassure the public that our military is fit to fight. So, with that in mind, do your part to tamp down demands for enhanced service support in these areas; be it from staff or patients."

It was clear from Roderick's tone and demeanor that neither discussion nor dissent was permissible and a quick pivot to more mundane business matters reinforced the folly of pursuing the issue. Lloyd left the meeting with an inexplicable unease and pondered silently if the new narrative papered over the extensive emotional descent blanketing the country.

Nadene was preparing dinner when her somber husband arrived. She immediately noticed the gloom and debated whether or not to inquire but after a few moments deliberation pushed ahead, "You seem a bit down. Did something happen at work?"

Lloyd hesitated before responding by remembering the non-disclosure agreement but dismissed the concern since Nadene was his most trusted confidante. "Colonel Roderick summoned the leadership to his office for an impromptu meeting but before saying a word had each of us sign a non-disclosure agreement. I can tell you quite honestly that I considered leaving the room instead of signing that form but in the end, my curiosity overcame concerns and I signed it."

Lloyd paused before proceeding, walked to the refrigerator, and removed a soft drink. Resuming his place at the table he took a long drink of the cool beverage and resumed his monologue. "It has become obvious to nearly everyone at the hospital that the medical clinics are far less busy, but patients are spilling out of the psychiatry waiting rooms. It's also apparent that after their initial psychiatric evaluation, a sizeable number are referred to the alcohol and drug treatment programs. Those programs have loudly and repeatedly requested additional support to handle the load, but those pleas have been ignored. At Colonel Roderick's briefing, he explained the silence as a directive from the highest echelons of government to downplay the emotional problems sweeping across the country. It all seems designed to protect government leaders from their failed policies and the resulting social harms."

A loud buzzer interrupted Lloyd. Nadene sprang to her feet and rushed over to the oven just as the faintest traces of smoke filled the kitchen. The smoke detector's anger grew louder as Nadene hurriedly removed the pizza from the oven and turned the ceiling fan on to dissipate the smoke. Lloyd opened several windows and the cross current eventually silenced the smoke detector.

Fortunately, Nadene rescued the dinner; burned but not charred. It was still edible and Nadene preferred her pizza very well done. In between slices of the pizza, Nadene prompted her husband, "What do you think about the emotional situation?"

With his mouth partially full, Lloyd swallowed before responding, "I must admit I see it at work and not just with the military healthcare beneficiaries. On several occasions, I've noticed alcohol breath from co-workers. I've debated what to do about it but except for two cases I too have ignored the issue."

"And what happened in the two cases you mentioned?"

"I know both of those two people quite well and figured that I could broach the subject with them," Lloyd admitted. "Both felt guilty about their increased drinking and sheepishly acknowledged that their spouses were concerned. Neither could make it through the duty day without alcohol and were secretly imbibing."

"Why are they drinking more alcohol," Nadene wondered.

"I asked them that very question and both responded with similar answers," Lloyd noted. "They both yearned for a detached numbness that would insulate them from the hardships imposed by the rationing. I think the alcohol helped them forget about their plight, at least for a short time, but it was coming at a great price. Both admitted problems in their marriage severely disturbed sleep, and fear that their drinking would damage their career."

Nadene nodded her understanding, "Sometimes I think that as sentient beings we are cursed with an awareness of our ultimate destiny and wonder if humanity would somehow be better off if we only lived in the present."

Lloyd laughed at the suggestion but upon noticing an evident frown clouding Nadene's face he hastened to apologize, "I wasn't laughing at you. I've had the same thought and was amused that we shared the same idea. It's just an absurd philosophical point anyway since we can't change the way we are."

Lloyd pushed his chair back from the dinner table, collected the plates, and placed them in the sink. He stared at Nadene still sitting at the table and wondered if she was still upset. As if to answer his silent query, she rose from the table and proceeded to wash the dishes. While doing so she matter-of-factly noted, "After work tomorrow I need to pick up a few things at the store. Do you need anything?"

"I don't think so," he responded after mulling the question over. "Would you like to pick up some sandwiches for dinner on your way back?"

"Sure," Nadene pertly replied, "I will get your favorite tuna salad sandwich along with a ham salad sandwich for me and a huge pile of onion rings!"

Nadene's visit to the local market was unpleasant. Barren store shelves reminded her of the ongoing, seemingly endless deprivation that was deepening with each passing day. Cosmetics, household supplies, and coffee were replaced with signs "Out of stock." She grabbed the few remaining items on her list and left the store filled with an abject fear of the future.

A despondent cloud darkened the mood at the military hospital. The staff was edgy; wary of leadership that seemed to be hiding important information. Behind closed doors, hushed voices verbalized various conspiracies ranging from looming staff furloughs to complete civilian outsourcing of military healthcare. Morale suffered accordingly along with a widening rift of distrust between staff and leadership.

Lloyd keenly felt the change. As a mid-level leader, his loyalties were divided between a staff that delivered the daily duties and a senior leadership seemingly out of touch with the currents of distrust flowing through the organization. Hospital patients felt the tension and were the inadvertent recipients of the staff's anxiety and anger.

Medical complications soared as did patient complaints and finally triggered an external review of the hospital's operations.

The unannounced inspection included both civilian and military healthcare surveyors. Over the next week, a comprehensive examination looked at medical records, surgical procedures, standard operating policies, environmental conditions, and interviewed staff and willing patients.

It was a complete whitewash. The final report extolled the hospital's safety, quality of care, and favorable comments from staff and patients. Lloyd was not surprised and related such to Nadene, "I know firsthand that staff and patients lodged many complaints and concerns with the surveyors. Many were reasonable assessments of a climate of distrust that hindered communications and prevented a proper evaluation of medical mistakes. The surveyors completely ignored that feedback and produced a report at odds with reality but designed to placate the public."

Lloyd's harsh analysis was for Nadene's ears only with one caveat, "I wonder if I should meet with Colonel Roderick," he mused. "Perhaps I could share what I am seeing and hearing. Colonel Roderick used to make the rounds throughout the hospital regularly but over the past several weeks he has been noticeably absent."

Nadene was far more risk-averse than her husband and her reply urged caution, "I do not think that would be a good idea. Colonel Roderick must know what is going on and sharing your thoughts and observations may not be welcomed."

After a moment's reflection Lloyd agreed, "I guess you are right. There certainly seems to be more risk than reward."

With the deepening worldwide miasma bursts of anger began coalescing around a theme of retribution, dissipating the political fog of pacification. The network news outlets intensified their belligerent campaigns and uniformly castigated the defiant outbursts as dangerous and destabilizing. This time though their efforts only fueled the nascent trend and soon large gatherings in communities across America demanded action.

Public opinion flogged the politicians and news media; reluctantly forcing the opinion managers to confront the uprisings. Year after year of soothing sophisms and social programming had presumably inculcated the prerogatives of the ruling class but the descent into deprivation awakened the public. The present crisis magnified the disparities between the leaders and ordinary citizens amplifying the clamor for change, leaving leaders deeply worried about the upcoming election cycle.

Vast sums of money filled the coffers of the status quo leaders and ferociously flowed to receptive newsgroups. Advertisements cluttered mailboxes, endlessly interrupted radio, and television programs, and adorned commercial vehicles with smiling faces and pithy messages. Paradoxically, the flood of adulation designed to drown opposition voices emboldened dissent as evidenced by swift and strong polling currents buoying nationalistic sentiment.

When all the votes were counted a tsunami of discontent swept the current leaders away and, in their wake, a resolute group of leaders surfaced with a clear mandate to right the ship of state. The new American President promised a mixture of relief and retribution in a rousing inaugural address to the nation. Reluctant and dispirited news organizations criticized the speech as incendiary but with their tattered credibility, it fell on deaf ears.

The new government leadership quickly consolidated power. Dovish leaders at all levels succumbed to the President's directives to install more aggressive management. Nowhere was this more prominently and urgently undertaken than with the Department of Defense, weakened in the President's opinion by lame leadership. The imposition of the changes bolstered the military's posture, strengthening morale and readiness.

Colonel Roderick could not be happier. The new President respected the military and was certain to prioritize their needs. Roderick's prophecy was soon fulfilled when swift legislative actions brought a steady flow of resources to the hospital. Like every other military unit in America Roderick now grappled with an embarrassment of riches denominated by personnel, equipment, and training.

One quizzical directive accompanied the hospital largesse. Senior military leaders ordered subordinate hospital commanders to make immediate plans to transition all nonactive duty healthcare to civilian facilities. Interrogatories hoping to rationalize the directive were regularly rebuffed by the President's team.

At work, Lloyd felt a buzz in the air. The prospect of personnel and supplies generated a strong emotional current that galvanized the staff; a powerful discharge that freshened the hospital's work environment. Despite the dynamic surge, Lloyd's secret doubts drained some of his newly created mental energy.

Lloyd revealed his private worries at dinner. Looking pensively at his wife he somberly began, "I guess I should be ecstatic. My every wish list at work is on the cusp of fulfillment. I have new civilian hiring authority, am expecting six new military staff, and what seems like an inexhaustible budget to procure supplies."

Nadene knew her husband's comments presaged yet unspoken suspicions and softy coaxed his further thoughts. "It does seem too good to be true."

"What set my imagination ablaze was the directive to transfer all non-active-duty care to civilian facilities," he mused. "A large staff of case managers will lead the effort so the work impact for my unit will be minimal, but I just wonder why we need to do this."

"What did Colonel Roderick say," Nadene pointedly inquired.

"Nothing really. The directive provided no explanation," Lloyd offered.

"So, what do you think is going on," Nadene wondered.

Nadene's question prompted Lloyd to share his thoughts. "We just elected new government leaders who campaigned on themes of nationalism and retribution. These are not pacifist politicians, and their subsequent actions are meant to signal strength and resolve. I think the military build-up is more than just meaningless posturing. Emptying the hospital of non-active-duty patients diverts space, resources, and staff to support mission essential readiness. In short, I think the President is preparing the military for war."

Before responding Nadene considered the implications of her husband's analysis and then agreed. "I think you are right. Western nations are hostages of both their failed diplomacy and an implacable enemy."

In actuality, the rogue eastern nation had already declared war on the western powers through a well-calculated and coordinated strategy of economic blackmail, terrorist tactics, and clever propaganda. Patience was a key element the enemy deployed that ran counter to the goal of the western nations to quickly resolve enmities and reclaim the tranquil status quo.

With a fully armed military thanks to the western benevolence, the enemy increasingly assumed an aggressive posture. Neutral neighbors appealed to the western leaders fearing a looming assault but aside from soothing words, their concerns were largely ignored.

Beleaguered neighbors remembered the independent island previously swallowed by the enemy along with the western nations' credibility. The only recourse for the small nations was a joint defense pact against their aggressive adversary but the ink was barely dry on the agreement before tragedy struck.

A multipronged lightning-swift attack completely surprised the five small countries. Hordes of well-trained soldiers fanned out across the lands, gobbling up territory and establishing local military control. Within days, the enemy's bristling military occupation subjugated the populations.

Western leaders predictably publicly criticized the invasions but privately wrung their collective hands bemoaning the inevitable need for a forceful response. The leaders debated and discarded economic sanctions as historically ineffectual but also conceded that their weakened financial position made imposition improbable.

Military leaders offered a range of options. Politicians debated the various scenarios applying risk-reward analysis to each but the principle sentiment favored a surgical strike that ostensibly would send the enemy a clear message denouncing their aggression. Such restraint it was argued by a slim majority of the western leaders would demonstrate resolve without provoking a tit-for-tat retaliation.

International news organizations paved the way towards deescalating the crisis by providing notice to the enemy of a looming military response; a gesture publicly promoted to prevent unnecessary damage and civilian casualties.

The United States abstained from the decision and insisted on an individual prerogative to act unilaterally. This rift created more animus against the lone dissenter than ire towards the enemy and hardened and affirmed the majority's sympathetic judgment. And so it was that the western bloc of nations minus one launched a discrete attack on the enemy's homeland. It was a disastrous intervention that failed in all respects and far from lessening tensions propelled the world towards a vicious global conflict.

Lloyd awakened at 5 am, his usual time, and sleepily prepared his morning coffee. Nadene soon joined him and set about making her tea and a light breakfast for both. She liked the heartiness of oatmeal and twenty minutes later a steaming bowl of cereal greeted her husband. Lloyd preferred his with a pad of butter while Nadene added some brown sugar.

As per their usual morning routine, Lloyd turned the television on to catch up on overnight news developments. The graphic scrolling across the screen riveted his attention with ominous urgent breaking news as a somber newscaster intoned midsentence, "it struck a densely populated area and hundreds of casualties are expected. Local officials are reporting massive infrastructure damage with collapsed buildings trapping unknown numbers inside. Even more worrying is the fact that the alleged errant missile struck during the busy morning hours. Leaders of the western nations have just issued a statement apologizing for the damage and lost lives claiming that a malfunctioning guidance system delivered the missile to the wrong location."

"Your oatmeal is getting cold," Nadene reminded her husband and at the same time recognized how inconsequential her comment was considering the news.

"I know," he quietly replied and mechanically stirred his lukewarm oatmeal.

A jarring ringtone startled Nadene. Picking up the receiver she answered, "Lane residence."

"This is Major Jeffries calling from the hospital for Lieutenant Lane"

"One moment," Nadene replied while handing the phone to her husband.

Lloyd was not surprised when Major Jeffries resumed his call, "Colonel Roderick has ordered an emergency meeting in his conference room. Please come as quickly as you can."

After confirming his understanding, Lloyd turned to his wife, "I fear the worst now. Roderick has called an emergency meeting and I suspect it is in response to the missile attack. I doubt the enemy will be placated by an apology. I can only imagine a fierce counterattack."

Tension was palpable as Lloyd took a seat in the hospital commander's conference room and waited along with the other attendees for the 7 am meeting to start. Anxieties escalated even further when Roderick did not arrive on time and the minutes slowly passed by. No one dared say a word and the eerie silence aggravated the apprehension.

Colonel Roderick entered the conference room thirty minutes late and began his monologue with an apology, "First let me apologize for being late. Just as I was preparing to come in, I received a phone call that demanded my attention. It was from the Army Surgeon General. It was a brief conversation necessitated by his desire to personally speak with each hospital commander."

An enlisted soldier timorously entered the conference room pushing a cart with beverages and breakfast rolls. Roderick motioned for the man to enter and remarked, "Everyone, please take advantage of the light breakfast, and then I will continue."

In reality, no one wanted breakfast but in deference to the offer, they dutifully complied. Lloyd was last to get a cup of coffee but declined any further offerings and resumed his seat at the table.

Roderick took a sip of his coffee and softly sighed before continuing. "Earlier this morning the President put the armed forces on the highest alert. As you might have figured out the decision to transition all non-active-duty care to the civilian sector was a prelude to this announcement. I think the general sentiment expects an inevitable military response from our protagonist. The Surgeon General's brief comments hinted at such an outcome; now made more likely as the preliminary casualty reports from the errant missile attack are counted. Of course, the enemy will inflate the damage, but satellite imagery suggests the missile landed in a densely populated suburb of their capital city. It seems likely given the huge impact zone and reports of secondary explosions that the missile destroyed an underground cache of weapons."

Lloyd listened intently and in a conscious effort to relieve the mounting tension, took a sip of his cold coffee. The cold brew was distasteful and provoked a sour grimace which Lloyd instantly suppressed fearful that his expression would be misinterpreted.

Perhaps it was, for Lloyd noticed that Roderick's gaze seemed to linger in his direction.

The Hospital Commander scanned the faces of his audience and paused. Each person's visage betrayed their anxiety, but Roderick knew the worst was coming. "Even more concerning are early reports of a spike in radiation extending miles from ground zero. Western intelligence has confirmed this. This troublesome development will be exploited by the enemy and rest assured that we can expect accusations that the errant missile carried a nuclear payload. Of course, it did not but apparently, the underground munitions somehow did. Speculation is running rife with some analysts suggesting that the enemy intentionally detonated a small nuclear device for purely propaganda purposes."

The conference room phone rudely interrupted Roderick and jangled the nerves of everyone in the room. Lloyd hesitated for a moment hoping someone else would answer the phone but none did, expecting him as the nearest person to deal with the intrusive device. Lloyd timorously reached for the phone and responded, "hospital command conference room."

All eyes were on Lloyd as he waited for a reply. "This is metropolitan pizza. We ran out of pepperoni and are substituting some sausage. Is that, ok?"

Lloyd stifled a chuckle, but the traces of a grin remained as he replied, "Sure, that is fine."

"Ok," the disembodied voice returned, "we will deliver the pizzas to the conference room at noon"

Placing the receiver on the wall Lloyd toyed with the attendees' curiosity for a moment. Assuming a serious countenance Lloyd gravely declared, "metropolitan pizza ran out of pepperoni and will instead bring sausage pizzas at noon."

His deadpan routine completely surprised everyone. It took a few moments for the assemblage to process the incongruity of the phone call, but murmurs of laughter signaled an anxiolytic response.

Roderick used the inopportune phone call to happily dismiss the meeting.

Chapter Four – Treachery

Lloyd and Nadene looked forward to their mini-vacation even as the simmering global tensions reached a boiling point. Both wanted a respite from the endless barrage of bad news and an escape to the nearby seashore was the perfect tonic.

Hours of research helped Lloyd find a surprise destination and with a gleeful tone and a twinkle in his eye he teased his wife, "I looked everywhere for a hotel but not much was available. So, I spent some time at the hospital's tickets and travel office and settled for a remote bed and breakfast."

Nadene focused on the word "remote" and imagined an inland location that was miles from any beach access. "I was hoping for a beachfront hotel. It's so nice to open the windows at night and drift to sleep with the sea breeze."

His wife's disappointment stabbed Lloyd's sensibilities and now hobbled by the thoughtless joke he demurely produced a colorful brochure. "Take a look at this."

Nadene's face visibly brightened as she opened the brochure and scanned the contents. "Is this a lighthouse B&B?"

"Yes," Lloyd answered and then added. "This lighthouse was purchased by a historical trust and restored. Apparently, it was quite dilapidated, but the trust group modernized the lighthouse keeper's accommodations and several adjoining buildings and now rents the rooms. I was able to get the room on the top floor of the keeper's house which has access to a cupola. It also has a kitchen, and several grocery stores are just a few miles away."

"It sounds wonderful," Nadene exclaimed. "When should we leave?"

"The reservation is for three nights. I figure it will take four hours to get there. So, if we leave bright and early tomorrow, we can stop for some groceries and have dinner at the lighthouse."

Heavy rain greeted the travelers as they packed their car for the day's journey. Nothing could dampen their enthusiasm, but the weather forced more careful driving, and what should have taken four hours stretched insufferably to nearly twice the expected time. Multiple car accidents highlighted the peril of imprudence and reinforced the need for caution.

Just before noon pangs of hunger directed the wayfarers to a fast-food restaurant. It was an opportunity to relieve the monotony of driving and get a quick bite but neither wanted to linger being anxious to get to their destination before darkness obscured the landscape.

Nadene and Lloyd shared the driving chore which lessened the tedium. During her respites from the wheel, Nadene would close her eyes and soon fall asleep; an amazing transformation that Lloyd envied but could never replicate.

Dusk was descending when the intrepid pair parked at a grocery store just a few miles from the lighthouse. Dashing inside they mostly avoided the pelting rain and quickly set about securing provisions for their stay. The store was surprisingly well stocked with prepared meals and, after taking longer than planned, they settled on seafood entrees. Tasty-looking desserts added to their bounty and for late-night munchies, they grabbed flavorful bags of chips.

A short drive brought the travelers to their destination for the night; tired and hungry but eagerly anticipating their first night at the lighthouse. Their expectations were amply rewarded by the clean, tidy room filled with vintage nautical items. Centered prominently in the living room was a rough-hewn ship's hatch table; obviously, hand made many decades earlier. Lloyd spied a brass label attached to the side of the table and bending over, read aloud, "S.S. Rudolph Kauffman. That was a World War II Liberty Ship."

While her husband was examining the other nautical furniture Nadene was scrutinizing a collection of black and white photographs centered above the sofa. In one, a stern-looking man in a uniform stared vacantly at Nadene. Underneath the picture faded lettering identified the man as the first keeper of the lighthouse. Adjoining the keeper's image was a photo of a dour-looking woman, frazzled Nadene thought by the daily drudgery and isolation imposed by her husband's occupation.

Pangs of hunger reminded Nadene that the night's dinner was waiting a turn in the microwave oven. She selected two seafood pasta entrees and after putting both in the oven spent the intervening time unpacking their luggage.

A loud chime from the microwave oven signaled that dinner was ready and Nadene removed the steaming hot pasta dishes and gingerly placed them on the ship's hatch table. It was a delightfully delectable meal enhanced by the ambiance of the light keeper's house.

Neither wanted to succumb to their fatigue and a burst of enthusiasm propelled them both up the steep stairs to the cupola. Lloyd cautiously opened the door permitting access to the cupola and was greeted with a gusty breeze that nearly tore the door from his grasp. Nadene followed and the wind angrily whipped her long brown hair forcing her momentary retreat as she secured her tresses.

Once outside, a dim light shined through the Fresnel lenses in the lantern room; clearly installed for creating a romantic atmosphere and not for maritime navigation. Ever practical, Lloyd appreciated the light's illumination of the cupola's narrow circular corridor.

Once outside Nadene shuddered briefly as the cold wind swept her body heat away. Tightening her jacket in response, she cast her gaze across the inky dark black night and barely discerned the far distant lights of a ship. Far below, the ocean's roar and the effervescent whitecaps suggested high tide. Altogether it was a mélange of thrilling, somewhat spooky sensations.

The cold wind finally sapped the visitor's remaining reserves and the warm interior beckoned them inside; an entreaty they both affirmatively answered. Once inside, the day's long adventures compelled the travelers to admit their bone-weary fatigue and after opening the windows for a cross-breeze they snuggled under down comforters for the night.

Lloyd slept soundly and awakened thoroughly refreshed. For a moment he marveled at the night's uninterrupted slumber; a rare phenomenon for the man whose typical sleep was restless. With a spring in his step, Lloyd made his way to the kitchen and soon the pungent odor of coffee filled the room.

Lloyd poured a cup of coffee and quietly checked on his wife who was still sleeping soundly. Crossing over to the sliding glass door, Lloyd slid it open and relished the gush of fresh ocean air that rushed inside. The cool breeze stirred Nadene and rising from her slumber she joined her husband.

"Are you ready for breakfast?" the bleary-eyed woman asked.

"Why don't you have a cup of tea first," Lloyd offered in return.

"That's a good idea," she said and then turned her attention to making a pot of black tea.

"I will then quickly attend to my daily ablutions," a remark from Lloyd that evoked a quizzical look from Nadene as she poured a cup of tea and dragged a chair nearer to the open window.

Nadene sat quietly sipping her tea, watching the waves chase each other over the open sea and then collapse on the white sand. A noisy bird diverted her focus and she now watched its antics; darting to and fro presumably searching for a tiny tidbit.

The woman's reverie came to an end when her husband returned.

"Are you ready for breakfast now?" he queried.

"I suppose so;" although Nadene preferred her ocean view.

Nadene opened the pantry and removed a box of granola. She casually read the label and frowned at the calories in a small serving. Her husband liked granola, so he got a larger portion. With the respective beverages replenished they both sat down for a light meal.

"What would you like to do today?" Nadene wondered.

The ever-prepared man responded, "I thought we could go for a walk on the beach and then go to a nearby tropical garden. From what I read it has some excellent nature trails that wind through the extensive collection of plants."

"That sounds nice," Nadene simply rejoined.

Lloyd took notice of Nadene's half-hearted response and continued. "I figured we could have lunch at one of the restaurants near the garden. There are two seafood restaurants, a diner, and a couple of fast-food restaurants."

"Let's go to the diner," Nadene suggested.

"Ok, I think you will like it. It's a local favorite," Lloyd replied.

"And after lunch?" Nadene open-endedly asked.

"There is a craft fair about ten miles from here. It looks pretty large and seems to have many vendors selling unique artistic items." he offered.

Nadene visibly brightened at the prospect. She enjoyed craft fairs and voiced her excitement, "That sounds like a great way to spend the afternoon!"

The day's leisure began with a brisk walk on the beach. Numerous shells littered the beach and Nadene collected several perfect specimens. Like little balloons, jellyfish dotted the beach; forcing the amblers to cautiously avoid the nettlesome creatures.

Roughly an hour later Nadene and Lloyd returned to the lighthouse's parking lot and took the short drive to the nearby tropical garden. The lush oasis shielded them from the bright sunshine and was a quiet, welcome respite. Surprisingly, few people were in the garden which left Nadene and Lloyd alone as they meandered through the trails. Cascading waterfalls ornamented the gardens along with modern statuary. On their way out Nadene took a quick stroll through the gift shop and purchased a small souvenir.

Lunch at the diner was a disappointment. When they arrived an empty parking lot flashed a warning sign, but the hungry visitors overcame their trepidations, opened the door, and stepped inside. The restaurant was dark inside and after waiting several minutes Lloyd impatiently whispered, "I don't like the looks of this. There were no cars outside and it's dark in here. No one has come to seat us. I think we should leave."

Before Nadene could respond to her husband a woman peered from behind a partially opened door and anxiously declared, "We are closed. Please leave."

The plaintive plea irritated Nadene, "I wish you would have put a sign outside indicating that you were closed. In any event, can you recommend a nearby eatery?"

"No," the frightened woman answered and then resolutely closed her door.

Nadene and Lloyd reluctantly returned to their car. Both were glum, confused, and still hungry but the diner's closure sparked Lloyd to comment, "She seemed rather frightened."

Frustration replaced irritation with Nadene, "I was looking forward to a nice lunch. Let's just drive down the main road and find some fast food."

Her husband quickly acceded to the request and soon they were motoring along a principal highway. A cluster of restaurants hugged an interstate exchange, and like weary nomads crossing a desert and sighting an oasis, their hearts rejoiced in anticipation of relieving their hunger.

It turned out to be a mirage, not in the classical sense of a perceptual disorder but sharing with it the same profound disappointment accompanying a cruel trick. It was not their senses that betrayed them, quite the contrary.

"None of these restaurants look open," Lloyd noted after driving past three buildings.

"This is weird and a bit scary," Nadene added.

"It looks like a convenience store may be open," Lloyd hoped while pointing to a small building.

"Well, it does have some cars parked out front. I guess we can get something for lunch there," Nadene said.

Lloyd took a side road for a closer look and confirmed the presence of three other vehicles. Just as he drove in, a person opened the store's door and disappeared inside.

"It looks open. I think we should get some gas before we go inside," he suggested.

Nadene was more interested in satisfying her hunger, "Ok, but I will go inside and see what we can get for lunch."

They briefly parted company while Lloyd filled the car's gas tank. He congratulated himself on getting gas since the car was nearly empty and the price was reasonable. Lloyd quickly scanned the other empty pumps and decided not to move the car; briskly walking the short distance to the store's front door.

Once inside, Lloyd looked for his wife and found her peering at a small collection of sandwiches. She was not happy with the selections and voiced her discontent. "None of the sandwiches look particularly good. I found one that was soggy and another with mold. I think we would be better off getting some peanut butter, crackers, and some chips."

"Ok, let me get some soft drinks," Lloyd said, barely concealing his frustration.

Lloyd and Nadene glanced disapprovingly at a forlorn picnic table at the far edge of the convenience store and decided to eat their meager meal in the car. Despite the day's travails, they both refused to emotionally succumb and enjoyed their lunch.

With a full tank of gas and their hunger satiated Lloyd resumed the day's agenda and headed to the craft fair. It was midafternoon when they left the convenience store and with another hour's drive, Nadene suggested an alternative. "Why don't we skip the craft fair. We can take another walk on the beach and explore the lighthouse."

With a puzzled expression, Lloyd tested her resolve. "Are you sure? I know you were looking forward to the craft fair."

"I was but it is getting late. I like the lighthouse and the ocean. Plus we have the makings of a really good dinner," she conceded.

Lloyd accepted her decision and turned the vehicle back to the lighthouse. While Nadene was changing clothes for the stroll on the sandy beach Lloyd aimlessly turned the television on. Given their isolated location he did expect to receive many stations and a list of channels on the table confirmed his suspicions.

Flipping through the channels produced nothing but static. Lloyd inspected the coaxial cable and finding nothing amiss returned to the channel search. Nadene returned and watching her husband fiddle with the television innocently inquired, "Did you find a good channel? It might be nice to watch a movie with dinner."

"I've been through the channel list," he said while motioning towards the document on the table. "Not a single station comes in."

"Oh, well," Nadene sighed. "Perhaps after we come back from our walk the television will cooperate."

The ocean breeze blew their gloom away as they walked along the beach. High tide gobbled up most of the dry areas forcing the pair to walk single file to avoid getting wet. Even so, a pounding surf unleashed cool sea spray that slowly soaked their clothes. It was an exhilarating experience but after an hour's walk, they turned around and headed back.

The return trip was treacherous. They miscalculated the high tide's reach and soon were wading in ankle-deep water.

Nadene good-naturedly but with a touch of concern noted, "I wonder if we will need to swim back. The tide is rising fast."

Lloyd heard the undertone and suggested, "We are almost back. Let's race back. I will give you a head start."

Nadene bolted past her husband splashing and laughing as she conquered the waves. Lloyd waited for a minute and then dashed forward, overtaking his wife but then slackening his pace to remain a few steps behind. Now thoroughly soaked but enjoying every moment of their escapade they tiredly climbed the steps to their lofty abode.

Dinner preparation took about thirty minutes during which time Lloyd again tried to find an operable television station. Like before, his efforts were in vain, but he decided on another tactic.

"Nadene," he asked, "Will dinner be ready soon?"

"In about twenty minutes," she replied.

"I am going to check with the onsite manager about the television. I will not be gone long," Lloyd promised.

As it turned out, his excursion to the manager's cottage was both unproductive and short. The manager was located a short walk from the lightkeeper's house and as Lloyd approached the building the absence of a vehicle and the shuttered blinds suggested that the tenant was gone. A small, hand-lettered sign fluttering in the breeze on the building's door attracted his attention. One word was scrawled in large, angry, block letters on a piece of paper – CLOSED.

Lloyd walked around to the back of the building and peered through the partially closed shutters. It took a moment for his eyes to adjust to the dark interior but after careful scanning, Lloyd speculated that the closure seemed permanent. His conjecture seemed more certain after observing the chairs in the dining room sitting precariously on a table and yawning cabinet doors displaying vacant shelves. The haphazard arrangement suggested that the erstwhile occupant had left in haste.

Dusk was robbing the day's light and Lloyd's mood darkened in tandem with the dwindling illumination. His thoughts gravitated towards the day's other frustrations that were united by a common theme, peoples' inexplicable, seemingly fearful disappearances.

Nadene was setting the table when her husband returned. Turning towards him she inquired, “What did the manager say?”

Lloyd wondered if his revelation might frighten his wife but after quickly deciding otherwise, he answered, “The manager was gone. There was a crudely lettered closed sign on the door. I managed to peek inside, and it appeared as if the manager left rather quickly.”

“This has certainly been an odd day,” Nadene blandly concluded.

Lloyd started to share his ominous analysis of the day’s events but stifled the impulse in deference to the sumptuous meal on the table. While enjoying their dinner, a cool breeze from the open windows wafted across the table and the distant sea, now placated with low tide, rumbled quietly in the background.

Coffee, tea, and generous slices of key lime pie were the perfect ending to the night’s dinner. Lloyd cleared the table while Nadene peered out the window; dimly lit by the crescent moon. On the distant horizon, she could barely discern what appeared to be a flotilla of ships speedily crossing the expanse.

Nadene greeted her husband the next morning with a surprising request. “After breakfast let’s take a walk on the beach and then head home.”

With a perplexed expression, Lloyd probed his wife’s suggestion. “We paid for tonight’s stay. Are you sure you want to leave?”

“I have this strange feeling that something is wrong. Yesterday, stores were closed, the manager of this property apparently left in a rush, and we can’t even get a television station,” she complained.

Lloyd nodded his head in agreement but offered an alternative. “These are mysterious, but we have not taken a vacation for months. I would prefer to leave tomorrow as we planned. We still have plenty of food for today and we can take two long, leisurely walks on the beach.”

Nadene stared at her tea; lost in thought as she considered the options and then with conviction proposed, “Let’s make this our special day and have a picnic on the beach.”

“That’s a great idea,” Lloyd exclaimed.

With a newfound eagerness, they busily prepared the meal. Generously loaded tuna salad sandwiches went first into Lloyd's backpack, followed by corn chips, cucumber slices, seedless grapes, a box of chocolate cookies, and bottles of flavored water. Lloyd hoisted the bountiful cargo and securely fastened the backpack as they headed out the door.

Brilliant sunshine welcomed Nadene and Lloyd, lifting the morning fog and their spirits. Lloyd glanced at his watch and suggested, "We can walk for about two hours and then find a spot for our picnic."

Squinting in response as she surveyed the landscape Nadene replied, "I think we could walk forever. I don't see any end to the beach."

For the most part, they said little to each other during their journey. Nadene simply enjoyed wading in the shallow, cool water as a soft breeze fluttered her hair. An occasional crab scurried across the sand but otherwise, the beach was devoid of the usual animations from birds and humans.

Lloyd avoided the water, preferring the firmer sand. Small shells abundantly cloaked his path and crunched with each step. Aside from that sound and the cresting waves, it was eerie quiet.

Their diminutive shadows, shortened as the sun beamed directly from overhead, prompted Lloyd to break a lengthy silence. "I'm famished. Are you ready for lunch?"

Nadene stopped and while slowly looking around replied, "A little further ahead I see a group of palm trees. Maybe we can find some shade there."

Approaching the little cluster of trees afforded them little relief from the intense sunlight but a gathering of dark clouds promised otherwise. Lloyd shielded his eyes and scanned the sky "It looks light a storm is developing. I think we should have time for our picnic before it rains but we may get soaked on the way back."

Nadene helped Lloyd remove the backpack, after which she spread a large towel on the sand. A freshening breeze curled the edges and blew some sand on the towel; the weight of which paradoxically prevented further movement.

They both sat facing the water and watching the sky lose its bright blue color as the distant clouds moved closer. Their long hike was a famish-inducing trek, and they relished the sandwiches and chips. Unfortunately, the backpack transmitted Lloyd's every step to the contents, traumatizing the grapes which bled their purplish juice. Had there been any birds he would have considered leaving them behind but seeing none he returned the mash to the backpack.

"Maybe we should head back", Lloyd suggested, "We can sweeten the trip with our cookies."

Nadene laughed as she gathered up the towel while surveying the clouds, "Perhaps I should leave the towel out. We may need it pretty soon."

With a sense of urgency, they began their journey back to the lightkeeper's lodge, their pace quickened by the impending inclement weather and an angry surf roiled by the storm. Booming thunder and spears of lightning gave notice that the menacing storm was approaching.

Lloyd counted the seconds that passed between the lightning and the thunder and turning to Nadene said, "I counted 10 seconds between the flash of lightning and the thunder. If I remember correctly, you then divide that number by five which suggests that the lightning is two miles away."

"We passed a small gazebo-like building this morning Nadene remembered, "I think we are pretty close."

Nadene had a remarkable sense of direction and rarely got lost. She remembered little details and could use them to navigate unfamiliar terrain. Lloyd lacked this gift and particularly welcomed Nadene's proposal.

They both scanned the shoreline impatiently looking for shelter, but the darkening sky hampered the search. Wind-whipped drops of rain spotted their clothes and pressured them both to start running. Nadene stumbled momentarily but as she regained her balance she exclaimed, "I see the building! Hurry up and follow me."

Lloyd sprinted alongside his wife, and they ducked inside the welcoming shelter. A loud clap of thunder shook the little building, almost as if the storm were angry at their escape. Torrents of rain followed as the occupants watched nature's drama. Lloyd reached into the backpack and removed two candy bars and handing one to Nadene commented, "I'm glad you remembered this little building."

Twenty minutes later the storm ceded the sky to the sun and the ocean sparkled in appreciation. Nadene and Lloyd sallied forth, playfully thanking their little building's hospitality. The storm-freshened air invigorated the walkers and hastened their trip; a journey soon rewarded as they sighted the lighthouse.

As they ascended the steep shoreline leading to the lighthouse Nadene noticed a thick, black, plume drifting towards the heavens. Pointing towards the sight, she asked her husband, "Lloyd, do you see that? It looks like smoke."

Lloyd looked to the distant horizon and confirmed Nadene's observation. "Let's take a look from the lightkeeper's cupola. There is also a pair of binoculars up there so we can get an even better view."

Nadene agreed and they bounded up the stairs to their lofty perch. Gusty winds, remnants of the recent storm, greeted the pair as they gained the cupola. Lloyd cautiously wound around the circular platform and reaching into a recess removed a pair of binoculars. "It looks like a ship is burning and sending those thick spirals of smoke upwards."

"Let me take a look," Nadene anxiously plead.

Lloyd handed the binoculars to his wife and awaited her analysis. After gazing at the distant horizon for several minutes Nadene concluded, "It is indeed a ship. I think it is a Coast Guard Cutter. I can just barely see the ship's insignia against the red background."

Nighttime obscured their vision except for a yellow glow that dimly illuminated the burning ship. The cold wind argued for their retreat and once inside Lloyd wondered, "Maybe we should call the police and let them know what we saw."

With Nadene's acquiescence, Lloyd removed the telephone's handset from its cradle and after listening for a few moments tiredly noted, "The phone is dead."

In a feint-hearted attempt at humor, Nadene replied, "Well, we wanted a quiet getaway and it seems that everyone and everything is cooperating."

They both agreed that the mysteries would remain unsolved until they returned home. Setting aside their curiosity until then allowed them to enjoy their dinner.

Nadene awoke earlier than usual the next morning and quickly prepared their morning meal. After packing the suitcases, they decided to take a last stroll on the beach. High tide lashed the sandy shore and a brisk wind hurled spray at the pair. As they traversed the narrow path untouched by the crashing waves Nadene and Lloyd both searched the sea for the burning ship.

"I don't see the ship anywhere," Nadene concluded.

"I guess it sank," Lloyd mused, "I hope everyone got off safely before it went down."

They walked hand-in-hand for another hour before turning around. Clambering over a wind-driven dune brought them back to the lightkeeper's house and a few minutes later they were on their way home.

The return trip differed remarkably. Long lines of traffic and scattered accidents marred their drive to the lighthouse, but the reverse journey was void of vehicles. Mile after monotonousness mile passed by without any traffic. With the gas gauge nearing the halfway mark, Lloyd eased the car into an off-ramp and headed towards a cluster of gas stations.

Nadene was napping but awakened when Lloyd stopped at a gas pump. She lazily looked at the surroundings and commented, "It certainly looks deserted."

"It is," her husband acknowledged, "but I hope the pumps still work."

Lloyd examined the pump and noting that the lights were on, slid a credit card into the machine. With a sigh of relief, Lloyd saw the pump come to life and placing the nozzle in the car he fully fueled the vehicle.

While Lloyd was filling the gas tank Nadene wandered around; a desultory search that left the woman convinced that the property was abandoned. Peering across the highway she spied a similarly vacant restaurant and was silently thankful that they had the makings for a decent midday meal.

Since their return trip was not marred by accidents and heavy traffic, they both decided to stop at a nature park roughly halfway home. Nadene wanted to postpone their arrival home, hoping to linger in the relaxing moments of the mini vacation.

The nature park was empty just as they expected. Lloyd parked the car under the obliging canopy of a large tree, opened the trunk, and removed the makings of their lunch. He placed the food and drinks on a picnic table near their car after which Nadene prepared the meal. A few scattered clouds added texture to the azure sky and the sun's warmth countered the cool, light wind. All-in-all it was a delightful wayside stop.

After lunch, Lloyd studied the park's trail map. "Nadene," he announced as a prelude to further comment, "There are some interesting trails. One of them parallels a small stream before heading uphill to a large waterfall. It's about a two-mile round-trip hike and I guess it would take us about an hour."

Nadene liked waterfalls and the walk through the verdant forest added to her eagerness. "That sounds nice," she enthusiastically quipped.

A soft, babbling, stream accompanied their trip to the waterfall while the dense vegetation reluctantly admitted patches of sunlight that created iridescent patterns on the ground. Chirping birds happily flitted from tree to tree adding their joy to the serene landscape.

The ascent uphill was steep but numerous switchbacks lessened the labor. Their efforts rewarded Nadene and Lloyd with breathtaking views of the surrounding countryside and the rumbling water as it furiously funneled through a rock crevice before hurling over the precipice.

Having conquered the mountain, they lingered near the waterfall before heading down to the cascade's plunge which terminated in a shallow pool. A rocky traverse, mottled by rivulets, invited the daring duo nearer. After examining the terrain Lloyd declared, "I think we can get much closer."

Without waiting for an answer Lloyd stepped gingerly from one dry patch to another before stopping a few meters from the falling water. Nadene followed, carefully approximating her husband's path, and was soon near his side. Both were now close enough to feel the pounding turbulence and cool spray as the water made its triumphant landfall.

"I could stay here forever," the woman exclaimed.

Lloyd too was enjoying the natural spectacle, but his progressively damp clothes urged a retreat from the waterfall. "Nadene, I think we need to leave. I'm getting soaked."

Nadene laughed, unfazed by her soggy attire. "My clothes will dry on the way back, but it is getting late, and we should head back."

The trek to the car was delightful and as they departed the trail the full force of the sun returned, no longer masked by the dense canopy. Nadene offered to drive the remaining distance home which was an invitation Lloyd readily accepted.

Neither could explain the sense of foreboding that greeted their return home. The preceding day's tranquil aura quickly unfolded; seemingly in tandem with unpacking the luggage from the all too brief trip. Memories of seaside sojourns and lush landscapes withered with the dry back-to-work reality.

Lloyd glanced at the clock and quietly sighed. "It's getting late, and I need to get up early tomorrow. No more lounging around."

Nadene juxtaposed his comment with her husband's unbending routines. Lloyd was an early riser and invariably was out of bed at 5 am. Even late-night delays in getting to bed did not upend his schedule nor his energy. Every day began with intensity and purpose so "lounging around" to Lloyd was equal parts anathema and absurdity. Reconciling the contradiction relied on a nuanced analysis of "no more lounging around," which when translated by Nadene meant the return to his stress-laden job.

Her thoughtful insight guided a response, "I do not return to work for another day so I thought I would get some groceries tomorrow and have a welcome home dinner."

Lloyd visibly perked up in response to Nadene's suggestion. "That would be a very nice treat after work tomorrow!"

Sleep maliciously denied Lloyd a restful night. Shortly after midnight, he surrendered to insomnia, ceding the bed to his wife as he wandered around their home. After parting the vertical drapes, he peered out, expecting to see streetlights illuminating adjacent roads and buildings but strangely there was only a vast expanse of inky darkness.

Lloyd's first thought was a power failure, and he tested his theory by switching the porch lights on. Two brilliant orbs of light pierced the darkness. As he turned away from the drapes Nadene quietly entered the room and with a quizzical expression asked, "Lloyd, why aren't you in bed?"

"I was just tossing and turning around. The more I tried to fall asleep the worse it got so I gave up," he replied.

"I saw the porch lights. Did you see something outside?" Nadene wondered.

Lloyd explained, "When I first looked outside it was pitch dark and I guessed that the electricity was off. That's when I turned the porch lights on."

Nadene yawned, and unimpressed by the mystery returned to bed. Lloyd followed and after another restless hour finally succumbed to dreamless slumber.

Lloyd's internal clock awakened him at 5 am. His troubled sleep robbed the man of his normal ebullience, but two strong cups of coffee restored the homeostasis. While Nadene prepared breakfast Lloyd took a quick shower and donned his uniform. Now neatly attired, he joined his wife for a robust meal of pancakes, maple syrup, and scrambled eggs; washed down with another cup of coffee.

"Would you like me to drive you to work?" Nadene suggested.

Normally Lloyd would have demurred, but the drive together prolonged the vanishing vacation. "Sure," he acquiesced, "that will give us another twenty minutes together. I should be able to have lunch at the hospital with you too."

Nadene quickly accepted her husband's proposal, "Lunch sounds great!"

Lloyd suppressed his anxiety. The twenty-minute drive to work was an enjoyable reprieve from the expected problems at work, even though his absence was counted in three days. Nadene drove the car to the hospital's front entrance and kissed her husband and reminded him that she would return for their lunch date.

Lingering outside long enough to see his wife disappear as she returned home, he then entered the hospital, walked past the information desk, and went to his office. As expected, his inbox overflowed with documents requiring responses. Before tackling the beckoning papers, Lloyd alerted the administrative assistant of his arrival and his intention to whittle the workload down.

A phone call interrupted Lloyd's single-minded focus and with evident irritation, he answered, "This is Lloyd. How may I help you?"

"Colonel Roderick has called for an emergency meeting at 1 pm," his administrative assistant announced.

"Ok, thank you for letting me know," Lloyd replied.

"Another emergency meeting," he muttered to himself. "I wonder what Roderick will say this time."

Setting his speculation aside, Lloyd resumed the task at hand and once again was immersed. The morning shed ninety minutes before Lloyd completed reviewing and signing the document trove. Emerging from his office he checked in with his staff and together they made the rounds; a combination of socializing with the soldier-patients, identifying needs and intervening as required to expedite clinical and administrative prerogatives. A short staff meeting always followed the morning rounds. Lloyd quickly reviewed the notes taken during the walk-around and doled out staff responses based on their contents.

Lloyd returned to his office just as the phone rang. "Hello, this is Lloyd. How may I help you," he answered with his habitual greeting.

"Did you forget your lunch date?" Nadene asked. "I am waiting for you in the lobby."

Lloyd looked at his watch, surprised at how quickly the time passed before he enthusiastically replied, "I'll be there in a minute."

Nadene smiled when her husband approached; a beaming countenance reflecting her inner pride in his professional appearance and military bearing. "I'm famished and looking forward to cafeteria food," she replied with a wry laugh that betrayed her honest opinion of the hospital's fare.

Lloyd smiled in return and promised, "You will love the menu. Monday is their spaghetti special."

Nadene frowned, expecting a mediocre pasta but then conceded. "Ok, let's get two spaghetti specials."

The lunch was quite tasty and after jointly conceding their apprehension, Lloyd reviewed his morning activities. "Nothing much of interest this morning but Colonel Roderick wants all leaders together for an emergency meeting at 1 pm."

"Do you have any idea what the emergency is?," Nadene cautiously inquired.

"Nobody I met with earlier has any idea, but folks are nervous," he admitted.

"Well, you better be on time," Nadene warned. "It sounds like something important."

Lloyd was never late for a meeting, but the admonition prompted the man to consult his watch, and reading 12:50 he responded, "I guess I should make my way to the conference room. Thank you for coming over for lunch – even if it was just hospital food!"

As it turned out Lloyd was the last person to claim a seat in the hospital commander's conference room. His conspicuous arrival garnered the gaze of those already seated but no one said a word. After he sat down, Lloyd looked around the table but by now everyone was avoiding eye contact and pretended preoccupation with notepads or coffee cups; a not-so-subtle mask disguising their anxiety.

Colonel Roderick joined the group precisely at the appointed time and without hesitation broke the nervous silence. "Thank you for coming," he deferentially began, "I will not hold you in suspense nor will I sugar coat my comments. These are perilous times that require frank disclosures."

His opening remarks presaged bad news. Lloyd's heart raced in anticipation and discreetly looking across the table he noted other reactions to Roderick's ominous opening. A palpable restlessness seized some while a stiffened posture among others betrayed their resistance to any observable emotional response.

Roderick continued, "The President has declared war against the eastern enemy. This came after consultation with senior members of Congress. All military absences are revoked along with that Presidential directive. In a surprise announcement, the President castigated former administrations that eviscerated military appropriations that severely diminished our nation's offensive capabilities. As the President noted, recruitment and retention have suffered in consequence and severely eroded military readiness. Our commander-in-chief is mobilizing all national guard units and reserve elements. Anyone who is receiving military retirement or disability pay will be ordered to undergo a fitness for duty evaluation. As you can imagine that stipulation will substantially increase our workload. Orders directing personnel to report for a fitness evaluation will begin immediately and must be completed expeditiously. It is worth noting, that noncompliance with the President's order will result in termination of all military entitlements."

Roderick paused for a moment letting the gravity of the situation sink in but then he turned to Lloyd and said, "Lloyd, I am placing you in command of our newly constituted Fitness for Duty Board. Similar FDBs will be launched across the country and guidance from the Surgeon General's Office will support the effort. As a hospital, we must pivot and prioritize clinical activities to ensure that the FDBs provide comprehensive examinations that can activate eligible service personnel."

Lloyd blushed at Roderick's promotion, a behavioral characteristic the man rarely experienced. Uncertainty momentarily gripped the man as he pondered a response. Should he remain silent or voice his understanding? Lloyd opted for the latter and simply replied, "Thank you, sir, I look forward to the challenge."

Colonel Roderick smiled imperceptibly while adding, "It will be a challenge for all of us, but I have no doubt we will succeed."

The brief exchange between Roderick and Lloyd lessened the room's tension as the mutual respect between the two men took central stage. It was a brief reprieve as Roderick resumed his monologue. "The other surprise announcement is closely related to the mobilization of the National Guard and Reserves. Even with those assets, the President is convinced that the enemy's vast military force could quickly defeat our depleted troop strength with catastrophic consequences. Tonight, the President will address the Nation; outlining the threats and the sacrifices we must face. He will review the unprovoked submarine attack off our coast that destroyed two Coast Guard Cutters and a cruise ship two days ago and led to his decision to declare war. The loss of life on the cruise ship alone is estimated at over four thousand innocent civilians. Of course, all active-duty military forces are now on the highest alert and the President will inform the Nation of the mobilization of all reserve forces."

Roderick paused briefly, a momentary delay that piqued Lloyd's curiosity. His inquisitive nature was satiated when Lloyd digested the Commander's main entrée. "The President will describe the enemy's strengths and our vulnerabilities as a prelude to conscripting all able-bodied men and women between the ages of 18 to 35. The first phase of the draft will develop the infrastructure to identify and notify the prospective individuals. After that, civilian doctors and allied health professionals will perform physical and mental examinations consistent with current policies and procedures. The President expects the draft to start supplying recruits within three months."

The gravity of Colonel Roderick's comments weighed heavily on the attendees; with falling spirits mirrored in their grave visages. Even after Roderick invited an open discussion among the leaders, silence reigned as each person sought cover in their private thoughts.

Sensing that any discussion was unlikely persuaded Colonel Roderick to conclude the briefing. Members slowly drifted out of the conference room and Lloyd was among the last to leave when Roderick stopped him, "Lloyd, please join me in my office."

Lloyd was lost in thought like the others attending the briefing and Roderick's request startled the man. "Yes, sir," was the most he could muster in response.

Roderick disappeared into his adjoining office and quickly taking a seat motioned for Lloyd to do the same. Lloyd was now doubly uneasy; his twin discomfitures revolving around the recent meeting and now the unexpected invitation to the Commander's office.

"I wanted to begin planning for the Fitness for Duty Board, otherwise known as the FDB, since we need to be up and running very quickly," Roderick opened the discussion.

A wave of relief washed away Lloyd's anxieties as he turned his attention to the business at hand. His response was focused, "As we begin to set up operations, I think my current staff is sufficient, but we will need expedited access to all clinical services. When the demand grows, we will need additional help to process the fitness for duty evaluations."

Roderick agreed with the interim assessment and added, "I will order all clinical activities to prioritize all referrals from the FDB. I also have some good news for you. Along with your added responsibility, I am asking the Surgeon General to support your promotion to Captain. You were in the secondary zone for consideration, but I am hoping you will be promoted early." With the impromptu meeting concluded, Lloyd thanked Roderick for the unexpected recognition and the two shook hands warmly.

Lloyd could not shake the gloom that darkened his mood upon leaving Roderick's office. Even the prospect of promotion and new responsibilities failed to lighten the atmosphere but like the sun dispatching the morning fog, Nadene's sunny disposition greeting her husband in the hospital's lobby warmed his soul. Taking her hand in his, they quickly departed.

Once in the car, Lloyd suggested they stop at a quick-service restaurant for a takeout dinner. Loaded with sandwiches, onion rings, and drinks they then resumed their journey home. Casual conversation accompanied the feast at home with Lloyd studiously avoiding any mention of the afternoon's revelations.

With dinner now a memory, Nadene reminded her husband, "I go back to work tomorrow. I will drop you off at the hospital since I go in later than you." Her suggestion was the usual arrangement that most efficiently made use of their one car.

"The President is addressing the nation tonight in a televised speech," Nadene abruptly tendered, offering her husband the opportunity to expand the discussion.

"Yes, I learned about that this afternoon at Roderick's meeting," he tentatively offered.

"How did the meeting go?" his wife quizzed.

Nadene's query unleashed the emotional torrent Lloyd held at bay. "It was mostly bad news. The President will announce his decision to prosecute a full-scale war against the enemy. The trigger was the submarine sinking of two Coast Guard Cutters and a passenger cruise ship."

His wife gasped as she remembered peering through binoculars perched on the lighthouse's parapet just two days ago.

"So, the Cutter we saw was destroyed by a torpedo," she openly mused in amazement.

"Yes, along with one other cutter. But the tragic loss occurred when the enemy torpedoed a cruise ship. Around four thousand people were killed in that attack," Lloyd added.

"Why hasn't this been publicized in the news media?" Nadene wondered.

"I can only guess they are waiting for the President to address the matter, perhaps fearing a widespread panic," her husband speculated.

"Maybe that explains the mysterious evacuation we saw in the coastal area. Those people must have figured out what happened and fearing more of the same fled the area," Nadene surmised.

Her husband agreed, "I think you are right but there must be more to this story. I just can not fathom a burning ship spooking that many people. What do you think?"

Nadene mentally rolled her husband's theory around before replying, "Maybe, the submarine surfaced and was visible or perhaps some of the crew came ashore?"

It was plausible conjecture and Lloyd agreed, "that may be true. This attack may have been designed to test coastal defenses. If that is true, then the sinking of the cruise ship might have been a cruel deception concealing the enemy's true intention to begin a ground invasion."

Taking a rest from the day's momentous events allowed Lloyd and Nadene to catch up on their leisure reading while waiting for the President's evening address to the nation. Lloyd enjoyed reading novels written by Horatio Alger while his wife preferred mystery stories. For the next two hours they both voraciously flipped pages; entirely immersed in their respective books.

Almost by accident Nadene noticed the time, set her book down, and said, "The President's talk should be starting soon."

Lloyd reluctantly stopped reading, set his book aside, and turned the television on. A pontificating news commentator was filling the gap while awaiting the President which stimulated Lloyd to comment, "It will be interesting to hear the reporter's editorializing after the President speaks."

A camera panned away from the reporter just as the President approached the dais. His solemn mien portended the serious declarations. The President began his discourse by summarizing the enemy's aggressions and then peremptorily invoked his authority as commander-in-chief to declare war. In obeisance to the law, the President noted that he would submit his emergency order for consideration and adoption by the US Congress.

Looking straight into the camera as if appealing to every viewer the President stated, "These are perilous times, and our way of life is under assault. We will prevail but our enemy is a determined foe and for us to succeed we all will contribute and sacrifice. To that end, I am ordering all National Guard and Reserve forces to active duty. Along with our current active-duty personnel, these brave men and women will be the backbone of our military response."

The President paused, strode from the podium, crossed his arms, and looking weary continued, "The enemy has a well-disciplined force with enormous numbers of personnel and weapons. Our Nation's factories will be retooled to supply the military but that is not enough. So, tonight, I am asking Congress to join with me in revitalizing our Nation's Selective Service System to ensure all eligible men and women between the ages of 18 to 35 are recruited as soon as possible. I am also asking our medical associations to support the process by volunteering to examine eligible recruits per fitness for duty procedures."

Fifteen minutes passed in the blink of an eye as mesmerized citizens absorbed the President's address. With a subdued, "God Bless America," the President concluded his remarks. Pre-selected members of Congress followed and added their comments; all of which supported the President's proposals.

Lloyd had little interest in hearing the members of Congress and instead asked Nadene, "What did you think of the President's speech?"

"I think we are on the cusp of Armageddon," she pensively replied.

Nodding his head in agreement, Lloyd added, "I do indeed think we are staring into the abyss. I am particularly pessimistic about the President's appeal for shared sacrifice. This country has relied on military volunteers for decades and the public-at-large is not accustomed to or prepared for the rigors and deprivations of war."

After exchanging their soliloquies, Nadene and Lloyd resumed watching television with a keen interest in the news media's analysis. The current news commentator's animated behavior and breathless expostulations continued unabated. "The President declared war without exhausting diplomatic efforts. The sinking of three ships simply does not justify committing our nation to war."

Lloyd consciously tuned out the commentator's animus, scarcely believing the perspective given the months of aggressive acts that preceded the recent loss of life when the enemy destroyed three ships. Despite his deep reservations, he returned his attention to the commentator and was again rewarded with further remonstrations.

"If the President believes war is inevitable the US Congress should repudiate his efforts at expanding the military. He can fight his war with volunteers." the commentator pressed.

With this declaration, Nadene quipped, "It seems clear to me that the reporter objects to the President's reliance on the Selective Service System to beef up the armed forces. The reporter looks like she would be within the age range under consideration for conscription."

A panel of like-minded guests joined the commentator in a round table discussion. All agreed that the President's resort to compulsive military service was unnecessary, arguing that the volunteer force was more than adequate to prosecute the conflict.

Lloyd rose from his seat and approaching the television asked, "Nadene, do you care to see anymore?"

His wife responded, "Change the channel. Let's see what the other networks are saying."

With a sigh, Lloyd complied. He fully expected much of the same vitriol and was not disappointed. As he surfed through the channels it became evident that while the faces changed the message did not. Repeating his previous request but with more finality, he said, "I think we can safely conclude that the news media objects less to war than the prospect of their participation."

Lloyd arrived at the hospital earlier than usual the day after the President's speech to begin the transition to his new job as director of the FDB. Shortly after arriving Colonel Roderick joined him, bringing two steaming hot cups of coffee.

"Late last night I received the Surgeon General's Guidance on establishing the FDBs. It relies on existing medical fitness standards so it should be straightforward. The real unknown is the numbers. We do not have a good idea of how many individuals we will need to process." the Commander noted.

For the next several hours Roderick and Lloyd huddled together hammering out a standard operating policy that would provide the FDB's structure. When finished, Roderick had the new policy sent throughout the hospital and the two's next step was a relaxing lunch in the hospital's dining facility.

"What did you think of the President's address to the nation last night?" Roderick inquired.

"Pretty much what I expected," Lloyd replied and continuing, "but I was a bit taken back by the news media's fierce denunciation. Their opinions were remarkably consistent in condemning the draft."

"I think the news media's opposition is just the tip of the iceberg. As they continue their drumbeat, I would imagine that the social resistance will gather momentum. In the end, though, I think the president will prevail, the Congress will begrudgingly comply, and the Selective Service System will begin processing eligible recruits." Roderick sagely suggested.

Warships soon dotted America's coastline while a large naval task force made its way to the enemy's shores. Bombers and fighter aircraft were also repositioned and awaited orders for their missions. The critical shortage of personnel hampered a full-throttled response but the President hoped the initial military response would provide a deterrence, or at least a delay, in the enemy's aggression as America desperately repopulated the ranks.

Curiously, the enemy remained silent in the days following the declaration of war. Speculation ran the gamut from the enemy being intimidated to other opinions that more ominously imagined the calm as preceding the storm. Favoring the first assessment was an apparent lack of urgency from the enemy; there were no visible troop movements or changes in their offensive posture.

News outlets welcomed the enemy's restraint and used the observation to broaden their attack on the President's plans to invigorate the Selective Service System. Some members of Congress wavered and the final vote authorizing the plan passed by only one vote: unleashing a monumental verbal tirade from disaffected journalists and celebrities.

Lloyd's FDB struggled as a trickle turned into a torrent. Roderick directed more staff to support the effort but this depleted other clinical activities. Much the same occurred at other FDBs around the nation but the surge promised relief in the coming weeks as the newly activated service members deployed to combat and support units.

Like others, Lloyd was mystified by the enemy's apathetic attitude and shared his puzzlement with Nadene, "It's been two weeks since the President declared war. During that time Congress supported the expansion and mobilization of the Selective Service System and we have positioned naval forces and aircraft in the enemy's backyard."

"According to the news media the enemy was all bark and no bite but that ignores their multiple aggressions. It seems like they fundamentally oppose the President's declaration of war for fear of being drafted themselves." Nadene suggested.

"That certainly seems to be the case, but I cannot believe that the enemy is so easily deterred. Perhaps part of their strategy is relying on the President's opponents to weaken his approach and blunt our Nation's capacity to respond." Lloyd offered.

"Intentional or not, their cabal may succeed in supporting the enemy." Nadene griped.

"Our enemy is shrewd," Lloyd believed and then thinking further, "My memory keeps drifting back to our seaside excursion. In three days, we went from traffic jams and fellow vacationers at the ocean resort to empty buildings and vacant highways. It seemed like an entire hundred-mile stretch was deserted until we crossed the bridge spanning the bay on our way back home."

"But if that is true then why have we not heard about this?" Nadene asked.

"Remember, that right after the President declared war, we sent troops to defend our coasts, both onshore and offshore. Once in place, military security probably prevented any further discovery of any irregularities. And the news media is not interested in reporting this." Lloyd concluded.

Nadene kept quiet at work. Other librarians at the college did not support any of the President's decisions, including the declaration of war and most decidedly not the draft. Numerous times her colleagues did their best to draw Nadene into the political diatribe; fishing for a response but Nadene avoided the bait. Without even a nibble from Nadene, the other librarians quietly ostracized the woman, not knowing her sentiments but suspecting "she was not with them."

Freedom from contentious political discussions offered Nadene compensatory benefits. She was able to focus on her job and being unburdened with angst and anger, habitually bore a pleasant, cooperative attitude. The other librarians did not understand her behavior, but they did resent it. On the other hand, the library's patrons appreciated Nadene's cooperative mindset, and many expressed their satisfaction in the obligatory customer comment box. Those tokens of solicitude only hardened the other librarian's negative opinions.

Lloyd and his staff were exceedingly busy processing National Guard and Reserve service members for active duty and consequently had little time for political discourse. If they had indulged, it would be supportive of the President's directives. Having that view helped deflect the occasional, but not insubstantial, complaints brought to their attention from disaffected individuals receiving their fitness for duty examinations.

Malingering was a valid consideration as artful dodgers challenged clinicians with deceitful diagnoses. Lloyd responded by devoting more Inservice training to the subject which resulted in roughly one in twenty individuals suspected of malingering. Much the same was observed at other FDBs with a patchwork quilt response.

The Army Surgeon General signaled the alarm when fully twenty percent of eligible individuals failed the fitness for duty examination, seriously undermining the mobilization. It was estimated that half that number succeeded in their malingering.

Early on, Lloyd had a plan and approached Roderick, "Our statistics are trending towards an increase in suspected malingering. We cannot prove it and because of the current regulations that require the fitness for duty decision to be expedited, we are forced to disqualify questionable cases. I would like to propose that instead of rendering a hasty opinion we develop an intensive, inpatient clinical program to conduct more comprehensive examinations."

Roderick was intrigued but counseled, "That is a great idea but it would require the examinee's orders be modified to allow an extended, inpatient evaluation. Let me approach the Surgeon General with your suggestion."

Later that afternoon Roderick called the Surgeon General and discussed Lloyd's suggestion. The following day, The Surgeon General directed all FDBs to immediately implement an extended diagnostic pathway for complicated cases. The instructions allowed each facility the flexibility to develop its programs consistent with the local resources.

Dissension, driven by a persistent partisan media, descended across the country. Isolated pockets of protest received outsized coverage deceitfully doctored to magnify their influence. The strategy effectively aroused larger segments of public opinion opposed to the war and the draft with the news media's inflammatory rhetoric igniting smoldering passions. Peaceful protests turned violent with complicit reporters dutifully documenting the turmoil.

Lloyd turned the television off following the evening news and with a furrowed brow exposing his disgust he remarked, "It's been two weeks since the President set the wheels of war into motion and the enemy has not responded. I am beginning to wonder if part of their strategy relies on our civil discontent to undermine the war effort."

Nadene nodded her head in agreement but wanted to change the topic. There was no disagreement between them, but she believed the barrage of negative news was emotionally corrosive and avoidance offered the only protection. "The news is so depressing," she said, "I prefer to talk about something else."

Her frank response initially irritated Lloyd but he quickly recognized the communication rut that was developing regarding the subject and shifted the conversation. "Why don't we go out for dinner tonight?" he proposed.

"It's Friday night you know and might be busy. We can get a pizza instead and bring it back home and watch a movie."

Lloyd agreed and called a local pizza restaurant after which they made the short trip to get their dinner. If Nadene thought she could counter, at least momentarily, the current toxic news she was mistaken. As the pair parked the car and walked towards the restaurant's door a neatly lettered sign boldly informed customers, "Military service members NOT welcome."

The sign angered Lloyd and without a word, he returned to the car. Nadene followed and while simmering she was not boiling and counseled, "Let's get our pizza and leave. We just won't come here again."

"Ok," he reluctantly said and while tacitly agreeing with his wife added, "Do you mind if I stay in the car? I might be tempted to say something inside."

"No problem," she casually replied.

Nadene and Lloyd enjoyed their Friday night dinner and looked forward to a quiet, relaxing weekend. They were just settling in for the early night sleep when the phone startled them. For a moment, Lloyd considered ignoring the offending instrument, but his conscience dictated otherwise and with a groan, he answered, "This is the Lane residence."

"I was so preoccupied today that I forgot to mention that my wife is hosting a small get-together at 6 pm tomorrow and we hope you can join us." Lloyd was now fully alert and recognized the anonymous caller as Colonel Roderick.

Nadene yawned as her husband simply replied, "We would be delighted."

It was a short conversation at the conclusion of which Lloyd announced, "That was Colonel Roderick. He invited us to dinner tomorrow." Before Nadene could reply he impishly added, "And ONLY military service members are welcome!"

Chapter Five – Research

Lloyd was worried. Nearly a month had passed, and the enemy remained strangely quiet. During that interlude, declining numbers at FDB's across America signaled the looming closure of the programs. Eligible National Guard and Reserve service members plugged gaping holes in the depleted military, but their relative lack of experience and enthusiasm subtracted from mission readiness.

Weeks of placidity weakened the tenuous resolve generated by the President's declaration of war. The President's opponents interpreted the enemy's seeming tranquility as a peaceful gesture de-escalating the conflict and taking to the airwaves, they demanded reciprocity. From their media pulpits, forceful words denounced the provocative military mobilization with especially harsh rhetoric criticizing conscription.

Public opinion, never fully in favor of the President's position, retreated as the news media's onslaught intensified. Cameras captured civic discontent, nurturing the media's narrative of a unified opposition. Politicians swayed as the ill winds buffeted their initial convictions. Congress responded to the gust of negativity by debating the President's position and reconsidering previously appropriated funds. A particularly vocal group vowed to eliminate the draft.

Congressional review satiated the news media's hunger for reversal of the President's policies and restive rallies paused in response to their dampened stridency. The connection between the two was fodder for Congressional debate with the President's allies claiming the news media and their acolytes were recklessly fomenting public discontent. Of course, the President's opponents viewed the matter differently, arguing that the pause in civic unrest signaled support for their position.

Nadene noticed a change in Lloyd. His long hours managing the FDB exacted an emotional toll financed with poor sleep and edgy irritability. Both improved as the workload decreased prompting Nadene to suggest, "Now that the FDB is winding down maybe we can celebrate by taking a weekend trip."

"That sounds like a good idea." Lloyd responded, "Do you have any ideas?"

"About three hours north there is a drive-in theater. They are having a 1950s science fiction movie marathon. It gets dark around 7 pm so the movies start then and run until 2 am the next day. I figured we could stay overnight at a local hotel." Nadene offered.

"That is a great idea!" Lloyd exclaimed, "And the weather is just right – as long as it does not rain."

"I knew you would like the idea. I already made a reservation at a hotel a few miles from the drive-in theater. We can leave Saturday morning and visit some antique shops, have lunch, and check into our room before we go to the drive-in theater."

Lloyd appreciated his wife's thorough planning and with that in mind he asked, "What restaurant did you pick for lunch?"

Nadene coquettishly replied, "What makes you think I found one?" and after a suitable pause continued, "Well, I did come across a possibility. Next to one of the larger antique stores is an old mill converted into a restaurant. They grind their flour and specialize in gourmet sandwiches."

"I can hardly wait. It should be a wonderful weekend." Lloyd replied.

Saturday morning greeted Nadene and Lloyd with a soft breeze and cloudless, blue skies. It was perfect weather inviting open car windows and as Lloyd navigated the car the cool draught warmed their spirits. Their first stop filled the car with the aroma of hot coffee and breakfast biscuits procured from a fast-food restaurant.

In between tasty bites the travelers traded witty badinage which lightened the drive's tedium. Even so, the endless expanse of the gray highway married to its boring verdant foliage, and unadorned with distracting billboards, prompted Nadene to consider an alternative.

"It's a long drive but it may be more interesting if we take the back roads. We can take the next exit," she suggested.

Lloyd glanced at his wife and smiled. "It is a boring drive," he conceded and squinting down the road, "I can just now see the exit sign."

The car's tires squealed as the driver exited the highway a bit too fast before coming to a stoplight. After what seemed an interminable wait the green light granted permission to proceed and Lloyd eased the car around the corner and onto the secondary road. Acres of young cornstalks crowded both sides of the road and extended to the horizon.

Rounding a corner, a few houses and scattered farm equipment dotted the rural landscape. The mid-morning sun foreshadowed the spiking temperature and the highway's heat ripples urged Lloyd to close the car's windows and turn on the air conditioner.

"I can't imagine living in this area without air conditioning," Nadene said.

As if in response to her comment, a dry funnel-shaped wind danced across the highway and deposited a thin layer of dust on the windshield. "A dust devil," Lloyd announced as he cleared the windshield.

Topping a slight rise dimly brought a distant town into view and suggested a welcomed respite from their travels. Glancing at the car's gas gauge Lloyd commented, "We have about half a tank of gas. Let's stop in town and get some gas and cold drinks."

It was a small town with one gas station. Several cars were patiently waiting their turn at the two gas pumps and Lloyd joined the line. After topping off the tank, Lloyd parked the car to the side of the small convenience store and along with Nadene, they went inside.

Nadene quickly scanned the store and spotted the soft drink dispensers. Lloyd wandered through the store's narrow aisles casually examining the small collection of assorted snacks. While doing so he caught snatches of conversation apparently from local farmers, "It hasn't rained in weeks and these hot, dry winds are killing our crops. The corn futures are going through the roof – I just wish I had some to sell."

Switching drivers was Nadene's choice as Lloyd slipped into the passenger seat and placed the two drinks in their respective cup holders. A dry stream bed passed by as Nadene took a sip of her drink and commented, "It doesn't look like it has rained in a long time."

Miles of dry farmland rolled by with driver and passenger both preoccupied with private thoughts. Lloyd broke the silence by noting, "We should be near the hotel soon. Did you want to have lunch before we go antique shopping?"

Glancing at her watch she said, "I guess so. It's almost noontime."

Passing by the night's hotel they both scoured the local environs for a quick lunch before settling on an unpretentious restaurant. Their attention was drawn to the weather-worn building by the nearly full parking lot. Nadene guided the car into the remaining space and with a hint of despair wondered, "It looks busy. I hope we can get a table without a long wait."

Just as she finished parking, a small group of people left the restaurant increasing the probability of quick service. Entering the restaurant, a cacophony of diner's voices introduced the restaurant to Lloyd and Nadene and after a brief wait, they added to the noisy throng. The menu was lazily leaning against a napkin holder and Lloyd grabbed two, handing one to his wife.

Nadene marveled at the reasonable prices and after studying the offerings they both selected fish and chips. While waiting for their meal, Lloyd roamed the room examining the antiques decorating the restaurant, and discovered that many were for sale. Most were vintage kitchen tools including what appeared to be a Catalan flatware set in a pleasing butterscotch hue.

Shortly after resuming his seat, the server placed two heaping platters of fried fish and French fries on the table, along with coleslaw and tartar sauce. Nadene gushed, "What a mountain of food! The fries are even battered and seasoned. There is enough food here for two meals."

Lloyd agreed and when the server returned, he said, "The food is amazing! More than we can eat right now though. Do have some containers so we can take the rest with us?"

The server chuckled, "Almost everyone has the same request. I will bring you two large Styrofoam boxes."

Nadene carefully filled the two containers and they proceeded to leave the restaurant, pleased with their pick. On their way out they asked for directions to the best local antique shop and were soon making their way across town.

Ramshackle buildings on the edge of town with rusty farm implements littering the premises were their first clue that this was the antique emporium. Walking inside, a musty odor assailed their senses and narrow aisles with shelves packed with antiques was a cornucopia of delights.

A collection of vintage motion lamps attracted Lloyd's attention. Waving to Nadene, they both watched the Econolite lamps, entranced by the brightly colored animations produced by the bulb's heat slowly spinning the cylinder. Nadene carefully examined one lamp's scene of an old mill with flowing water and looking at the price wondered, "Maybe they will consider an offer."

In response, Lloyd hunted for an employee and spying one asked, "We would like to buy the old mill motion lamp. What is your best offer?"

Haggling back and forth reduced the price by ten percent. Nadene paid for her treasure and securely placed the lamp in their car's trunk. It was mid-afternoon now and she suggested, "Let's check into our hotel room. We can unpack, freshen up, and then go to dinner."

Going to the hotel room was in order but Lloyd demurred further. "I am still stuffed from lunch and want to leave room for the movie theater's delights."

"So am I," conceded Nadene, "and I want to enjoy the popcorn too!"

The drive-in theater was about fifteen minutes from the hotel, but Lloyd allowed twice that time, a prudent measure as it turned out. "I did not expect a line to get into the theater," he said with dismay.

"It looks like there are ten cars ahead of us but it is not dark yet and I doubt they would start the movies with this many people waiting outside," Nadene suggested.

Fortunately, the line dwindled quickly, and Lloyd drove the car to a space in the middle of the theater's parking lot. Dusk was draping the sky at this point and the large screen flickered to life with cartoon admonitions to visit the snack bar before the movies started.

Nadene left the cozy confines of their car and made her way to the snack bar, joining a line of similarly motivated movie patrons. Her wait was rewarded with two large boxes of popcorn and two soft drinks.

They both settled in for the night's movies expecting to replenish their popcorn during an intermission. Partway through the first movie Lloyd noticed a bright orb of light and turning towards his wife and pointing above the screen said, "Can you see that light above the screen?"

Nadene responded by directing her gaze in the direction indicated. "Yes, but its color seems to be changing. When I first saw the light, it was bright red but now it seems to be fading. I suppose it's fireworks."

The momentary distraction was soon forgotten as popcorn and movies took center stage once again. Three movies later Nadene suggested they skip the last show. It was well past midnight and a tired Lloyd agreed.

After a leisurely breakfast, they began their early trek back home. Nadene plotted a longer, more circuitous path not wanting to retrace the same route, but she was disappointed by similarities with the first excursion. As the sun rose it awakened an angry wind, roaring across the road, buffeting the car, and scattering debris. An errant plastic bag mischievously swooped from afar and clung tenaciously to the passenger's windshield. Nadene cautiously opened her window, dislodged the uninvited guest, and sent it flapping heavenward.

Lloyd watched with amusement as Nadene gave the heave-ho to their erstwhile visitor, a welcome diversion from the tedious and tense driving. At his present, cautious speed he mentally estimated their time of arrival home around 6 pm.

Nadene suggested they stop for dinner on the way home which her husband readily agreed to. Of course, that delayed their return trip and they arrived just as the sun was inviting the evening sky. After unpacking, Nadene commented, "It seemed like we were gone longer than just one overnight stay."

Lloyd agreed and sighed, "Maybe we should take more mini-vacations but tomorrow we go back to work."

An alarm rattled noisily awakening Nadene from a deep slumber. Her husband was in the kitchen making the morning beverages and when Nadene sleepily joined him he admitted, "I got up about twenty minutes ago. You looked so tired last night that I did not want to awaken you, but I forgot about the alarm clock. I normally end up turning the alarm off since we are both awake before it goes off."

Nadene kissed her husband goodbye as he jumped out of the car and walked swiftly to his office in the hospital. Opening the office door revealed a bright red flashing light on his telephone and urging Lloyd to retrieve the message, "This is Colonel Roderick. Stop by my office when you get in."

Roderick's peremptory tone alarmed the listener, but Lloyd quickly responded and was soon seated in his boss' office. Faultlessly polite, Roderick invited Lloyd to share a cup of coffee with him and then said, "Later today the US Congress will vote on the President's proposal to expand the Selective Service System to all individuals 18-35. I have reason to believe that both chambers will narrowly approve the resolution. If so, it will require that we transition the FDB to become a military entrance processing station to assist in the national recruitment effort. I think the lessons learned from the FDB will be helpful, but I am concerned that there will be overt and covert resistance from sizeable numbers of dissatisfied individuals."

Lloyd listened attentively, absorbing the magnitude of the looming project, and then predicted, "I think you are right. The draft system will endanger many Americans who have been comfortably spared military service. This social shelter suborned complacency and self-absorption; both of which will probably accompany the recruits to the processing stations."

Roderick did not respond to Lloyd's gratuitous analysis but instead returned to the practicalities of processing the putative recruits. "Give some thought to the staff and other resources you may need. I would expect malingering in every form imaginable so be prepared for that as well. Let's meet tomorrow after the resolutions are voted on. Perhaps, I am wrong, and Congress will not authorize the expansion."

Puzzled by Roderick's dismissive attitude Lloyd left the meeting crestfallen at the apparent slight. With his best poker face hiding the chagrin Lloyd assembled his closest confidantes and shared the gist of Roderick's thoughts, omitting the contretemps.

In an ironic twist, two of the attendees broached the same general thoughts Lloyd shared with his boss. He nodded in agreement, quietly pleased that others shared his concerns.

Congressional debate on the President's emergency proposals continued throughout the afternoon without resolution. Most of the heated rhetoric scorched the Selective Service System's expansion and with the President's support fading his opponents sensed victory and called for an evening vote.

Lloyd consulted his watch, adjourned the meeting, and absent-mindedly left the hospital, waiting outside for Nadene. Raindrops bounced off the street and distant peals of thunder warned of more to come. Lloyd regretted not listening to the weather report and without an umbrella was a prisoner of the portico, increasingly occupied by an ever-increasing host of people jostling to and fro.

Relief arrived when Lloyd spied the familiar automobile with Nadene at the helm and plunging through the burgeoning crowd he made his appearance visible to the driver. Nadene briefly double-parked and awaited her passenger, who sprinted the short distance and quickly scrambled inside.

"You're soaked," Nadene said with a smile. "There's a towel in the back seat."

A thunderous boom shook the car, and a simultaneous bolt of lightning struck an adjacent electrical transformer as Nadene piloted the car from the hospital. Streetlights, traffic signals, and buildings instantly darkened, severely complicating the journey home. Nadene cautiously approached unguarded intersections and when clear she scooted quickly across.

"I hope we have power when we get home," she said with a sigh.

Lloyd was more pessimistic, "I have not seen any lights since we left the hospital."

"We will know soon," Nadene predicted as she parked the car.

Armed with umbrellas they walked across the parking lot and entered a dark house. Lloyd fumbled for a flashlight in a kitchen drawer and directed the beam towards the white ceiling which dimly illuminated the interior. "We don't have power," he glumly concluded and then more brightly remembered, "Fortunately, we have a gas range so we can have a hot dinner."

Nadene called the electric utility company and a recorded message informed callers that crews would begin restoring power when the storm passed. Heavy rain, mixed with hail, signaled that the storm's fury was not abating anytime soon. Resigned to the darkness, Nadene set about making the night's dinner.

Lloyd and Nadene usually watched the evening news during dinner but bowing to the present circumstance, they relied on a battery-operated radio to fill the void. Before the newscast began a lengthy round of commercials filled the air but finally their patience was rewarded.

"Observers were stunned," the announcer began, "When Congress narrowly passed the President's war plans. The Selective Service System's expansion was fully funded by the Congressional vote and according to the resolution authorities will immediately begin administering the law."

Interrupting the announcer, Lloyd recalled his conversation with Colonel Roderick and briefed his wife. "Earlier today I had a meeting with Roderick where he predicted both this outcome and the vast network of military entrance processing stations that would be needed. Our hospital would be one of the sites and Roderick asked me to start planning for that eventuality."

Evolving from facts to opinion, the announcer breathlessly commented, "This reckless vote authorizing the draft is unconscionable. Why are we militarizing America when no threat exists? The so-called enemy has a diplomatic peace envoy reaching out to our leaders but the President refuses to meet with them."

Lloyd turned the radio off in what he knew was a meaningless gesture dismissing the announcer's ascendant hyperbole. "I can only imagine that this inflammatory rhetoric will ignite people's passions," he said to Nadene after silencing the radio.

With few exceptions, newspapers, television, and radio reports condemned the march to war and with plausible deniability stealthily encouraged mass resistance. Protests erupted across the nation denouncing the draft with scattered violence marring the message. Even so, as a juggernaut unleashed, the Selective Service

System moved forward, tossing resistance aside and engineering a network of military entrance processing stations.

Lloyd's newly constituted processing unit started receiving potentially eligible recruits within days after Congress approved the expansion. The initial cohort surprised Lloyd: and he shared his testimonial at Roderick's leadership meeting, "I was expecting opposition and anger but this batch of recruits have been polite and cooperative. And so far, there were no disqualifying medical conditions among the group."

Heads nodded in support around the table in response to Lloyd's assessment, but Roderick bucked the trend, "The leading edge of this wave of recruits consists of more compliant individuals but I think we need to prepare for a larger group of the unwilling and disagreeable. An untold number of individuals may avoid the Selective Service System registration, but the law passed by Congress includes an enforcement mechanism. Local police will arrest draft dodgers. Once detained, they will have the option of registering or remaining incarcerated for what could be the duration of the declared state of war."

Roderick's analysis proved correct. News media stoked rebellion with weaponized words attacking one enemy – the President's policies. Violent clashes followed, gathering force as police started arresting the non-registrants. Faced with incarceration a small but vocal group cast their lot in jail, hoping their moral position would inspire others and provoke a constitutional challenge to the draft law.

Popular draft resistance might have succeeded but for the enemy's intervention. In what some considered a blunder and others a shrewd maneuver, the enemy's leader counseled his country, "I am withdrawing our diplomats from the United States. We have tirelessly attempted to reason with their leaders but received only bluster and blame in return. As you know, two weeks ago we were accused of destroying a civilian airplane near Washington, DC. What you do not know is that America's President banned news media coverage claiming authority under the declared state of war. We believe that the tragic loss of life, around a thousand individuals, was the American President's blunder in unintentionally shooting down the aircraft believing it was ours. The American's continued belligerence and meritless allegations leave us no choice. We are now, regrettably, in a state of war with the United States."

"That must have been the bright light we saw at the drive-in theater," Nadene speculated.

"Yes," her husband agreed while turning off the television commentator's subsequent opinions.

"I also wonder how this will affect popular resistance to the draft," Lloyd added.

Over the next few days, Lloyd noticed a trend beginning with standing room only in his military entrance processing service's waiting area. Part of the capacity came from compliant individuals heeding the Selective Service System's call, but police escorted a more recalcitrant group.

The staff of health care providers and support personnel efficiently examined the medical status of the recruits and early statistical reports culled by Lloyd indicated nearly 20 percent were unfit for duty. Leading causes of disqualification included morbid obesity and substance misuse,
with substance misuse confirmed through secondary gas chromatography-mass spectrometry analysis.

Lloyd presented his statistical findings at a Hospital Commander's Meeting, "preliminary results from our military entrance processing service indicate that 20 percent of eligible recruits are medically unfit. I have discussed our findings with several other regional facilities, and they are reporting roughly the same figures. What I find interesting is the frequency of disqualifying substance misuse."

A pause followed while Lloyd waited for any questions. Roderick leaned forward in his chair and with a bemused look asked, "Why do you find the rate of substance misuse puzzling? I think it is common knowledge that alcohol and drug abuse are widespread."

Lloyd shifted uneasily in his chair and directing his gaze around the conference table remarked, "Yes, of course, you are correct. Substance misuse is common but that is not the puzzle here. When I drilled deep into the laboratory data, I discovered a curious result in our screening urine drug tests. As you know, urine drug tests are screened with immunoassays for rapid results. Urine specimens that screen positive are subject to confirmatory testing with gas chromatography-mass spectrometry."

Again, Lloyd paused, and an impatient Roderick implored, "So, what is curious?"

In response, Lloyd replied, "Nearly 30 percent of the submitted urine specimens screened positive for a peculiar, unknown substance. Subsequent testing with gas chromatography-mass spectrometry confirmed opiates in only five percent of the samples. The remaining 25 percent had morphine levels well below the 2,000 nanograms per milliliter cutoff required for a positive test. I also anecdotally found that the clinical records used similar words such as lethargic, apathetic, indifferent, inattentive, and poor memory to describe the recruits."

The Director of the Hospital's Clinical Laboratory echoed Lloyd's monologue, "It seems we have significant numbers of false-negative screening test results and when those samples are subjected to further chemical analysis, we find this previously unidentified compound. I have never seen anything like this."

Roderick turned to Lloyd and suggested, "It seems you have stumbled onto a real mystery. Perhaps, this is an isolated finding, but it may be worthwhile to check with other military entrance processing stations. I know you are busy, but I also know you are an inveterate investigator so I hope you can follow up on this as soon as possible."

Lloyd assured Roderick that he would pursue the matter as time permitted but the crush or recruits in the coming days prevented his full attention. The matter receded even further to the background when the enemy's declaration of war transitioned from words to deeds.

The public's first hint of something amiss was the closure of transportation routes to the mid-Atlantic coast. Aerial photography from news helicopters showed a stream of military vehicles snaking their way eastward before government authorities peremptorily closed the airspace, effectively grounding civilian aircraft. With access to the mission denied, reporters substituted speculation for information and amid the news blackout could not enlighten their viewers.

Nadene remembered their prior vacation to the eastern shoreline and connecting the dots between current events and her past observations opined, "The strange events when we were at the light keeper's house and the military now streaming towards that area makes me think that what we saw last month was a preliminary assault by the enemy. They were testing our coastal defenses."

Always impressed by his wife's perspicacity, Lloyd exuberantly and mirthfully endorsed her analysis, "I think you should be in charge of military intelligence!"

As it turned out Nadene's prescient remarks were accurate, a reality revealed a day later when the President delivered a terse, brief homily to the nation. "The enemy has taken their aggression to the next level after months of unprovoked attacks. Yesterday, the enemy landed a large contingent of special operations forces from a submarine group and engaged our forces in combat. Efforts are underway to evacuate the local civilian population, but submarine missiles have destroyed many roads and bridges in the area. In response to this craven attack wantonly targeting civilians, I have ordered a counterattack. We will respond forcefully to this incursion but for security purposes, I cannot provide any detail. My fellow Americans, these are perilous times that test our resolve and way of life. The enemy will be ruthless in their quest to conquer our nation and a large naval task force is approaching our eastern shore. Now is the time for every able-bodied American to lay aside prejudice and politics and support our Country; remembering that united we stand and divided we fall."

"DEFCON 1" stared defiantly on the television screen boldly proclaiming the Nation's highest alert level mandating maximum military readiness. America's defense readiness condition, otherwise known as DEFCON, had never reached the highest pinnacle but the enemy's presence on the eastern coast and their massive firepower demanded the reaction. Military planners did not underestimate the enemy's nuclear arsenal nor their determination to use it.

Exactly what DEFCON 1 would mean in terms of military action was a closely guarded secret, but the constant movement of ground forces was a clue to its massive scope. Civilian travel was severely restricted by the twin priorities providing military vehicles unfettered access to highways and fuel. Rationing was on the horizon but the immediate crisis and the military's thirst for fuel drained gas from civilian stations with pump after pump in the Mid-Atlantic region despondently empty.

Faced with facts, the news media reluctantly modified their stance, and while admitting the crisis, reassured listeners that American forces would quickly repel the enemy's isolated invasion. Implicit in the revised narrative was continued resistance to expanding the draft.

Non-deployed military personnel received gas for their vehicles, sufficient to allow daily roundtrip travel to their worksites. Fortunately, Nadene's library commute only added a few miles which did not exceed Lloyd's allowance. Others were not so fortunate and while homebound expectantly awaited the fulfillment of the news media's proclamation of a short war.

The enemy's invasion dramatically increased the military's response, exemplified by orders directing personnel to the eastern shore where intense fighting was demanding additional deployments. Based on the dwindling hospital staff Lloyd correctly concluded that American forces were suffering enormous casualties. Combat support hospitals sprouted like weeds but in doing so they depleted the military hospitals. Volunteers from civilian hospitals heeded calls for support and joined the military hospital's medical staff but not without engendering complaints of abandoning the public's medical needs.

With personnel displaced, deployed, and reassigned Lloyd's military entrance processing service struggled. He was not alone as other regional facilities buckled under the same constraints. Complicating matters further was another disturbing trend developing in the recruits. As news of the battlefield injuries and deaths trickled into the public's consciousness recruits visibly and demonstrably exhibited their fears; with pleas for military exemptions, malingering, and malfeasance exploding.

Lloyd's depleted staff was bogged down with recruit's feigning illness and in more desperate cases acts of self-mutilation. In too many cases, individuals miscalculated the lethality of their self-injurious behavior and died as a result. Other recruits expressed their disdain and fear of military service through criminal behavior; effectively replacing the frontlines with prison lines.

Military entrance processing stations epitomized a doorway to death for many eligible draftees, one they feared and were determined to close. Gangs of hooded individuals sporting defiant emblems of resistance started protesting and attacking Selective Service System employees and soon thereafter extended their assault to military entrance processing stations.

Nadene privately worried that her husband could be victimized by the angry mobs, a concern magnified by whispers and angry eyes from her neighbors. To Lloyd, she suggested, "It might be a good idea not to wear your uniform around the neighborhood. Tensions are running so high about the war and the draft that it may be best not to advertise your role with the Army – particularly in regards to your leadership of the military entrance processing service."

Lloyd read the worry in his wife's face and words and responded, "Colonel Roderick suggested that all military hospital personnel refrain from wearing their uniforms in public. I can leave home in civilian clothes, change into my duty uniform at the hospital, and revert to a civilian when I leave."

A noticeably relieved Nadene sighed, "That should help." And changing the subject she continued, "We are having one of your favorites for dinner, spaghetti, and meatballs!"

Overwhelmed is a word Lloyd would never use but the crisis in America required ever longer days at the hospital. Staff shortages complicated coverage and rumors of looming deployments kept everyone on edge. Lloyd expected to eventually receive reassignment orders but until then he plowed ahead, even finding a few spare minutes to research the unusual drug screen results.

Well-placed phone calls to regional military processing stations netted a trove of drug screen results. It was too chaotic at the hospital to study these data, so Lloyd placed the reams of paper in his briefcase and studied the materials at home. Nadene noticed the bundles and indirectly inquired, "That is a lot of paper you are looking at."

"Yes," Lloyd responded, "I am doing some research. A few weeks ago I noticed an unusually high number of false-negative drug tests that coincided with recruits exhibiting apathetic behavior and suffering from rather extensive memory loss. Clinicians at our hospital routinely assess recruits' cognitive function and the results, at least anecdotally, support my premise that an unknown illicit drug may be the culprit. So, I reached out to other hospitals and the treasure trove of papers before you are their responses."

"I can help if you tell me what you are looking for," Nadene enthusiastically offered.

"That would be great!" Lloyd ecstatically agreed and then offered guidance, "I have created a database with the entries I need. It's pretty simple but tedious. For each recruit, you will see the drug test results and a clinical summary of their medical examination. The cognitive test scores will be in the clinical summary."

Lloyd divvied the papers and gave Nadene a small packet, retaining the balance for his perusal. It was boring work and after an hour both were fatigued. It was past their usual dinner time and Lloyd retrieved a large can of mushroom soup from the pantry. "It's a bit late for dinner so I thought we could have a large bowl of hot soup and maybe some cheese crackers."

"I'm not too hungry so that sounds fine. I have not felt good today," she said.

Nadene never complained so her admission alarmed Lloyd, "Are you sick?"

"My stomach has been upset all day and my lunch refused to stay down," she said with a lame attempt at humor.

"Maybe you should go to bed early?" Lloyd suggested.

"I think the soup might be helpful, but I will skip the crackers. After dinner I will go lie down," she quietly replied.

Nadene awakened the next morning, refreshed and relieved. As an insurance policy, she avoided her typical breakfast and instead nibbled on a few dry crackers and a hot cup of green tea. Lloyd suggested she consider staying home but the resilient woman refused. On the way to work, Lloyd carefully monitored her behavior and seeing nothing amiss simply suggested, "Call me if you have any problems."

"I will but I won't," she cheerfully responded.

News from the eastern shore battlefield trickled from military public affairs, heavily filtered to preserve secrecy, and deny enemy intelligence. Sophisticated psychological operations further slanted and distorted coverage of the war but the calls for additional military personnel were loud and clear. Based on the military reports, American forces stalled the enemy's ground advance, and a static line demarcated the combatants.

The Pentagon's war command hesitated to send reserve elements to change the tactical situation harboring suspicions that the enemy would attack elsewhere. Certain members of Congress, those who vigorously denounced the Selective Service System, insisted on deploying additional resources to swiftly defeat the enemy, arguing that a decisive loss would dissuade further aggression.

Public and congressional resistance melded, creating a toxic mix that threatened civil unrest even while American forces battled the enemy. Right on cue, the news media surrendered to the agents of discontent, stirring the bubbling brew fomenting social strife. Sensing dissension that jeopardized the war effort, the Pentagon responded with half-measures.

Troops in America's mid-west states received orders to the eastern shore battlefield. Military assets in the southern states remained on high alert but in place. As soon as the enhanced military contingent assumed positions on the eastern shore the enemy pivoted and stealthily removed all but a small ground force.

The President's irremediable critics hailed the apparent retreat as proof of their convictions, but it was a short-lived victory dance. Lying in wait in the Gulf waters, the enemy launched a massive, combined operation with furious naval and air bombardments pounding the deep southern states. Panicked citizens fled the area snarling highways and preventing a rapid military response.

Enemy forces relentlessly pushed forward, and scattered reports spotted warships on the Mississippi River. Amphibious units attacked installations on the River, paralyzing commerce and occupying key facilities.

The President huddled with senior war planners crafting a counterattack. America's potent air forces took to the skies targeting the enemy's warships and embedded ground positions. Deadly munitions illuminated the night as both sides traded fire. Precision-guided ordnance dented the enemy's capabilities, but American losses were staggering, both in terms of aircraft and personnel.

Hastily assembled combat support hospitals tended to the wounded. Clinicians sorted patients balancing medical resources with estimates of survivability; a process resulting in a disproportionate number of expectant casualties. War's lethality strained mortuary affairs as the dying outnumbered the survivors.

Rumors of the enemy's battlefield atrocities hardened the public's resolve in decidedly different ways. Among individuals supporting the call to arms and defending the country the enemy's apparent brutality increased their nationalistic fervor. On the other hand, the enemy's ruthless behavior supported their demoralizing and fearmongering campaign.

One important result of the enemy's rapid battlefield successes and psychological operations resulted in vulnerable recruits going underground to avoid military service. Law enforcement could not arrest the fugitives quickly which hampered national efforts to blunt the enemy's advance. Losses on the battlefield even drained the reservoir of optimism among much of the American military personnel adding to the Country's peril.

General Order Number One issued from the Department of Defense strictly forbids the use of alcohol or illicit substances in the areas of combat operations. Resources and the exigencies of war permitting required combat commanders to support random drug and alcohol biochemical testing. Field expedient methods used included urine screening immunoassays for drug use and alcohol breath testing devices. Commanders referred all positive test results to their combat support hospitals for further diagnostic assessment.

Diversion of military persons suspected of alcohol or drug misuse for further assessment to the support hospitals negatively impacted combat readiness. A typical army unit lost upwards of twenty percent of its soldiers for a routine three-day drug and alcohol evaluation. Of that total, five percent were placed on medical profiles and reassigned to a medical management unit while receiving treatment.

The influx of soldiers needing drug and alcohol treatment swelled Lloyd's medical management unit and additionally spurred opportunities to study the vagaries of illicit substance test results. Converging data points increasingly supported Lloyd's hypothesis of a relationship between the false-negative test results and the unusual chemical substance that occurred in tandem with specific behavioral changes; principally manifested by emotional indifference and complete anterograde and partial retrograde amnesia.

Lloyd meticulously gathered and analyzed mounds of data and with Nadene's invaluable assistance compiled an impressively detailed report. Confident that his findings revealed an important trend he decided to submit the preliminary results for Colonel Roderick's review. A week would pass before Lloyd could speak with his boss; a delay used to perfect his presentation.

"Colonel Roderick will see you now," his administrative assistant said.

Lloyd arose from his chair and entered Roderick's office greeting the man, "thank you for meeting with me today," he said.

Roderick swiveled in his office chair and smiled in response, "I look forward to learning about the results of your research. I know you have been very busy, and I appreciate the extra time spent on this ad hoc project."

Beaming in the glow of the unexpected compliment, Lloyd opened his briefcase and handed Roderick a summary of his findings, replete with statistics and charts. The recipient closely examined the documents during which time Lloyd remained quiet. Nearly twenty minutes elapsed before Roderick broke the silence. "This is quite interesting and potentially actionable. Just to make sure I understand your research can you provide me with a synopsis?"

"Yes sir," Lloyd began, "I examined the clinical records of 2,000 service members. Of that total, 500 came from our hospital and the remainder from mid-Atlantic regional facilities. From each record, I gathered basic demographics, medical conditions, prescribed medications, drug screening immunoassays, and secondary analyses, and neuropsychiatric test results. If you look at the tables and charts you will see the relationships among the variables. I have highlighted statistics related to cognition and drug tests. As you can see there are statistically significant findings correlating false-negative screening drug tests with our mysterious chemical detected in secondary laboratory analysis and the multiple dimensions of impaired cognition; specifically impacting both recent and to a lesser degree remote memory tasks, limited emotional expressivity, and intense desensitization. I calculated the effect sizes which in every instance exceeded 0.80; suggesting, as you know, a strong relationship between these variables."

After the briefing, Roderick leaned back in his chair, closed his eyes, and deeply contemplated Lloyd's study. Anxious minutes later he asked, "Lloyd, what are your recommendations?"

"These might well be considered preliminary findings which in the normal course of research would probably benefit from a longer period of study," he cautiously offered.

"These are not normal times," Roderick blandly noted homing in on Lloyd's conditional comment.

"The other thought I had considers the drain on personnel when the false positive tests force commanders to evacuate the individual to the combat support hospital for detailed evaluations. Based on the numbers I am seeing only five percent of that group are ultimately medically profiled for treatment. That means that a lot of folks are needlessly being pulled from combat operations," Lloyd concluded.

"I agree with that," Roderick added but then insisted, "What is your best recommendation based on your data?"

"Aside from their peculiar behavior which tends toward the insensate, I did not see any evidence of performance degradation in combat. Numerous clinical records annotated a commander's lamenting the loss of such soldiers and embracing behaviors they interpreted as stoic; unflappable in combat and indifferent to the hardships."

"I can see how commanders would value those traits," Roderick mused.

"With that in mind, one approach might position clinical resources with expertise in substance use disorders closer to the combat units. Instead of removing service members with positive drug screens from their assigned units, the forward-deployed clinicians would make decisions based on their actual day-to-day performance. Clinicians would consult with commanders throughout the process. We know that roughly one-third of screening drug tests will be false negatives and given the importance of maintaining unit cohesion I would argue that a new clinical model that supports combat is imperative," Lloyd determined.

Roderick stood up and walked towards an open window. With his back to Lloyd, while gazing outside, he said, "Prepare a command brief as soon as possible. Be succinct, present your research, and provide at least two proposed courses of action. I will review it and then we will get on the Surgeon General's calendar."

"I can have a draft on your desk in two days," Lloyd stated and sensing the meeting was over quietly left Roderick's office.

On the way home Lloyd was pensive and his wife was reluctant to query his mood. The impasse yielded when Lloyd cleared his throat, "I had the meeting with Colonel Roderick today."

Without waiting for Nadene to prompt him, Lloyd reviewed the meeting in detail, including his suggested courses of action. He ended the monologue with Roderick's plan to brief the Surgeon General. On the surface, the high-level briefing seemed complimentary and appropriate in light of Lloyd's autonomous research, but Nadene grew concerned with political pitfalls that could rapidly turn to his disadvantage.

Nadene answered the phone call at home from Colonel Roderick, "Hello, this is the Lane residence."

"Good evening, Nadene. I hope everything is well with you. If Lloyd is free, can I spend a moment with him?" he graciously asked.

"Of course, let me go get him," she cheerfully replied.

Lloyd was outside retrieving accumulated mail from the last several days. Mail delivery was spotty because of frequent road closures and many times the mailbox was empty but this time Lloyd retrieved a few crumpled, discontented letters addressed to "current occupant". Without even examining their contents he threw them into a nearby trash container and walked briskly back home.

Nadene heard the front door open and sang out, "Colonel Roderick called. He waited a few moments but then asked that you telephone him back."

"Did he mention why he called? " Lloyd inquired as he dialed Roderick's phone number.

Before his wife responded, his boss answered the telephone, "Lloyd, thank you for calling back so quickly. I just received word from the Surgeon General that he wants to meet with both of us tomorrow morning. Let's meet in my office and my driver can take us to his office."

"Yes sir, I will bring several copies of the briefing documents. I would imagine there will be others attending the meeting," he concisely added.

Lloyd astutely speculated that the Surgeon General would invite others to the briefing but he was surprised with a conference room of twenty individuals, mostly military but some serious-faced civilians. Upon seeing the group, Lloyd quietly suggested to Colonel Roderick the need for more briefing documents, who in turn asked the host for a slight delay in the briefing to accommodate the crowd.

Colonel Roderick took a proffered seat near the Surgeon General while Lloyd strode to the podium, assembled his briefing documents, and awaited the Surgeon General's cue. The Surgeon General opened the meeting with platitudes and promises of medical support for the war; bromides offered for consumption to the high-ranking government attendees. After this political preamble, the Surgeon General introduced his guests, which confirmed their eminent positions.

With a wave of his hand, the Surgeon General directed everyone's attention to the podium and after a brief introduction asked Lloyd to begin. Lloyd's shaky opening comments betrayed his anxiety, but he quickly suppressed his nervousness and completed the briefing by suggesting two courses of action. "These data strongly suggest relationships between false-negative drug tests, a unique chemical compound, and specific behavioral attributes. In terms of proposed courses of action, I might mention two. We could broaden the research, gather more data, and postpone any further decisions. On the other hand, the war effort would benefit from clinical interventions that reduce personnel evacuations from the area of combat operations."

Lloyd thanked the audience for their attention and expectantly awaited questions. Typical briefings usually included spirited discussions and pointed interrogatories, but the group remained remarkably tight-lipped. Lloyd shifted uneasily imagining some faux pax, an awkwardness alleviated when a stern voice from an impeccably attired civilian intoned, "Speaking on behalf of the President, I am directing the second course of action be adopted as a pilot program. Captain Lane will develop and command this project and with the concurrence of Colonel Roderick will provide regular updates to the Surgeon General. I would especially commend Captain Lane for his work and in recognition, the President approved his promotion to Major, effective immediately."

Lloyd wobbled imperceptibly, visibly blushed, and humbly sputtered, "Thank…thank you for your confidence."

Colonel Roderick rose from his chair and signaled for Lloyd to accompany him as the pair left the conference. No one else stirred which for some inexplicable reason troubled Lloyd. The evanescent alarm faded through distraction as both men reviewed the briefing and contemplated the way forward.

"The Surgeon General will authorize additional resources for the pilot program. Based on our previous discussions, Lloyd, it seems reasonable to augment the forward-deployed battalion aid stations with addiction-trained medical personnel. We should also develop a training program to educate existing assets and military leaders in the area of combat operations," Roderick advised.

"I can begin working on that immediately," Lloyd suggested.

"I need to carve out some extra time for you to do this. As a major now, you can transfer day-to-day operational control of the medical management unit to the officer on your staff best suited to carry on. I will also provide a military vehicle and driver to facilitate your command consultations in the combat areas on the eastern shore, "Roderick said.

Nadene joined her husband at the hospital as usual and the couple began their journey home. She was bursting with curiosity and impulsively blurted out, "You haven't said a word about your briefing!"

"I was waiting until we got home," he remarked in a rejoinder that left her unsatisfied.

"With all the travel disruptions it takes us twice as long to get home now. Can't you share what happened?" she pleaded.

Lloyd looked at his wife and read the perturbation on her face, pondering how to package his answer. After an annoying pause, he decided to lead with the best news, "At the end of the briefing a civilian advisor to the President lauded my research and announced my promotion to Major."

"That's wonderful!" Nadene exclaimed, "but you certainly deserved the praise."

Lloyd smiled and continued, "As you know I presented two courses of action and the resolute decision favored the pilot program. I was charged with developing and directing the program. Colonel Roderick will coordinate the additional support and he placed a vehicle at my disposal."

"Why do you need a vehicle?" Nadene apprehensively asked.

"I will need to occasionally travel to the area of combat operations to monitor the program and provide field training to the military leaders," he offhandedly added.

Nadene squirmed in her seat, tightened her hands on the steering wheel, and with her face darkening nervously questioned, "Won't that be dangerous?"

Lloyd allayed her fear, at least for the moment, "I do not expect I will need to go there very often, and anyway the most pitched warfare has moved to middle-America."

Once at home the subject received no further discussion with Nadene and Lloyd ensconced in private thoughts. Lloyd pondered practicalities, such as designing a leadership training program and recruiting medical personnel to staff the project. The man relied on a reservoir of optimism that irrigated his self-confidence and motivation. He also expected Colonel Roderick's full support which would remove barriers that might prove impassable otherwise.

Lloyd's wife deemed the new reality a mixture of perils and pride; with the former pressing heavily on the latter. She believed that the advancement to Major and the Surgeon General's trust in Lloyd's abilities was a positive development but nagging worries about the political, programmatic, and personal perils he faced curbed her enthusiasm. Although fully aware of the national crisis, Nadene had taken comfort in her husband's stability at the hospital; safely isolated from the din of war but this new development challenged that belief.

The next morning Nadene drove her husband to work but the journey was different as neither seemed inclined to their usual morning banalities and frivolities. A pensive air filled the vacuum with a contemplative climate as the travelers sought subconscious, silent shelter.

Nadene absent-mindedly tapped the brakes too forcefully, jarring both occupants, as she parked the vehicle outside the hospital. With a sliver of iciness in her voice, she said, "Let me know when I should pick you up."

Her cold, perfunctory tone shattered the stillness, but Lloyd was in problem-solving mode and oblivious to the emotional undercurrents. "I should be ready at the usual time," he advised while exiting the car and failing to kiss her goodbye.

A new office greeted Lloyd's promotion and prospects; normally a welcome development but as he scanned the surroundings his flushed face advertised more than disappointment. Forlornly sitting askance in the middle of the space was a shop-worn desk and a telephone with its cord dangling on the floor. No chairs graced the interior and a pile of paper in the corner seemed to mock the man. Checking his impulse to angrily react, Lloyd took a deep breath and stuffing his resentment cooled off with a hot cup of coffee in the cafeteria.

Lloyd aimlessly pondered the swirls of steam rising from his coffee and wondered if the same was visibly emanating from him. His chuckling at the mental picture attracted oblique embarrassing glances from passersby and motivated the man's return to reality. Time passed too quickly while Lloyd was daydreaming, culminating in a tardy arrival for a meeting with Colonel Roderick.

"Please forgive my late arrival," Lloyd apologized to his boss without further explanation.

"I was getting ready to send out a search team," Roderick humorously responded; an uplifting comment that relieved Lloyd's heavy guilt-ridden thoughts.

Lloyd affected a smile and then pivoted, "I have prepared a briefing outline for the leadership training. It is simple. I just need to explain the project and solicit their support in capturing data."

Roderick reviewed Lloyd's work and after a lengthy pause enthusiastically appended his approval in bold letters on the cover. "I will send this up the chain for additional comments, but you can begin preparing for travel to the area of combat operations. Get your required training and equipment."

Anticipating the approval, Lloyd casually admitted, "I begin my training tomorrow and that should be completed in a week. Getting the field equipment, driver, and vehicle seems more challenging but I can work on that today."

The meeting ended when Roderick received a phone call, apparently unpleasant as the man turned toward Lloyd and while frowning gestured toward the door. Lloyd quietly left the office and with a sense of urgency escalated his field-bound efforts. He was partially successful in securing the diver and vehicle, but a shortage of personal gear hampered his plans. At best he could expect the equipment in a week.

Military censors rigorously controlled news from the battlefields but their best efforts could not conceal a troublesome trend; the enemy was advancing and gobbling up vast tracts. With a positive spin, the military's public briefings minimized the territorial losses while alluding to the imminent implementation of secret strategies.

Unhappy and suspicious with the constraints imposed by the military, inspired a small cohort of investigative journalists to seek answers elsewhere. These journalists considered casualties a proxy for battlefield success, reasoning those lower losses correlated with victory. It was an imprecise yardstick but when historically compared to prior wars offered some semblance of scientific analysis. Prime targets for data acquisition naturally led the reporters to military healthcare facilities.

Lloyd had his first encounter with an investigative reporter while waiting outside the hospital for Nadene. His attention was drawn to a commotion near the hospital's front door where a small knot of employees surrounded a tall man. The man was fashionably attired with a dark blue pinstriped suit, coordinated bowtie, and a brown Fedora with a prominent red and white hatband.

Like a snowball traveling downhill, the clump grew larger as the man slowly moved away from the front door and more people joined the group. The assembled throng snaked its way towards Lloyd who strained to hear the man's voice above the crowd. It soon became clear that the man was a reporter, "I work for Syndicated Universal News, otherwise known as SUN. I came here today hoping to meet with the hospital leadership. Unfortunately, Colonel Roderick refused to meet with me citing security and patient privacy. I have instead arranged a town hall meeting tonight with the families of patients."

Lloyd instantly connected the offending phone call in Roderick's office with the reporter's request. While remembering the incident, Lloyd watched the man enter a waiting news van, and once inside he lowered a window and speaking to the crowd said, "Please join me tonight at 7 pm at Constitution Hall. The event will be recorded and nationally televised."

Traffic came to a halt in front of the hospital with police inexplicably clearing a path for the television station's van. Nadene narrowly avoided the debacle, but persistent pedestrians, hobnobbing after the reporter left, urged caution as she gently eased her way to Lloyd still waiting outside.

The drive home was uneventful. A police siren screamed in the distance, escorting the news media's van, and helped clear the traffic. What normally took an hour was traversed in half that time.

Lloyd postponed any talk of his deployment until after dinner, figuring it would upset his wife. The extra time was spent cogitating on the coming conversation, which incidentally reduced his anxiety. With the table cleared and the dishes washed Lloyd finally broached the subject, "I discussed my plans for the demonstration project with Colonel Roderick. He endorsed the leadership training and extra clinical support I requested. I now have a driver and a vehicle. The only hang-up is my military gear which should be available in a week."

Nadene expected her husband's imminent deployment, but his announcement still startled her. She detected a tone of excitement, almost an eagerness, in his voice that troubled the woman.

"When will you leave?" Nadene responded in a leaden voice, devoid of emotion she valiantly struggled to suppress.

"I have some leeway since my gear is not ready. Once I receive my equipment, I can make firm plans but my best guess is about 7-10 days," he said.

It seemed too sudden and like a levee buckling with floodwaters her emotions surged and with a tear trickling forth and a tremble she said, "How long will you be gone?"

Lloyd mentally castigated himself, his best intentions failing miserably. Somehow, he imagined that his calm demeanor would reassure his wife but sensing otherwise he tried to mitigate the damage, "I will only be gone a week. That will give me plenty of time to complete my command consultations and launch the new drug screening program. I do not expect this to be in a hazardous area since most of the combat activity has left this area."

Lloyd hoped this additional disclosure would relieve some of Nadene's concern and perhaps it did. Reflexively, the woman reasserted her mental balance, only momentarily upset and with a concerted calm demeanor replied, "I do not think the hospital can do without you for much longer."

Lloyd smiled at the suggestion and added, "I will be able to call you from the field. As I said, we have secured much of the area since the enemy moved most of their forces to the mid-west."

Nadene welcomed that news, "Just make sure you call me every night!"

Both slept soundly and awakened refreshed the next morning, ardently avoiding any further discussion of the deployment. A weekend preceded Lloyd's departure and during the commute to the hospital Nadene steered the conversation in that direction, "Will you have any free time this weekend?"

"Of course," Lloyd replied, "Do you have any plans?"

"I will do some research at the library today. We have seen pretty much everything in the area that is still accessible," she replied as the car came to a stop outside the hospital.

With a kiss goodbye, Lloyd left Nadene and sprinted inside. Once again, a heavy sensation enveloped the woman as she watched her husband disappear with a bounding stride. A few minutes later she parked the car at the library and slowly walked inside, hailed by another librarian's voice, "Christie called in sick. Can you cover the front desk?"

Nadene thought about ignoring the request and was on the verge of protesting by offering the chore to the voluntary part-time library aide, but she capitulated after calculating the possibility of blowback. "I can cover the front desk until noon, but I have a doctor's appointment at 1 pm," she lied.

Without waiting for a response Nadene seated herself at the front desk and despite her despondency greeted the few patrons that arrived. Library attendance suffered enormously as the war drained interest but what little remained was focused on current events and curiously, books about drug use dominated the reader's interest.

Between the scattered visitors, Nadene researched local attractions but soon concluded that most were inaccessible given their proximity to the hostilities. Taking a break from the front desk, she wandered through the library's holdings and spying a collection of video movies eyed the various titles. Many were timeless classics and appealed to the woman's fascination with film-noir.

Nadene decided on a weekend movie marathon and selected a half-dozen detective titles. Noon was now fast approaching and in preparation for leaving she placed the movies in a large bag and jauntily thanked the library aide, whose rueful response belied her acceptance.

No movie marathon is complete without popcorn, Nadene thought, and with that in mind, she used her free time to purchase an ample supply. Soft drinks and an assortment of candy joined the popcorn as Nadene drove home.

Nadene heard the phone ringing as she unlocked the door and rushing across the room, she breathlessly picked up the receiver and responded, "The Lane residence."

"Is this the lady of the house?" a familiar voice mirthfully asked.

"Is that you, Lloyd?" she coyly asked.

"Guilty as charged," the man playfully added. "I called the library, but they said you left for a doctor's appointment. I did not remember you have an appointment so I guessed you were playing hooky and might be at home."

"Guilty as charged," his wife said with a laugh. "But I figured out what we could do this weekend. We can have a movie marathon complete with buckets of buttered popcorn!"

Nadene filled in the details mentioning the movie titles but before finishing Lloyd interrupted her, "I almost forgot why I called you. I decided to leave a few hours early so we can get a head start on our weekend."

"Oh! That's wonderful, I will leave right now!" she exclaimed.

Chapter Six – Jeopardy

America was on the brink of defeat. The enemy's resolve and reserves spread like malignant cancer, first along the mid-Atlantic coast and then through the heartland. Vital organs of commerce succumbed, choking supply chains. Military forces attacked the metastatic growth, but weakened through decades of political and public neglect, faltered.

Military censorship applied a bandage to the bleeding, but leaks told a different story. Isolated reports surfaced implying widespread demoralization and rampant desertions among members of the armed forces. Hospitals hemorrhaged staff diverted to the war, suffered supply shortages, and faced an increasingly hostile mix of patients and their families.

Journalists tapped discontent, sympathetically interviewing wounded service members complaining of poor treatment in a sentiment echoed by family members. Dreadful, maiming battlefield injuries assaulted viewers' sensitivities, intensifying a nascent clamor encouraging America's capitulation.

The confident enemy recognized the political gap between the President's policies and peace activists and driving another wedge between the two, proposed terms for surrender. News reports magnified the benefits: America's military forces would be spared further losses, families reunited, business activities resumed, and reconstruction would repair the battlefield scars.

A closer study of the enemy's propositions revealed troubling demands. A provisional government would assume control, staffed by the enemy's military field leaders. The enemy did not mention the fate of the current American administration nor what policies the provisional government would implement.

Academic pundits appeared on television extolling the virtues of the enemy's plans, but everyone waited for the President's response. In an address to the nation, the President bluntly declared, "The enemy proposed unacceptable terms of surrender. America will never renounce our independence, but dark days lie ahead. We face a ruthless enemy, perpetrating unconscionable atrocities, and attacking nonmilitary targets. Their campaign terrorizes civilians with inhumane cruelty that constitutes war crimes. We will not negotiate, and we will win this war!"

Glimmers of battlefield success bolstered the President's determination. The enemy's ground assault stalled as American forces attacked enemy supply lines and concentrated their firepower on advanced elements, inflicting massive damage.

Winter in the mid-west worked to America's advantage when an early ice storm spread across the battlefield. Surprisingly inept, the enemy miscalculated the weather, further slowing their momentum and giving American troops an edge.

Unit morale improved when the seemingly invisible enemy stumbled but desertions remained stubbornly high. Occasionally, military police arrested a deserter and commanders would prosecute the accused service member. Desertion in time of war was a capital offense and courts-martial uniformly awarded the death sentence hoping the stern punishment would stem the tide.

Military authorities privately acknowledged the futility of deterrence. Prisoners sentenced to death were removed from the battlefield and transported to eastern state penitentiaries where lengthy legal appeals would delay and almost certainly deny execution.

Both military and civilian officials did not have the resources to arrest but a tiny number of deserters. Emboldened service members calculated the odds of arrest against a battlefield death and chose the former, confident their decision would go unpunished.

Emotional casualties of war depleted the ranks even more than desertions. Recruits unaccustomed to military discipline and the harsh realities on the battlefield succumbed to depression, anxiety, and traumatic stress. In response, forward-deployed aide stations operationalized well-known principles of combat stress management.

Initial management of combat's emotional casualties focused on proximity, immediacy, and expectation. Proximity ensured field-based treatment interventions that spared evacuations to more distant combat support hospitals. Immediacy was a two-pronged philosophy that rested on quick identification of debilitating emotional symptoms and once identified, a few days of psychosocial support at the aid station. Aide staff fulfilled the third step of treatment with a clear, unequivocal expectation of the intervention's success and the service member's return to their unit.

The time-honored management of combat stress faltered. Overburdened aide stations could not handle the relentless stream of emotional casualties and returning service members to their units within the mandated three days proved impossible. The crisis quickly reached a boiling point with the pressure vented through mass evacuations.

Evacuees consumed scarce combat support hospital resources nominally for medical and surgical care, upending unprepared staff. Clinicians soon recognized a disproportionate influx of patients with substance use disorders, particularly the use of sedatives such as alcohol and opioids. Hospital staff ostracized the group and segregated their swelling numbers to hastily erected tents outside the main hospital complex.

The personnel picture concerned military leaders. Desertions and emotional casualties were draining service members from both support and combat units, imperiling the war effort. With seemingly limitless soldiers, the enemy could reverse America's hard-fought battleground gains.

Military leaders yearned for a solution but deep pockets of popular resistance to the war hamstrung their efforts. Anti-war clinicians freely conjured medical excuses for potential recruits and those less scrupulous did the same for payment. The President's critics in the news media shrilly lambasted the war and shaky politicians straddled the divide.

War leaders resurrected an American Civil War practice and suggested the Selective Service System authorize substitutions. The legislation would create a network ostensibly connecting substitutes who would assume the military obligation of draftees in exchange for a monetary payment. Opponents succeeded in derailing the proposal citing a financial inequity that favored the well-to-do.

Six months of war squelched voices hoping for a short war. A stagnant atmosphere prevailed now with the enemy firmly entrenched and American forces blocking further territorial gains.

Army leaders fretted that spring weather would reverse the dormant conditions and they implored the Nation's politicians for resources. The prospect of warmer weather did not thaw frosty politicians who turned a cold shoulder to the Army's requests.

Politicians traded discordant dialogue, dysfunctional through delay and demagoguery that netted no action. Dithering guaranteed field conditions would suffer as political paralysis spread, immobilizing decision-makers. Military morale declined, even among the most enthusiastic service members who began openly questioning their role in a war that lacked Congressional and public support. It was another ominous turn affecting America's future successes on the battlefield.

Lloyd viewed the political news with trepidation, but his imminent deployment acted like a shield deflecting the unease. Time seemed to compress as the departure date grew nearer, adding urgency to each step and displacing less important matters. Obsessively, he checked and mentally rechecked his plans, worrying that anything neglected would scuttle the pilot project.

An eastern shore tactical operations center was Lloyd's destination for the one-week field exercise. Forewarned in advance, he expected an austere environment and planned accordingly. Leadership training was a central component of the trip and Lloyd procured all the necessary presentation props. A whiteboard easel and tripod would suffice as a visual aide and plastic three-ring binders securely bound supplemental resources including an outline of the presentation and additional reading materials. Lloyd expected an audience of ten individuals, a small group but ample for the pilot project.

To gauge the training's relevance and receptivity, Lloyd created a pre and post-test survey. Respondents would answer questions before and after training touching on basic facts about alcohol and drugs, signs and symptoms of misuse, methods of detection, and management options. Another section would seek the attendees' recommendations for future presentations.

Lloyd expected a skeptical crowd based on his experiences with command briefings and similar training exercises. Mental health topics in general, and drug and alcohol misuse in particular, guaranteed some eye-rolling responses. Far from discouraging the man, Lloyd engaged the cynicism by predicting the behavior and challenging the stigma.

Years of experimentation with different styles convinced Lloyd that military audiences preferred interactive presentations. His were full of questions inviting and, in some cases, awakening attendees for their thoughts. Lloyd's give and take talks avoided the danger of denouncement delivered by a pretentious physician preaching practices to a military audience.

The other part of Lloyd's pilot project required coordination with the combat support hospital. Three additional clinicians, quickly trained in relevant substance misuse management, would augment the hospital's new mission. Lloyd aimed for seamless integration and immediate employment. Together with the hospital leadership, these new clinicians would launch the pilot project and collect data for later analysis.

Lloyd trained the three clinicians destined for the combat support hospital. All three were experienced army nurses who volunteered for the assignment. Their training included relevant military regulations, the pharmacology of alcohol and drugs, physical and behavioral manifestations of misuse, biochemical testing, and management approaches. Lloyd also expected the small cohort to collect and tabulate specific research data.

Between the two imperatives of leadership training and clinical programming, Lloyd anticipated the latter to be less contentious. The Surgeon General's support and Colonel Roderick's guidance limited potential friction with the support hospital but for the combat leadership, successful training hinged on Lloyd's appeal.

Lloyd's military driver was a seasoned sergeant familiar with the eastern shore battlefield who could safely navigate the man to the tactical operations center. He was an affable, loquacious man with firsthand knowledge of the military audience members Lloyd would soon meet with.

A weekend movie marathon preceded Lloyd's field trip. The quiet interlude was a time for relaxation and introspection. Nadene knew her husband's thoughts focused on the pilot project and interpreted his wrinkled brow, inattentiveness, and tight-lipped behavior as evidence of concern colliding with confidence.

With that in mind, she asked her husband, “Do you have everything you need for the trip?”

“I think so,” he tentatively answered. “I have all the briefing materials organized and packed. The driver should meet me here. The three nurses are traveling with a larger group bound for the combat support hospital and should hopefully be there the day following my arrival.”

“You have spent an incredible amount of time developing this program,” Nadene firmly concluded, “and based on what you have shared with me, I am certain your trip will be successful.”

Nadene’s placidity was covertly orchestrated, masking her inner unrest, in a determined effort to minimize her husband’s worries. She empathically reasoned that her anxieties would burden and distract Lloyd, needlessly complicating his mission.

“What will you do when I am gone?” Lloyd asked, not realizing perhaps how the tangential question tread on Nadene’s feelings.

“I will go to work as usual. When I come home, I will miss you but look forward to your phone call. I have some reading to catch up on too,” she answered with affected nonchalance.

“Calling every night should not be a problem. My driver tells me that the officer’s quarters have telephones and currently there are no military restrictions preventing communications with immediate family members,” he offered.

Nadene stiffened ever so slightly at the official-sounding response, hoping for a more intimate rejoinder from her husband, but she ignored the unintended indifference, “I’m glad to hear that. I know you will be busy but call me anytime you are free.”

“We can’t have popcorn for every meal,” Nadene added as she changed the topic.

“Let’s get a pizza for dinner,” Lloyd suggested and with that, they both avoided any further talk of deployment.

On Monday, Lloyd confirmed his travel plans for Wednesday, and with the help of his driver, he loaded the military vehicle with his training materials and combat gear. He also expressed private satisfaction with the nurses’ departure plans and with a feeling of relief that came from the extensive preparation, he contentedly awaited the big day.

Colonel Roderick was preoccupied during the days preceding Lloyd's departure but late on Monday afternoon he surprised the man with an impromptu visit, "Do you have a moment," he inquired, standing informally outside Lloyd's office.

"Of course, I am glad you stopped by," Lloyd frankly admitted.

"I trust everything is arranged for your field trip?" Roderick asked, fully expecting the man's organization would leave no stone unturned.

"Yes, sir, as far as I can tell," Lloyd deferentially replied, "and I have double-checked everything."

"Very good. If you need anything give me a call. If you have time, I would also appreciate an occasional update," he added but before Lloyd could acknowledge the request Roderick revised, "You can skip the field updates. I can await your return and until then good luck!"

Nadene did not sleep well on the eve of her husband's departure and arising early set about preparing a bountiful breakfast. She had been hoarding a small package of stone-ground grits for just such a special occasion and with the extra morning time, she also made a small batch of biscuits. Her secret ingredient for golden biscuits was butter blended into the batter and the same copiously greasing the baking pan.

While the biscuits were baking, Nadene grated cheddar cheese for an omelet but decided against adding onions after inspecting the sole bedraggled specimen in the pantry. With a sigh, she threw the onion in the trash and looking up spied her husband approaching the kitchen.

"You're up early," he stated and admitting the obvious. "I did not sleep well either."

With a faint smile, Nadene replied, "I thought you might like a hearty meal. You will have to wait a whole week to enjoy my cooking!"

"I must admit that I do not look forward to a week of meals at the combat support hospital but that will make your next entrée even more delectable," Lloyd honestly concluded.

The oven's chime signaled Nadene, beckoning her to remove the biscuits. Heat spilled into the room as she opened the oven door and removed the hot, golden brown biscuits. Setting them aside, she turned her attention to cooking the omelet, generously loaded with cheddar cheese.

Lloyd buttered the biscuits while Nadene toiled over the stove. Noticing that the omelets were finished, Lloyd said, "I will pour the hot tea now. By the way, what is in the pot?"

Nadene carefully placed the semicircular omelet on a plate and after sprinkling cheese on top turned towards her husband and with a twinkle in her eye, "Several weeks ago I found a package of stone-ground grits at the store and scooped it up. I know it is your favorite and was saving it for a special occasion."

She filled large bowels with the precious cereal and placed a large dollop of butter and grated cheese on top. The steaming mixture was placed on the table along with the biscuits and omelet. It was a wonderful meal.

Lloyd expected Sergeant Beckman, his military driver, to arrive at 9 am. After breakfast, he cleared the table and while Nadene washed the dishes, he collected his personal belongings and placed them near the door.

Nadene was increasingly anxious as the clock counted the minutes remaining before her husband's departure. She knew that military proprieties would take precedence when her husband's military driver arrived and with that in mind tenderly said, "I will miss you. Please be careful."

Lloyd kissed his wife and reminded her, "Don't forget. I will call you each night."

A firm knock on the door interrupted the romantic interlude, and in response, Lloyd briskly opened the front door. Standing on the threshold was a tall man, impeccably attired in a combat uniform with a warm smile and the faint odor of tobacco greeting Lloyd.

"Top of the morning, sir," Sergeant Beckman exclaimed. "Are you ready for our expedition?"

The man's infectious smile animated Lloyd who lightheartedly rejoined, "I am indeed, and before we leave let me introduce my wife, Nadene."

Beckman strode inside and towering over Nadene while shaking hands with her politely added, "It is a pleasure, ma'am. And don't you worry about a thing. I am a good driver and will take care of your husband!"

Nadene muffled a laugh but genuinely appreciated the kind remark, "Thank you Sergeant and make sure you take care of yourself."

Beckman noticed the small suitcase and leather folder by the front door and without waiting for an invitation seized both and disappeared outside. For different reasons, Neither Lloyd nor Nadene prolonged the doorway departure and simply exchanged a voiceless hug. Nadene wistfully followed her husband outside and watched him clamber inside the military vehicle and with a wave of goodbye returned inside.

Lloyd estimated based on the distance, rough roads, and military checkpoints that it would take the better part of the day to arrive at the tactical operations center; the exact location of which only Beckman knew. As they left his home, the Driver inquired, "would you like to stop and get a cup of coffee?"

"Sure," Lloyd lamely agreed, remembering his many cups of tea and figuring the man needed the beverage.

"I know just the place," Beckman volunteered.

Military vehicles were common sights and occasioned no curiosity, a scene replicated when Beckman parked at a rundown-looking restaurant with a tangle of people waiting outside. Incongruously, a crudely lettered sign proudly proclaimed, "Best Coffee in the World". Lloyd privately doubted the advertisement but joined the crowd, growing larger as more cars disgorged their occupants.

Fifteen minutes later Lloyd paid for two large containers of coffee and walked back to the vehicle gingerly sipped the brew after which the observant Sergeant asked, "What do you think, sir?"

"I must admit I had my doubts, but the coffee is good," Lloyd conceded.

Beckman expertly guided the vehicle from the crowded parking lot and remarked, "We will be traveling on secondary roads until we get to the bridge across the river. It should take about an hour but we should get some gas before we proceed across the bridge."

The only navigable approach to the eastern shore battlefield was a pock-marked road, scarred from intense combat operations. Gas would be unavailable on that stretch which led to Beckman's wise counsel. It would also be the last opportunity to procure any last-minute provisions.

Both driver and passenger were mostly silent, each consumed by their thoughts. Lloyd alternated between rehashing his schedule, memorizing his presentations, and wondering how Nadene was doing. Beckman was singularly focused on leaving the eastern shore after depositing his fellow traveler and the glum necessity of a return trip one week later.

Traffic thinned as the pair approached the bridge spanning the river, an early warning of the conditions ahead. Just before making the traverse, Beckman drove to a military depot and fueled the hungry vehicle for the last portion of the journey. It took nearly an hour to accomplish the mundane task since a long line of military drivers stretched for nearly a mile before them.

"I'm glad that's done," Lloyd's exasperated driver fumed as he headed towards the bridge.

Beckman's frustration spilled over again seeing the endless line of military vehicles snaking their way to the bridge and with muttered expletives, he apologized, "pardon my colorful language, sir."

Lloyd smiled, "It does look like we will be spending some time waiting to get across the bridge."

Stop and go, bumper to bumper, and breathing diesel exhaust added to the misery of the delay. Nearly two hours passed before the bridge's checkpoint came into view. Military police thoroughly inspected each vehicle and required all occupants to temporarily exit, accounting for the long lines.

Hot and tired, Beckman finally stopped at the checkpoint, and obeying instructions, they both left their vehicle. Lloyd watched from the side as the military police examined every nook and cranny. A fully armed soldier, obviously bored with the repetitive chore, wandered over to Lloyd and casually observed, "We don't see many two passenger vehicles."

Lloyd faced the woman and offered, "I have a special assignment at the tactical operations center and later at the combat support hospital."

Security prompted Lloyd's vague response, and the soldier understanding the ambiguity, changed topics, "The lines are like this all day and night."

"It must be tiring work," Lloyd sympathized.

Before she could respond, Beckman hollered, "Let's go, sir. We've been cleared."

Lloyd climbed in and Beckman joined the cavalcade slowly moving across the long bridge. A wide, blue river scintillated under the bright sun and merged in the distance with white, puffy clouds on the horizon. Lloyd pondered the expanse, a peaceful expanse contradicting the fleet of warships poised to counter the enemy's aggression.

Approaching the bridge's terminus revealed another checkpoint, a seemingly unnecessary imposition after their four-mile trek. Mercifully, this was a short stop as the military police simply asked for personal identification.

Lloyd handed his military identification card and a copy of his orders to the military police officer, "I see you are heading to the tactical operation center. Just be advised the roads are rough and there are several more checkpoints."

Beckman acknowledged the warning and looking at his watch asked, "How long would you estimate it will take?"

"Maybe three to four hours but you should arrive before dark," the policeman ventured.

After leaving the bridge, Beckman drove a few miles but then left the main convoy, choosing a more direct route to the tactical operations center. It was indeed a rough passage with the bomb scarred road forcing caution and the three to four hour estimated time of arrival out of reach.

Hunger pangs reminded Lloyd of the long passage of time since breakfast, and he congratulated his prior prudence buying two box lunches at the military depot's convenience store. Since leaving the main road their only company was the endless forest of pine trees with no evidence of human habitation.

"Would you like to stop somewhere and have lunch?" Lloyd posed to his driver.

Beckman countered, "Yes, sir, I would like lunch but if you don't mind, I would prefer to keep on driving. I figure we have several more hours of daylight and we might just manage to arrive before dark."

Lloyd agreed and placed one of the box lunches within the driver's reach. The sandwiches were cold and slightly soggy but neither voiced any complaints. Potato chips and chocolate chip cookies rescued the meal.

Shortly after lunch Lloyd alerted Beckman to an obstruction in the roadway. The driver cautiously slowed as he neared an improvised gate stretching across the highway. After coming to a complete stop, two military policemen approached their vehicle and imperiously inquired, "Where are you bound for?"

Irritated by their tone, Beckman quipped, "Not for a picnic," while simultaneously providing military identification and travel orders.

After scrutinizing the documents, the military policeman peered inside the vehicle and asked, "Are you, Major Lane?"

Lloyd affirmed his identity and received in return, "The commander at the tactical operation center is expecting you. Please proceed."

Beckman waited while the two military policemen wrestled with the makeshift gate and then, with a wave, continued the journey. As they left, the sun was resting on the horizon and the tall trees blocked the fading light, heralding the advent of nighttime.

In the distance, a dim glow stood against the darkness. "I think that is the tactical operation center," Beckman guessed while pointing at the light.

Drawing nearer to the orb confirmed his conjecture and just outside the perimeter, a sentry flagged the vehicle to stop. After the now routine security check, the sentry directed Beckman to a remote parking location.

Lloyd climbed out, stiff from the long drive and happy at the prospect of leaving the noisy vehicle behind. They both walked a considerable distance guided by their destination's warm illumination and then entered the large mobile command post. Several faces turned in their direction but only the senior officer greeted the pair.

"We have been expecting you, Major Lane. My name is Colonel Davidson, commanding officer for this area of combat operations. I am sure you and your driver are tired. We have accommodations for you both nearby and then tomorrow we look forward to learning more about your mission."

Lloyd thanked Colonel Davidson and offered his interest in working with the command staff. At the short meeting's conclusion, a junior officer escorted Lloyd and Beckman to their quarters. A vague fear invaded Lloyd's thinking, now alone and free of the day's distractions.

Dark clouds threatening rain greeted Lloyd the next morning. Pelting drops attacked the man making his way to chow and darting inside the mess tent he noticed the empty tables. Assuming a tardy arrival, Lloyd nervously glanced at his watch, and feeling somewhat reassured that six o'clock was still early, he approached the cafeteria-style line.

Pushing his tray towards the compact steam table revealed a rather sorry-looking amalgam of eggs, bacon, and what appeared to be oatmeal. Field coffee dispensers and a small condiment bin hugged the steam table but most obvious was the absence of a cook to ladle the food.

"Hello, is there anyone here?" Lloyd loudly voiced.

Faint stirrings from the cooking area hinted at human habitation followed by the languid appearance of a short, stocky soldier who tersely demanded, "What would you like?"

Oatmeal was not one of Lloyd's favorites but when surveying the alternatives, he chose the pablum, imagining that butter and sugar might improve the cereal. Two pieces of toast and coffee completed the fare. Before sitting down, Lloyd asked the mess cook, "Where is everybody?"

"Breakfast hours are 4 to 6 in the morning. Most come early," the man perfunctorily replied.

After breakfast, Lloyd returned to his quarters and reviewed the training outline. While placing the handouts in neat piles a familiar voice requested admittance, "May I come in, sir?"

"Yes, please do so," Lloyd said to his erstwhile driver.

"I just wanted to let you know I will be leaving now. I will return in six days for the trip back. And – good luck on your training with the command!" Beckman airily added.

Lloyd thanked the man and then returned to his morning preparations. Another hour must pass before he could begin the program which provided an opportunity to visit the briefing room. Looking outside before venturing forth confirmed a pause in the morning's rain. Lloyd sauntered over to the portable building serving as the training site and cautiously entered the vacant structure, mentally positioning his presentation easel and handouts in their imagined locations.

Lloyd once again returned to his quarters, gathered his props, and just as the clouds unleashed a torrent, he darted inside his home for the day. With everything situated Lloyd idly waited at the speaker's podium for the audience.

A rising babble of voices heralded their arrival. They noisily entered the building taking scant notice of Lloyd. Colonel Davidson was the last to enter and instead of taking a seat he strode to the podium beside Lloyd and rapped vigorously on the wooden structure. All eyes turned to Davidson who ceremoniously introduced the speaker, "I am pleased to introduce Major Lloyd Lane who comes with the highest recommendations of the Army Medical Department. As I understand it, Major Lane will be introducing a demonstration project based on his groundbreaking research which promises to steady personnel losses. Please pay close attention, take notes, and ask questions."

Scanning the audience revealed pockets of indifference. Some of the officers conspicuously exposed their apathy in Lloyd's presentation with heads hunched over esoteric documents. In the back of the room, two non-commissioned officers with expressionless faces stared at Lloyd with unblinking eyes, seemingly on the verge of a somnolent collapse. Colonel Davidson took a seat in the front and seemed unaware or perhaps unconcerned about those behind him. Lloyd was reassured by several officers seated near their commanding officer, seemingly eager to hear the presentation, along with Davidson's apt-appearing attention.

Lloyd thanked Colonel Davidson for the introduction as he stepped away from the podium and distributed the handouts. Standing squarely in front of the audience Lloyd began, "Let me first thank you for attending this presentation. I know you are busy and perhaps some of you may think this is a waste of time."

Directly labeling the leadership disinterest created a stir. Davidson chuckled at the speaker's audacity, buried heads rose from their resting places, but the two in the back remained placidly immobile.

"Now that I have most everyone's attention let me categorically declare that your contribution to this program's success may be instrumental in winning the war," Lloyd proclaimed and then pausing for emphasis continued. "Boots on the ground, sailors on ships, and fully staffed aircrews will win this war but as you well know we are bleeding service members."

"So how can we fix this?" Lloyd wrote in large block letters on the dry erase presentation easel and turning back to the audience declared, "We must staunch the flow!"

"Easier said than done you think, and I agree, but let me describe my idea," Lloyd explained and then he continued his monologue. "As you know, I am the director of a medical management unit with subsequent duties supporting the mobilization of reserve and drafted personnel. From both, I began noticing a curious behavioral trend documented by our clinicians consisting of memory loss, profound emotional detachment, and insensitivity to pain. Now I must admit I was intrigued and being a researcher at heart I set about exploring these observations. Almost by chance, I discovered a relationship between the behaviors and drug test results and not what you might expect."

To emphasize the punch line Lloyd returned to the easel and wrote "FALSE NEGATIVE" and voiced, "If nothing else, please remember those two words."

"Our clinicians suspected that the behaviors mentioned were related to illicit drug misuse, but routine drug screening proved otherwise. In any event, the clinicians concluded that the behaviors were medically disqualifying and referred the individuals for more extensive diagnostic evaluations which delayed and, in many cases, denied the individual's future role as an active-duty service member," Lloyd noted.

"But I unearthed a curious finding when digging deeper," Lloyd teased and continued. "Secondary analysis of the screening drug test results identified a peculiar compound present in those individuals exhibiting the behavioral triad of memory loss, emotional insensibility, and remarkable resistance to pain. Insensitivity to painful stimuli was the most recent discovery and again it was only through serendipity that I reviewed repetitive reports of benumbed, injured soldiers."

Colonel Davidson raised his hand and once acknowledged by the speaker inquired, "What do you know about this compound, for example, where did it come?"

"Great question," Lloyd complimented and then continued with his best answer. "I have requested the assistance of a research laboratory and further analysis is underway. At this point little is known about how the chemical affects humans, but I believe we will have more information in the coming weeks. Tracing the source of the chemical is also unknown but Colonel Roderick requested the assistance of epidemiologists."

Before taking a mid-morning break Lloyd explained biochemical drug testing in greater detail. He justified this deep excursion as a prelude to enlisting the leaders' support in the next phase of his presentation, hoping that the scientific foundation would bolster his case. Scanning the group, Lloyd observed the audience mentally drifting, and their eager exit when he announced a thirty-minute intermission confirmed their lack of interest.

Lloyd remained in the empty room during the break and reviewed his notes. Colonel Davidson was the first to return slowly followed by others. Resuming his post at the podium, Lloyd noted that the two lethargic members originally hiding in the back were absent.

"Tomorrow I will travel to the combat support hospital and after discussions with hospital leadership, launch the demonstration project. The new staff assigned to this project will conduct comprehensive assessments of individuals exhibiting the behavioral cluster of memory loss, emotional detachment, and pain tolerance. Data derived from these assessments will be collected and studied," Lloyd said.

"I need your help identifying service members that exhibit the behavioral symptoms," Lloyd pleaded. "Included in your handouts is a detailed description of what to look for but an acronym might be helpful."

Turning to the easel Lloyd wrote in large letters, "T-A-D" and then explained, "The T stands for tolerance, meaning the individual's high pain tolerance. The A stands for amnesia which refers to any profound loss of memory and the D stands for detachment meaning emotional detachment as suggested by an inability to express emotions."

Colonel Davidson interrupted the speaker and asked, "What do we do if we suspect a service member has TAD?"

"Refer the service member to the combat support hospital's TAD Triad clinical research project," Lloyd simply answered.

"And what happens then?" Davidson answered in follow-up.

"The TAD Triad Team will conduct an extensive clinical and epidemiologic assessment. They will also determine the service member's fitness for duty and make the appropriate dispositions. That could include the return to duty, a medical profile with specific limitations, or an evacuation from the area of combat operations," Lloyd elaborated.

Lloyd noticed a stirring among the group and guessing it might relate to the referral process added, "We will make every effort to render fitness for duty decisions within three days and I hope that most will return to active duty."

His response did not change the tense atmosphere. Lloyd initially speculated that the group's anxiety stemmed from anticipated personnel losses, but his answer did not quell the room's disquiet. Sensing that further efforts to tame the turmoil would be ineffective he decided to end the briefing on a positive note, "Thank you for your attention. As the project moves forward, please share your thoughts and I will keep in touch with Colonel Davidson."

Except for Colonel Davidson, the room emptied quickly. Lloyd folded the presentation easel and collected a few stray handouts and was on the verge of leaving when Davidson approached him, "You noticed the tension."

"Yes," Lloyd agreed. "I guessed wrong though. I thought they anticipated huge personnel losses."

"I won't deny that was part of the group's unease but when they thumbed through the symptom referral checklist, I think they recognized some of their colleagues," Davidson frankly concluded.

Lloyd accepted the Commander's consideration but decided against furthering the discussion, remembering the two absent glazed officers. Responding tangentially, Lloyd said, "I need your support to ensure that all service members who meet the behavioral criteria are referred for further assessment."

Colonel Davidson agreed and the two parted company. Lloyd returned to his quarters, deposited his props, and decided to take a stroll before lunch. Just before the serving line closed, Lloyd entered the empty area, retrieved a tray, and with a simple meal, took a seat by himself.

Lloyd had the balance of the day free after packing for tomorrow's journey to the combat support hospital. Leisure reading filled the void until dinner when the man brought a sandwich and chips back to his quarters. Keeping his promise, he reached for the telephone and called Nadene.

Five times the phone rang and then suddenly it went silent. Perplexed and concerned, Lloyd dialed the number again, unconsciously holding his breath in anxious anticipation. With the seventh ring, a familiar voice answered, "The Lane residence. May I ask who is calling?"

"Guess who this is," Lloyd teased.

"I've been looking forward all day to your call! Is everything all right?" Nadene worriedly asked.

"Yes," he replied. "I am through with my briefing here and tomorrow I travel to the combat support hospital. Really uneventful. For the most part, the leaders seemed polite but disinterested which is pretty much what I expected. How are things at home?"

"The electricity comes and goes and now the telephone is doing the same. I was afraid you would not be able to get through," she lamented.

"I did have some difficulty," he admitted. "But I do have some good news. Looking at my schedule I should be coming home sooner than expected. I built in some extra time allowing for inevitable setbacks but so far it's been smooth sailing."

"That is good news!" his wife exclaimed.

For the better part of an hour, they continued but the phone connection was increasingly tenuous as loud crackles and echoes competed with their conversation. Bowing to the phone's frailty, they reluctantly bid each other a good night, promising to speak again tomorrow.

Colonel Davidson arranged Lloyd's transportation to the combat support hospital. The trip was roughly an hour distant, but checkpoints prolonged the journey and Lloyd arrived mid-afternoon. He made his way to the hospital commander's office and after brief introductions, they toured the facility. The next day's plan included meeting the TAD Triad Team members and a short presentation to the hospital's staff.

After parting company with the hospital commander, an enlisted soldier escorted Lloyd to the officer's quarters. Dusk was setting in but just enough light remained for Lloyd to hike around the hospital complex. An old mobile kitchen supplemented the hospital's nutrition resources and its dim interior lighting captured his attention, bringing the man's hunger to the forefront.

With his dinner in hand, Lloyd returned to his quarters, determined to call Nadene. Fortune favored his efforts as the phone call went through without a glitch and seizing the occasion he cheerfully announced, "I am sitting in my spacious room at the combat support hospital with a hot gourmet meal!"

Nadene chuckled, "It sounds like a vacation resort, but I think you exaggerate."

"A little," he agreed. "But it is better than my last stop. Tomorrow I meet the staff and if all goes well, I should be wrapping things up. I can then get a ride back from here sparing Sergeant Beckman the effort."

"That sounds great. We can celebrate your return with a real gourmet meal!" Nadene exclaimed.

Lloyd's expectation of an early departure shortened the phone call and after hanging up he retired for the night. Midway through the night loud vehicle traffic awakened the man and peering outside he saw ambulances clustered near the hospital, a stark reminder of the war.

A dull, heavy, dark day greeted Lloyd as he strolled across the grounds to the hospital's dining area. It was here, over breakfast, that the TAD Triad Team would join him. Armed with his light meal Lloyd spied the small group at a distant table and smiling broadly as he approached them, he took a seat in their midst.

Lloyd knew them well having recruited the nurses from a cadre of volunteers. They were bright, eager, and particularly interested in clinical research. Lloyd enjoyed training the small group and looked forward to a successful project. Over the next several hours they huddled together reviewing the clinical procedures and research methodologies that would guide the nurse's work over the next few weeks. Lloyd had every confidence that their work combined with the laboratory's research would clarify the mystery chemical and its behavioral impact.

With their meeting concluded, Lloyd filled his coffee cup and made preparation for the staff briefing. In many respects, it mirrored the leadership briefing with an emphasis on recruiting support for the project. Lloyd anticipated more interest and questions so he condensed the talk to allow extra time for a more interactive discussion.

The hospital commander introduced Lloyd who in turn did the same for the TAD Triage Team members. He began his presentation by reviewing the casual connections detected between pain tolerance, amnesia, emotional detachment, and the chance discovery of a unique chemical compound. As Lloyd explained, "This project has two prongs. The TAD Triad Team will conduct extensive, focused, and rapid assessments of service members referred for evaluation based on the presence of the behavioral triad, and the Team will also collect demographic and epidemiologic data. The second prong relies on laboratory research elucidating the pharmacologic properties of the mystery compound."

Pausing for a moment to allow questions yielded none but during the interlude, Lloyd studied the audience. Perhaps it was just a coincidence the man mused but this large group shared similarities with the leadership group. The staff seated in the front rows seemed attentive but nearly a quarter of the attendees, scattered throughout the room but more concentrated in the back, appeared to be in various stages of unresponsiveness. Some were asleep while others vacantly stared into space.

Miffed by the disrespect but mindful of his mission, Lloyd partially subjugated the former by discarding the monologue momentarily. Leaving the podium, he walked down the central aisle and standing before a dazed officer said, "Captain, let's assume that after completing an assessment that the TRIAD Team confirms the behavioral symptoms. How would you determine the service member's fitness for duty?"

The officer eyed Lloyd with an expressionless stare and slowly replied, "I don't know."

Brushing the response aside, Lloyd returned to the podium and answered the question, "Determining fitness for duty is the primary outcome desired for this project. Fitness for duty would depend on the degree of impairment. For example, if the memory loss were circumscribed and the soldier able to perform their job then emotional detachment and tolerance to pain would be less important."

Coming to the end of the presentation Lloyd reminded the audience that the TAD Triad Team would be available for future questions and would provide regular feedback. "Are there any other questions I can answer?" Lloyd said as he prepared to depart the room.

"Yes, I have one," the hospital commander remarked. "How long do you anticipate the project to last?"

"One month should provide sufficient data given the anticipated number of referrals. The laboratory is working on the same timeline. I will then analyze data and prepare a briefing for the Surgeon General with suggested courses of action," Lloyd succinctly replied.

After the meeting, Lloyd planned for his return home. A quick call to Nadene alerted her to his pending arrival and with a sense of relief he settled in for a good night's sleep.

The return trip was uneventful, mirroring as it did the previous passage. Lloyd arrived late that night and thanking the driver jumped from the vehicle. Instead of unlocking the door he knocked quietly and waited for a reply. A few minutes passed without a response, prompting Lloyd to knock more vigorously and simultaneously ring the doorbell. To his relief, he heard shuffling inside and soon the door opened to reveal a sleepy woman.

Upon sighting her husband Nadene squealed with delight. "I was so worried!" she exclaimed. "I waited until midnight and then fell asleep on the sofa. When I heard the doorbell, I thought I was just dreaming."

"I thought you might be asleep," her husband admitted. "Nothing unusual happened on the return trip - it just takes forever, and I did not want to startle you."

Nadene was now thoroughly awake and after she made some tea Lloyd sipped the brew and spent the next hour talking about his short field trip. She listened intently and did not interrupt until Lloyd concluded his summary at which point, she mentioned, "Earlier today Colonel Roderick called. He knew you were returning but he seemed very anxious to speak with you. I offered to take a message, but he said the matter was too sensitive to discuss on the telephone. He even hinted at waiting for you here!"

Lloyd's face instantly darkened, "It must be serious. I wonder if I should wait until tomorrow."

Nadene suggested, "He only lives a few miles from here. He seemed so impatient that I would recommend you let him know you are back. He can then decide what to do."

In response, Lloyd reached for the telephone and dialed his boss. At the first ring, Roderick's booming voice greeted the caller, "This is Colonel Roderick."

Lloyd looked at his wife as he answered, "Sorry to phone you so late but Nadene said you called earlier."

"I did," he replied and with a sense of urgency added, "I would like to come over now. Is that alright with you and Nadene?"

"Yes," agreed Lloyd, "we look forward to seeing you shortly"

Roderick abruptly ended the conversation and Lloyd could imagine the man dashing out the door. Turning to Nadene, Lloyd said, "Roderick is coming over now."

An imperious knock at their door signaled Roderick's arrival. Lloyd sprinted the short distance, opened the door, and greeted his boss. Dispensing with the customary social exchange, Roderick strode to the dining room table and without a word removed a folder from his briefcase conspicuously marked "Top Secret".

Breaking his silence, Roderick turned to Nadene and with an apologetic tone asked, "I know this sounds awful but what I have to say to Lloyd is classified."

Nadene understood and good-naturedly replied, "I know when I am not wanted! Just don't keep me locked up too long."

A wan smile briefly drifted across Roderick's face. As she left the room a backward glance showed her husband huddled in quiet conversation with Roderick and with the classified folder and its contents strewn over the table.

"First, let me thank you for keeping me up to date on your recent trip. It sounds like it was successful," Roderick began, "but that is not the reason I wanted to meet with you. It was wise of you to ensure that all research data was duplicated with copies to both of us."

"During your brief absence," he continued, "I received an urgent phone call from the research laboratory examining the drug test results identified in those individuals exhibiting the behavioral triad of memory loss, emotional insensibility, and insensitivity to painful stimuli."

Roderick handed the classified document to Lloyd who spent the next several minutes scanning the reports before concluding, "Based on the initial results from the research lab it seems that our mysterious chemical is a ketamine analog. As a potent dissociative drug that might account for the extreme depersonalization, memory deficits, and its anesthetic properties would explain the remarkable resistance to painful stimuli."

"But what we don't know," Roderick interrupted, "is the source of the chemical. I have not received any feedback from the epidemiologists attempting to trace demographic similarities among the service members exhibiting the symptoms triad."

"Perhaps," Lloyd conjectured, "now that we know more about our mysterious substance, we can get closer to answering your question."

"Right now, the research lab named the substance a jaw-breaking 'glutamatergic *N*-methyl-D-aspartate receptor antagonist with complex serotonin receptor subtype actions' based on the presumed pharmacologic mechanisms," Roderick said but then added, "we need a better name. One that will capture the essence of this substance in simpler terms."

Lloyd rose from the table and waves of fatigue washed over the man. "Would you like some coffee, sir?"

With a sympathetic look, Roderick recognized the man's waning energy, "I should have waited until you had a night's sleep. I just thought you would like to see the preliminary results. In exchange for my imprudence, please take the next two days off and recuperate!"

Lloyd thanked Roderick for the consideration, "I will be fine with some coffee and maybe one day to rest before I return to work. But getting back to your question about naming the chemical I do have a suggestion."

Teasing his boss, Lloyd momentarily dangled his answer while placing two steaming cups of coffee on the table. Roderick leaned forward, took a sip of the hot beverage, and hiding his interest casually remarked, "I'm sure we can come up with some ideas after you have rested."

"Just to prove I am still awake," Lloyd joked, "I have the perfect name for our chemical. By combining the three behavioral symptoms with the chemical's class we have triad merged with ketamine -and voilà- we have TRIAD-AMINE."

Roderick roared with delight, "That is perfect. Let's finish on that note!"

Standing up, Roderick asked if Nadene was still awake. Lloyd tiptoed into the bedroom and discovered his wife sitting in a corner reading a book. She noted his arrival and jovially said, "Are you here to release me?"

Lloyd returned to work the next day and was assailed by phone messages awaiting a return call. He recognized the number from the research laboratory, but five messages came from an unknown source. Intrigued by the latter, he listened to the voice recordings. All conveyed the same request, "Please call Dr. Giel at 477-9099. I have important information."

Lloyd detected a mixture of fear and urgency in Dr. Giel's voice. Before complying with the Doctor's appeal, Lloyd took a moment to ponder the possibilities. Hopefully, Giel had information about Triad-Amine but the Doctor's emotional tone worried Lloyd. His mind wandered from prosaic to problematic explanations but the matter could only be resolved by calling Giel.

Reaching into a desk drawer Lloyd retrieved a notebook and placing it beside the telephone proceeded to call Dr. Giel. At the first ring, a loud raspy voice demanded, "Who is this?"

The strident tone surprised Lloyd who mentally conjured the image of a pugnacious, bespectacled, bull-headed man. Quelling his annoyance with the man's evident arrogance, Lloyd simply replied, "My name is Major Lloyd Lane, and I am returning your several messages."

"I'm glad you called back so quickly," the man snarled.

"I called as soon as I returned from a field mission in a combat zone," Lloyd patiently replied; a crisp response that choked a fit of mounting anger.

"I am the Chief of the Toxicology Section at the Defense Research Laboratory," Giel proudly declared, "and personally conducted the chemical analysis of the glutamatergic *N*-methyl-D-aspartate receptor antagonist that also exhibits complex serotonin receptor subtype actions."

"It's a pleasure to speak with you and let me thank you for your expertise," Lloyd genuinely conceded, "please go ahead."

Lloyd could almost imagine Giel swelling with pride, but the man's brusqueness deflated that impression. "I only have a few minutes to talk with you," Giel rudely intoned.

"After analyzing hundreds of specimens, I can confidently conclude that the chemical in question is hitherto unknown in science," Giel positively stated, "but it shares some structural similarities with ketamine. You may not know this, but ketamine is a powerful anesthetic, and this new chemical is even more potent."

Lloyd ignored the subtle insult and instead encouraged Giel to continue. The man needed little prodding, clearly relishing the limelight. "The new substance seems to preferentially target certain specific neurotransmitters and anatomical regions in the brain. As I mentioned before, the new chemical is a glutamatergic *N*-methyl-D-aspartate receptor antagonist that also has complex serotonin receptor subtype actions. In time, I will be able to better differentiate the serotonin receptor types but in a general sense, those involved with pain mediation and mood are most likely. I also suspect other neurotransmitters are involved such as dopamine, gamma-aminobutyric acid, opioid and cannabinoid receptors, and neuroactive peptides."

"It sounds like a very complex chemical," Lloyd mused.

Giel sneered at Lloyd's remark, "All chemicals have complex biological actions."

"You mentioned that the new substance had discrete sites of anatomical activity in the brain," Lloyd asked, ignoring yet again Giel's belligerence, "can you elaborate on that?"

"Yes, indeed I can," the man boasted and then proceeded, "it seems abundantly clear through voltammetry what neurotransmitters are involved. I have identified the new substance's activity in the limbic system based on newly developed in vivo neurotransmitter tracking techniques conducted among soldiers who volunteered for the research study."

"The limbic system," Lloyd repeated for emphasis.

"Yes, the limbic system," Giel growled, "and I am sure you know nothing about it. So let me take a moment and explain it. If you look at a midsagittal section of a human brain two somewhat central arcs containing the cingulate gyrus, hippocampus, amygdala, and thalamus, comprise key structural components of the limbic system. The limbic system is very complex, and science still knows little about it. But we do know that these structures affect other parts of the brain to ultimately control our emotions, memory, and processing of pain."

Lloyd interrupted the monologue to inquire, "What about the nucleus accumbens?

The question surprised Giel temporarily upending a plebian view of his interlocutor, "Yes, the nucleus accumbens is part of the limbic system. It is also known as the behavioral reward center and plays a role in various addictions."

Lloyd was on the verge of asking additional questions when a peremptory remark from Giel interrupted him, "I only have a few more minutes."

"Thank you, Dr. Giel, for taking the time to speak with me. I would appreciate your thoughts on two matters," Lloyd politely responded and continued, "Is the new substance addictive and how long do the drug's effects on behavior last?"

"At this time, neither question has an answer, but some preliminary data suggests that the drug is potent enough to permanently alter brain function," he glibly noted.

Lloyd reasonably concluded that further discussion would only provoke Giel and with that in mind he again complimented the man, "Thank you for your excellent work and I hope to speak with you again at a later date."

True to character, Giel abruptly terminated the discussion. During their time together Lloyd took copious notes and with a sigh closed the notebook. Giel's attitude irked Lloyd but he shook his head as if to cast the sentiments aside, and seizing the notebook, left his office in the hope of meeting with Colonel Roderick.

Much to his surprise, Roderick was in his office and after a short delay welcomed Lloyd's unexpected arrival. Rising from his desk, Roderick looked tired, even haggard. He removed his eyeglasses, for reading only he mentioned on multiple past occasions, and walked slowly to the sofa. He gestured to his guest to join him and once seated opened the small adjoining refrigerator and removed two energy drinks and handed one to Lloyd.

Lloyd took a sip of the cold drink and without waiting for an invitation announced, "I spoke with Dr. Giel at the research laboratory earlier and wanted to share his observations."

Roderick smiled and mischievously asked, "How was the good doctor? His usual pleasant self?"

Lloyd grinned, "A remarkably puffed-up person!"

"That was my impression too," Roderick admitted, "but he is a competent scientist."

During their short meeting, Lloyd discussed Giel's findings at the end of which Roderick returned to his desk and called the Surgeon General. The officer was unavailable, so Roderick left a short message seeking another briefing to review the recent research.

Lloyd's first weekend home after returning from the combat field assignment was a low-key affair. Shortages of gas and empty retail shelves were problems Nadene wanted to avoid so the pair sheltered in place, creating a blissful bubble blocking contact with reality. Long forgotten board games and puzzles emerged from hibernation; previously relegated to irrelevance and banished to dark closets. Their newfound liberty reminded Nadene and Lloyd of simple, shared joys.

Unreliable utilities were common annoyances with both scheduled and random electricity outages a consequence of the war. Lloyd was an outdoor enthusiast, evidenced by a complete array of camping equipment. Included in the trove was a butane-powered portable stove. Given unpredictable utilities, the portable stove rose in prominence, fueled by surprisingly abundant gas canister supplies.

Lloyd cracked open a window in the kitchen for ventilation, and after screwing a butane canister in place, lit the stove and exclaimed, "Let's go home camping!"

Nadene reached into a cabinet and removed a frying pan. Turning to the refrigerator she opened the freezer, found the hamburger patties, dropped them in the pan, and handed both to her husband. In a few minutes, an inviting aroma wafted through the kitchen sharpening their appetites. Lacking hamburger buns, Lloyd gingerly placed the hot burgers on slices of bread. Nadene completed the treat by adding pickles, onions, a small squirt of ketchup, and she crowned the feast with another slice of bread.

Lloyd resumed contact with reality on Monday. With hints of dysphoria, he settled into his office and noticed the pile of papers neatly ordering his desk. A handwritten memo from Colonel Roderick lay on top and informed the reader, "Please review these reports in preparation for a briefing with the Surgeon General."

After initially disconsolately shuffling through the papers Lloyd's attitude shifted. The documents revealed detailed results from his TRIAD Team and other similar groups. As he perused the research it was abundantly clear that Triad-Amine was widespread, affecting one-third of service members with the characteristic indifference first observed many months ago.

Lloyd's previous speculations were reaching the point of certainty. The convergence of research laboratory and broad, field-based behavioral data minimized statistical error. Interestingly, after conducting their comprehensive assessments, TRIAD teams universally agreed that service members were fit for duty.

Digging deeper into the data, Lloyd discovered that despite the behavioral declivities, surveys from combat commanders uniformly praised the service members' stalwart military bearing and combat performance. Based on this chance finding, Lloyd imagined that the combat commanders prized the Triad-Amine-induced behavioral characteristics. From a commander's perspective, these were fearless fighters.

It was nearing 5 pm. Lloyd had been so immersed in reviewing the field reports that lunch slipped by unnoticed. He was stiff from the prolonged posture and arising from the desk chair stretched from side to side, relieving the discomfort. Grabbing his briefcase, he made for the door but an imperious phone call halted his progress.

"Major Lane," he glibly responded.

"Glad I caught you before you left," Colonel Roderick excitedly said, "I just received word that the Surgeon General scheduled our briefing next Monday."

"That's good to hear. I will prepare a draft in the next day or two for your review," Lloyd offered.

Preparing the draft briefing proved more difficult than Lloyd anticipated. Distilling reams of material into bite-sized nuggets required careful consideration. Like separating the wheat from the chaff, Lloyd's decisions sorted the data into two piles; that relevant to a concise briefing and the remainder discarded.

But it was not that easy. Lloyd first needed decisional guard rails. Should he focus the proposed courses of action towards extending the research and obtaining greater confirmation or accept the current findings as definitive? The former was probably more scientific he reasoned but the nation's precarious war footing argued for the latter. Lloyd figured the Surgeon General would prefer a briefing oriented towards the war and not one construed as a vacuous academic exercise.

After three days of arduous preparation, with erasures and rewrites cluttering his efforts, Lloyd submitted a draft to his boss. Lloyd was not pleased with his draft, still internally debating the ramifications. He rationalized his proposed course of action by acknowledging his advisory role as a staff officer, leaving potential implementation to senior officers and other government officials.

Colonel Roderick received Lloyd's draft and quickly scanned its contents. He too privately harbored reservations, but the political environment would not countenance more delays gathering data. In his mind, Roderick could hear the Surgeon General pointedly wondering "when would there ever be enough."

As before, a large group of individuals attended the briefing. Lloyd recognized many of the senior officers and political appointees but was unfamiliar with the smaller group of stiff, serious-looking civilian-clad personnel sitting in a neat row at the back of the conference room. All wore sunglasses and carried barely concealed handguns.

After introductions, the Surgeon General invited Major Lane to begin the briefing. Lloyd was more nervous than usual and scanning the audience only magnified his anxiety. Expectant eyes, serious and intimidating, bore through the man. Colonel Roderick was the sole oasis of propriety in the room and seeking refuge, Lloyd focused his gaze on that direction throughout the briefing.

Bullet by bullet, the briefing unfolded concisely documenting TRIAD Team observations, command surveys, and Dr. Giel's research findings. Lloyd introduced Triad-Amine as the moniker for the chemical.

Before continuing, Lloyd paused and invited questions. No one stirred and a dreadful silence followed. During those tense moments, Lloyd's gaze drifted across the audience, and perhaps it was his imagination, but the attendees' faces were blank, expressionless, and seemingly devoid of humanity.

"Based on these data," Lloyd concluded, "there are two proposed courses of action. The research can be extended to obtain greater confirmation or you can accept the current findings as definitive. The exigencies of war might favor the latter approach, particularly when viewed from the commander's perspective that service members testing positive for Triad-Amine are fearless fighters."

Chapter Seven – Foresight

Nadene immediately distrusted Professor Christopher Jonas. The man stood at the whiteboard and grandly lettered his name in bold script and then turned to face his audience. He was a middle-aged man with a pear-shaped face, thin lips, half-open snake-like eyes, oddly protruding ears, and graying hair parted in the middle and combed in equal parts to each side. Nadene imagined that his perfect coiffure consumed hours.

Jonas' posture was rigid and unbending, much like his personality. Adorning his body was a crisp white shirt, black tie with Half-Windsor knot emblazoned with a silver crest depicting two overlapping semicircles. His dark blue pinstriped jacket lay casually draped over the lectern. Matching trousers with a single gold stripe running the length completed the ensemble.

From his uniform, Nadene accurately calculated his position as a faculty member with Foresight University. A round, gold, gleaming medallion depicting an open book with distinctive silver semicircles decorated the man's shirt pocket. From this Nadene knew that the man was a government-decorated academician.

His first words cemented Nadene's first impression. "My name is Professor Christopher Jonas. I am a senior government academic and will be your principal lecturer. I expect you to be attentive, take notes, and be quiet. I will not tolerate disruptions, disagreements, or dialogue. You are here to listen and not question."

His high-pitched, squeaky voice annoyed Nadene with its imperious tone. "I will begin with a roll call," Jonas intoned, "simply raise your hand when I call your name. If I have questions, you will then, and only then, speak out."

Nadene cautiously looked around the room and recognized Mona and her husband Curt who was seated in the third row. "Curt," she thought to herself, "what an appropriate name for the man." Neither of the pair responded when Nadene made eye contact.

"Is Nadene Lane present?" Jonas asked while scanning the assemblage.

Nadene obediently raised her hand prompting her inquisitor to inquire, "Where is your partner?"

"My husband is a senior official with the Central Government Home Guard. He submitted a waiver of attendance which was approved," she replied while offering a copy of the document to Jonas.

With an arrogant wave of his hand, Jonas dismissed the offer and continued with the roll call. All other attendees were paired couples which inexplicably troubled Nadene. She wondered if her solitary status would attract more than curiosity.

After completing the roll call, Jonas distributed a spiral-bound notebook to each participant. On the cover block letters spelled out "Foresight Education Committee". Nadene absent-mindedly thumbed through the handout, briefly scanning the table of contents. Scores of empty pages eagerly awaited inky notes.

"I will be compressing this lecture series - more on that later - but for now our first lesson will review the history of Foresight," Jonas squeaked.

His raspy voice, like chalk scraping on a blackboard, made her skin crawl. "How," she wondered, "can I stand two hours a day for a week of this?"

"Let's begin with the derivation of the sobriquet Foresight," Jonas said, dramatically emphasizing each word along with a condescending smile.

Nadene covered her mouth smothering a laugh triggered by the man's lofty language. The man was a boorish cartoon, a two-dimensional pretentious caricature with an endless inflated ego. Jonas' vanity-induced blindness reminded Nadene of the central figure in Hans Christian Anderson's fable the "Emperor's New Clothes". Viewing the man in this manner paradoxically helped Nadene ignore his conceit.

"Your Central Government promotes policies ensuring a safe, stable, society," Jonas began. He then pivoted to the whiteboard and in large letters wrote, "FORESIGHT".

"Foresight is the guiding principle in all government policy decisions. We must look forward, predict beneficial social trends, and then sagaciously implement appropriate public welfare regulations. Your attendance at this specific Foresight Educational Symposium for Parents will ensure you make the right decision for your child's future role in our society. I trust you will do so after our time together," Jonas caustically declared.

Nadene shivered involuntarily at the man's veiled threat. She felt a sudden urge to hold Clio and Alexander, prompted by a mother's instinct to protect her offspring. She shook her head ever so slightly but sufficiently to cast the distressing scene aside but worried that her behavior would be detected by her tormentor.

Jonas was oblivious to everyone except himself and senior government officials. He was an obsequious man, deferential to the powerful and disdainful of those he deemed weak. Through his distorted lens, Nadene and the entire audience were inconvenient provincials the man was forced to contend with. His stern classroom rules minimized reciprocal behaviors and minimized close encounters with passable people.

To be fair, Jonas' deportment was emblematic of many Central Government officials. Their officious character was cultivated through an incestuous government mediocracy that favored, retained, and promoted individuals residing in a tight-knit band of so-called civil servants. Popular opinion derisively branded the group as the magisterial minions.

At odds with this group were individuals recognized for meritorious duty. Lloyd was among this small cadre, and he was keenly aware of the magisterial minion's Machiavellian morality. The minions detested Lloyd and others of his ilk, jealous of their accomplishments and diminished stature through comparison. Behind masks of congeniality and cooperation, the minions subtly undermined opponents through their unscrupulous cunning and manipulative behaviors. It was well known in minion circles that a supposedly friendly pat on the back was a prelude to figuratively stabbing an adversary.

Jonas thumped the lectern and with his mouth drawn tight cried, "Several of you are not paying attention!"

Attendees nervously looked around the room or hung their heads in dismay. Nadene locked eyes with the man in a defiant stare. For some unknown reason her calm rebellion rattled Jonas; evidenced by an embarrassing blush that colored his face. In a moment he regained some composure, but his softer voice suggested a deeper wound.

Jonas used the remainder of the first day's lecture to review the handout and embedded homework assignments. A muted musical alarm from his watch signaled the expiration of two hours. "Be on time for tomorrow's session," he unceremoniously demanded and with a speedy stride left the room.

"How was the first session?" Lloyd asked.

"Much as I expected," Nadene sighed, "a highfalutin little man cracking his whip to keep the cattle in line. On a positive note, he did suggest that the number of lectures would be reduced."

Lloyd laughed at her derogatory description, "Now you know what I deal with daily!"

"Oh, well," she dejectedly said, "maybe tomorrow will be better. The next three lessons cover the history of how we got to this miserable time."

"You lived through that time. There's little you don't already know but the purpose of those lectures is for indoctrination," he said.

"I'm really worried though. Jonas' objective is to force everyone's capitulation to the Central Government's position. This will not be an even-handed presentation," she sadly admitted.

"That may indeed be true," Lloyd acknowledged, "but the law unambiguously mandates free choice. Parents have the legal right to choose their children's future courses. Unfortunately, the tide seems to be turning against parents that defy the Central Government."

"Enough of this," Nadene said as she stamped her foot and began preparing dinner.

As a senior official, Lloyd enjoyed rations of both gas and food commensurate with his rank. By no means were either extravagant but Nadene and Lloyd were far from being overly self-indulgent. Tonight's dinner was a simple but satisfying plate of spaghetti with a tasty marinara sauce. Complementing the pasta was a mixed salad with blue cheese dressing, bright red cherries, and garlic bread, all washed down with sparkling mineral water.

They both relaxed after dinner watching television. Lloyd collected old television videos that predated the war, avoiding the current crop of propaganda-laden shows. The only exception was a nightly newscast.

Near the end of their movie, the television fluttered and then went blank, the victim of a distressed electrical grid. It was nearing 9 pm and with an air of resignation, the married couple retired for the night.

Midway into the night, Clio started crying, awakening Alexander who sympathetically started wailing. Nadene jumped out of bed and quickly discovering the wet diaper made the necessary adjustments. The contented child soon fell asleep, and the tired mother returned to bed. She wistfully wondered how her husband never awakened.

In the morning, after two cups of tea, buttered toast, and a bowl of cornflakes Nadene perked up. Her husband quaffed coffee and a stale donut, kissed his wife goodbye, and headed for the office.

Nadene arrived earlier for the second session of the Foresight Educational Symposium for Parents. She deliberately chose a seat in the front row and neatly arranged her notebook and pencil on the small desk. Five minutes later Jonas strode to the lectern and ignored the sole occupant in the room. Pretending to be busy, he aimlessly shuffled his papers and never once looked up from the podium. Nadene, meanwhile, studied the man intently which no doubt added to his uneasiness.

Once the room reached capacity Jonas switched the lights off and an image projector on. The screen burst into color displaying a high-resolution battle map. Jonas walked to the side of the screen and with a laser pointer in his hand squeaked, "This is an accurate depiction of the battlefield forces during the static phase of the war. Red lines indicate entrenched enemy ground positions west of the Mississippi River, stretching from Minnesota to Louisiana. Red lines also indicate the enemy's combined naval and army forces focused on the Chesapeake Bay area. It was rumored but never publicly acknowledged that enemy submarines patrolled the waters along the eastern shore and pacific coastline."

A roomful of pencils leaving traces on paper sounded like a swarm of buzzing bees. When Jonas paused the bees fled but furiously returned when he resumed his monologue. "Blue lines are the American forces," he said.

Directing the laser pointer for emphasis he continued, "As you see, the American line confronted the enemy east of the Mississippi River from Wisconsin to Mississippi and blocked their eastward ambitions. We also deployed troops in the Delmarva Peninsula blocking the enemy's westward advance. It was assumed that we had submarines patrolling the Gulf of Mexico as well as the Atlantic and Pacific coastlines."

Jonas abandoned the map and switched the lights on. Oddly staring at the ceiling, he added, "Both sides deployed their respective aircraft mostly in support of ground operations. The enemy liberally bombed our infrastructure and utilities, but American sorties aggressively responded and diminished the assaults."

"And so," Nadene thought, "the war bogged down with neither side able to advance. It was hoped that by attacking the enemy's extended supply lines that we could choke them to death. But our so-called allies never came to our defense but instead many covertly profited by selling weapons, food, and other products. They sabotaged our air blockade."

Jonas touched on the allies' nonresponse but offered a different story, "Naturally, we expected our mutual defense treaties to break the stalemate, but our allies could not respond. The enemy relentlessly threatened them with a nuclear holocaust if they supported America."

Nadene remembered those lame excuses of western leaders. In reality, though, decades of profligate social welfare programs depleted their military capabilities. Even if the political will had existed to support America their anemic armed forces could not. Embracing the enemy's threats was a convenient fig leaf behind which western powers hid their impotence.

The static war lasted six months during which time each side jockeyed for supremacy. Neither could gain an advantage until the enemy flooded their western Mississippi River strongholds with massive troop deployments. The enemy's central authoritarian government brooked no discontent and unlike their opponents could count on the news media for unwavering support. Therefore, there was no public backlash when the enemy expanded the eligibility criteria for compulsory military service.

America's military leaders long anticipated such a move and vigorously pushed for a commensurate response, but public opposition and the implacably opposed news media frustrated the military's efforts.

Nadene remembered her husband complaining about bureaucratic hurdles erected by career Selective Service System employees that reduced the flow of recruits to a trickle. Sympathetic civilian health providers issued countless flimsy medical disability exemptions further reducing the number of eligible troops. In a few, particularly flagrant examples, government authorities prosecuted physicians issuing fraudulent exemption certificates in an unsuccessful effort to deter the practice.

Despite the resistance, some new service members eventually made their way to battlefield units. But like pumping air into a punctured tire, the replacements could never overcome desertions which leaked personnel at alarming rates and left combat units operationally flat.

Enemy intelligence observed the decay and with fresh reinforcements launched a massive assault on Christmas Day. In a coordinated pincer movement, the enemy's combined air, navy, and army forces unleashed furious bombardments across the Delmarva Peninsula and Western Mississippi theater in a determined effort to crush American forces in a vice-like grip.

The enemy's surprise attack on Christmas caught America off guard. Before a meaningful counterattack, American forces reported a vast armada of enemy transport ships ferrying enemy soldiers and their equipment eastward across the Mississippi River.

Frantic American military leaders sought and received authority for a hastily designed air campaign targeting the enemy's floating forces. A shortage of aircrews hampered the effort, but a determined group of pilots soon headed towards the river. The pilots targeted the seemingly endless expanse of enemy ships while dodging incoming fire but on returning they collectively sounded gloomy notes. Yes, they exacted massive damage but far too many ships would succeed in disgorging enemy combatants on the eastern side of the river.

American forces in the eastern theater prepared for the coming onslaught. Intelligence reports and pilot observations suggested that the enemy was focusing their forces along a line stretching from Iowa to the southern portion of Missouri. The enemy hoped to puncture the thin, overstretched American position and then quickly connect with their westward-bound forces.

In two days, American military commanders successfully repositioned a sizeable presence to confront the enemy. What followed was the bloodiest warfare to ever stain American soil. Evacuated casualties overwhelmed hospital resources and legions of dead service members demoralized the military. Despite the dreadful cost of human suffering, the American military blunted the enemy's advance. Even so, the news media pounced and fecklessly blamed the President and inept military leaders for the sorrowful state.

"The war is lost," one of the most prominent television news reporters solemnly announced on an evening broadcast. Nadene remembered Lloyd's angry expostulation accusing the reporter of treason.

Yet, even more, damaging than the reporter's prediction of defeat was her appeal for an American surrender. "Too many lives have been sacrificed on both sides and now is the time for principled people to stop the slaughter. Our President and his closest advisors have led us to the brink of disaster. They must acknowledge the folly of their pretensions and for the good of all humanity cease hostilities. Our adversary promises a safe and orderly transition of power in exchange," she said.

The reporter continued, "There is little difference between our two governments. Any sober and thoughtful critique would reveal many positive features in the other side's government."

Studiously avoiding terms such as adversary or enemy she continued, "The other side indeed places a premium on group attributes while discounting individual choices. Their learned leaders, skilled in social and management theories, make decisions that benefit the entire country. Their policies promote social harmony and equality; one measure of which is the very low incidence of crime. On the other side, citizens are happy and prosperous. If not, there would be widespread rebellion."

At the time, Lloyd scoffed at the reporter's naivete. Dissent was not tolerated in the enemy's homeland. A vast security force relentlessly scrutinized their citizens' behavior, and the slightest evidence of discontent exposed the perpetrator to punishment. Untold numbers of individuals deemed more dangerous simply disappeared. Family members also suffered in tandem with the malcontents, a powerful social deterrent.

During her prolonged reverie, Nadene maintained the appearance of interest in Jonas' rambling discourse. Unfortunately, she did not take notes and Jonas pounced, "Are you bored?"

Her response floored the man, "Yes, I am."

Jonas' eyes open wide but before the startled man could respond Nadene continued, "My husband and I lived this history. My husband was in the military. Perhaps future iterations of this historical lecture could be delivered by those with firsthand knowledge."

Jonas was on the verge of banishing the woman from the room, but he hesitated. Many other attendees nodded their heads in approval and sensing complaints that might be lodged should he evict the woman, he swallowed his pride and declared, "An interesting proposal. I will bring the matter up for discussion at the next faculty meeting."

Nadene smiled politely and accepted the response with grace. Jonas looked uncomfortably at his watch but then jovially added, "We only have a few minutes left so we will continue with the third lecture tomorrow." He then peremptory turned his back on the class and left.

Leaving the classroom Nadene spied Mona and Curt. Rushing up to Mona she greeted the woman, "How are you doing, Mona?"

Mona hesitated and seemed inclined to ignore the woman, but Curt whirled around and angrily confronted Nadene, "You were incredibly rude to Jonas. The man is a respected faculty member with the Foresight Educational Committee. You embarrassed everyone." He then grabbed Mona by the arm and roughly steered his wife from the room but not before casting a menacing glare at Nadene. Curt's brusque behavior left Nadene feeling sorry for Mona.

Lloyd's senior postwar position with the Central Government Home Guard was in recognition of valuable services rendered during the war. His recent promotion to Colonel was more ceremonial than substantial but in the preceding months, a barely discernable trend emerged. His boss, General Roderick, was transferred to a new department in the Home Guard and charged with establishing a robust surveillance system that would track all participants completing the Foresight Educational Symposium for Parents.

Losing his closest confidante at the Home Guard was troubling but even more vexing was Roderick's replacement; a career civilian well known for her duplicity. Lloyd vividly recalled the scene from a few months earlier. He was attending a conference at the time and while absent-mindedly walking to a session was accosted by another attendee. "Are you Colonel Lane," the man whispered while standing inches from Lloyd.

"Yes," Lloyd said, puzzled by the man's secretive behavior.

"I heard that Louise Darden will be replacing Roderick as your boss," the man furtively said while scrutinizing passersby. "She was my boss for a year, and it was the worst job I ever had. She is incredibly intrusive, a micromanager, and exceedingly devious. To be forewarned is to be forearmed." After delivering the warning Lloyd's messenger melted into the crowd.

Lloyd's first meeting with Louise Darden seemed to confirm the messenger's warning. Darden was reading a newspaper when Lloyd met her. She was a trim woman, with short brown hair, a pinched face, and heavy, almost clownish, makeup. When Lloyd entered her office, she continued reading the newspaper for a few minutes; much to his annoyance. She finally set the paper aside and with a saccharine tone said, "So good to see you, Colonel Lane."

Lloyd doubted her confession but politely returned a similar greeting. Moments later Darden made a remarkable request, "I know you count General Roderick as one of your closest friends but going forward I suggest you sever that relationship. Roderick is not trusted by the upper echelons."

Stunned by the statement, Lloyd quickly recovered and replied, "I have known General Roderick for many years and will continue to value his counsel and friendship."

"As you will," Darden cryptically added.

The remainder of the first meeting was chilly. Darden concluded by asking Lloyd to represent her department at the next scheduled meeting of the Home Guard Counsel, the governing body that reported directly to the Secretary of the Home Guard. Lloyd agreed but was suspicious. Attendance at the high-profile assembly was the strutting ground for promotion and an absence presumably dimmed Darden's climb. Lloyd seriously doubted Darden's goodwill in ceding her appearance at the prestigious get-together.

Over dinner that night Lloyd shared his concerns with Nadene. She agreed that "something was afoot" and urged her husband to be on his guard. They both were upset at Roderick's transfer and the "upper echelons" loss of confidence in the man. "Perhaps," Nadene suggested, "we should telephone General Roderick."

"That's a good idea," Lloyd agreed.

Nadene made the call and after several rings, a female voice answered, "Roderick residence."

It was the familiar voice of Hannah, Roderick's wife who responded. Nadene greeted the woman and after exchanging pleasantries cautiously inquired, "How is your husband's new job going?"

Hannah decoded the concern and from long years of mutual friendship openly admitted, "David went to the grocery store but in his absence, I can frankly state that he is not pleased with the transfer nor the way it unfolded. He simply received a phone call telling him about the transfer. An administrative assistant later brought the orders and a detailed description of the assignment. In their essence, the documents directed David to develop an incredibly sophisticated system to track the activities of all parents who completed the Foresight Educational Symposium."

There was a pause during which Hannah had a fleeting apprehension about government spying but dismissing the concern as unfounded she continued, "David asked questions. He wanted to know why the government needed the information and how it would be used. Louise Darden downplayed the significance, stating it was solely designed to improve the Foresight Education Symposium for Parents."

Nadene gasped in astonishment, "Darden is Lloyd's new boss. He distrusts her."

"Your husband should be careful," Hannah cautioned, "the woman is ambitious and held in high esteem by the upper echelons of the civil service." Nadene thanked Hannah and promised to share the warning with her husband.

The third session of the Foresight Educational Symposium for Adults extended the history lessons. Jonas began with a dramatic flair, "The war was lost. Americans could hope for no better than a new stalemate with enemy combatants resolutely clinging to their new territorial gains."

Jonas then switched the lights off and presented a video montage of news commentators lamenting the battlefield reversals. The pundits, all of whom managed to avoid military service, offered endless, depressing conclusions. They criticized the Selective Service System's creaky administration and hypocritically blamed the widespread, fraudulent medical waivers.

Nadene watched and thought, "The pundits always found problems, but they never offered any solutions."

The video compilation consumed nearly the entire two hours. With just minutes left, Jonas announced that the Foresight Educational Committee decided to combine sessions four and five. Noticing the quizzical looks from some in the classroom he added, "The Committee wants to streamline this symposium. With that in mind, I will merge elements of sessions four and five. From what I understand, future iterations will either condense or eliminate the background history lessons."

Nadene quietly rejoiced. She would have been even happier if the sessions were even further consolidated. As she left the classroom she wondered to what extent, if any, Jonas would mention the contributions of her husband and General Roderick.

That night Nadene shared Jonas' comments with Lloyd and then noted, "If anyone could discuss how America's fortunes changed it would be you and General Roderick."

Nadene snuggled next to Lloyd and with a wistful, nostalgic mood asked her husband to revisit the momentous changes ushered in through his efforts. At first, he demurred, not eager to conjure up memories but his wife's gentle insistence overcame Lloyd's resistance.

"Ok," he reluctantly agreed, "but I will be interested to hear how my version compares to what Jonas will offer."

"It's a deal," his wife quietly said.

"Where should I begin," the man rhetorically wondered.

"How about the meetings with the Surgeon General?" Nadene suggested.

"That's probably a reasonable place, to begin with," he agreed.

It was 6 pm when he began his monologue. He repositioned himself on the sofa, momentarily disengaging from Nadene. Both were now at least physically comfortable although Lloyd's anxiety spiked as he began his trip through history.

"I remember a profound sense of unease, almost a fear, after the first meeting with the Surgeon General," he began. "It was the first occasion where I presented the preliminary results of my research, coined the term Triad-Amine, and firmly established the nexus between that substance and the behavioral triad. For the most part the attendees, senior military officers, and appointed civilian leaders seemed disinterested. A small group of civilians sporting sunglasses and carrying concealed weapons were seated on the periphery of the conference room."

"Why were you uneasy at the meeting?" Nadene inquired.

"At the time I did not know why. It was just a feeling. Almost like a subliminal message. There was no overt hostility. The closest might have been what I imagined was an impenetrable glower from the sunglass crowd. There were also no questions after my presentation," he concluded.

Nadene stood up and stretched, interrupting his recollections. "Would you like a soft drink?" she asked.

"Sure," he responded while standing, "a cream soda would be great."

Nadene retrieved two soft drinks from the refrigerator and poured the contents into glasses. She preferred ice with her drinks, but Lloyd did not, complaining that the ice diluted the beverages. Once both were again seated Lloyd continued.

"After the meeting with the Surgeon General, I huddled with Roderick. Curiously, he had the same foreboding impression about the sunglass sporting group but like me, he could not pinpoint the source. The mystery deepened when the Surgeon

General called him back to the conference room. We were preparing to leave when the summons arrived. I was not invited but instead waited impatiently outside. About twenty minutes later an ashen-faced Roderick emerged and taking me by the arm we hurried outside," Lloyd said, with glum residues accompanying the memory.

"Once outside, I asked Roderick what happened. In a whisper, he suggested I come by his house that evening. You remember that when I came home that night, I told you about the meeting and Roderick's mysterious request," he recalled.

"Yes, I remember being worried," she admitted.

"We both went to Roderick's house later that night. Hannah was expecting us and as the perfect host, she had some tasty nibbles and mineral water waiting for us. Roderick was not in the room when we arrived but entered about ten minutes later. Fortunately, you and Hannah filled the void with some aimless banter but we all anxiously awaited Roderick. He finally joined us. I remember he was dressed very casually and had regained his poise. After taking a seat and pouring a glass of the cold mineral water he pointedly looked at me," Lloyd recited.

"Let's dive right in," Roderick suggested, "and talk about that unplanned meeting with the Surgeon General. When I walked in, the conference room was empty except for the Surgeon General and the four armed civilians. I expressed my desire to have you in the room, but the Surgeon General denied that request while adding that I could brief you on details."

"I'm glad you were allowed to share the meeting with me," I simply said.

"I would have anyway," Roderick admitted, "but let me proceed. It seems that your presentation was simulcast to the president and his closest advisors. I knew nothing of this but told the Surgeon General that you should have been advised. In any event, the President discerned actionable elements in your briefing and wanted more information. The President wholeheartedly agreed with your assessment that additional research was unnecessary, and the focus should squarely be on supporting the war."

Nadene interrupted the speaker, "I think it was disingenuous to have the President and his inner circle secretly listening to Lloyd's presentation."

"Well, I could hardly object had I known," Roderick conceded. "But what followed next was startling. The Surgeon General revealed that the President wanted a private briefing and an opportunity to delve deeper. He wanted a small group consisting of the Surgeon General, Lloyd, and me. Aside from a security detail, no one else would attend."

Hannah rose from her chair and began filling everyone's glasses with the sparkling mineral water. While doing so she asked if anyone was hungry. Her question stimulated a self-assessment among the group and resulted in a collective affirmation. In response, Hannah went to the kitchen and soon thereafter the delightful aroma of popcorn filled the house. She returned with laden bowls of buttered popcorn; an odd but welcome treat given the serious discussions.

Roderick took a handful of the treat and while munching the popcorn continued, "I asked the Surgeon General how we should conduct the briefing. Based on the feedback he received it was to be an informal meeting." I was not sure what an informal meeting with the President meant but as you know we decided to be fully prepared with a detailed presentation.

Roderick and I had the required security clearance for the meeting, but members of the President's secret service staff still vetted us. In the days preceding the meeting, I gathered a briefcase full of data. Among the trove were findings from the ongoing command survey, military service member evaluations conducted by the Triad Teams, and up-to-date biochemical studies on Triad-Amine.

Roderick guessed that the Surgeon General organized the trip to Camp David. On the specified briefing day, we all three arrived at 5 am and waited in the Surgeon General's office for the military escort that would transport the small group. At 5:30 am an impeccably attired military driver announced her arrival and led the three officers to the waiting vehicle.

Roderick admitted that he had expected some sort of military conveyance, but the driver pointed to a nondescript van. Once everyone was seated, Roderick recalled a brief conversation from the driver who said, "Barring any road closures or other problems we should arrive at Camp David in about two hours." She then pointed to the backseat area, "You may notice the large storage container behind the back seats. I thought our early morning ride would be more pleasant with breakfast. Inside you will find hot coffee and breakfast sandwiches. Enjoy!"

I remembered this thoughtful touch and when Roderick paused, I added, "I remember hoping it was a positive harbinger of the forthcoming day's activities."

Roderick nodded and continued recounting the meeting. "The trip was uneventful, even boring. As I recall, there was very little talking and I was preoccupied with reviewing the data and at times passed documents to the Surgeon General and me. As we approached Camp David there was a noticeable military presence requiring presentation of our credentials at several points as we wound our way through the cordon."

"I remember being impressed with the rustic charm of the mountain retreat. It seemed so peaceful and informal, an anomaly in a world gone amok. Reality intruded when we approached the site for our meeting with the President. While I imagined a spacious, modern structure, we parked near a humble building reminiscent of a hunting lodge. Before exiting our vehicle two marines entered and performed a thorough security check. We were then escorted into the building's conference room. One of the marines politely directed us to three small name placards on the conference room's table indicating our seating assignments. We were advised that the President and his advisors would join us soon. While we waited, another individual placed bottles of water, coffee cups, and saucers around the table." Lloyd added.

"You must have been nervous," Nadene interjected.

"I think we were all nervous, mostly from not knowing what the President wanted," Lloyd said.

"As I think back on that meeting, my apprehension grew with each passing minute," Lloyd responded. "I think we waited thirty minutes for the President. When he finally showed up, we left our chairs and stood at attention. He smiled and gestured for us to take our seats. There were four others with him, including his Chief of Staff, the Secretary of Defense, Chairman of the Joint

Chiefs Staff, and the Director of National Intelligence. In retrospect, I often wondered at those not included in the meeting."

"After roundtable introductions, the President asked the Surgeon General to lead the briefing," Lloyd continued, "but the man seemed befuddled. He was a politician and took little interest in the complex details of the briefing. I remember his confused, worried countenance when the President asked for his leadership and his stuttering reply that I would lead the presentation. Pretty much for the remainder of the briefing, The Surgeon General sat hunched over the table, blankly staring at the handouts, and not uttering a word."

"I was surprised by the Surgeon General's behavior, but I had no time to dwell on it. I remember looking at General Roderick for guidance. He nodded for me to proceed. I handed the President and his advisors copies of the briefing and began my presentation." Lloyd recalled.

"I began with the chance observations I made connecting a mysterious substance with a triad of service member behaviors. Those replicable behaviors consisted of service members who were detached and unemotional, had significant memory deficits, and had remarkable resistance to pain. I hastened to clarify the service members experienced pain but they were indifferent to its presence."

"The President interrupted me after about five minutes," Lloyd recalled, "and asked me to focus on the commander survey results. I had everyone turn to Tab A in the briefing packet. Data was still coming in, particularly from the eastern combat zones where the treacherous conditions slowed responses from the field as well as delivering the data. What I referenced in the briefing were the most recent results. At that time, my staff and I had over 10,000 results from commanders in various sized military units. We figured that the results represented roughly 20 percent of the military, insofar as we could determine based on estimates of service members deployed in these areas."

"Why did the President focus on the command survey," asked Nadene, who until this time had been listening quietly.

"At the time neither Roderick nor I knew why," Lloyd replied to his wife.

Lloyd resumed after the exchange with Nadene, "The President seemed most attentive when Roderick discussed the commanders' global opinions about the military service members' duty performance. The earliest surveys showed a trend suggesting that service members afflicted with triad symptoms and testing positive for the mysterious substance were perceived by their military leaders as extraordinarily proficient. That finding was replicated in the much larger data set I presented at the President's briefing."

Lloyd paused and swallowed a large mouthful of the once cold mineral water and continued, "After I presented the survey results in mind-numbing detail the President rose from his chair and thanked the Surgeon General for arranging the meeting. He then directed the three of us to leave the area while the matter was discussed."

"We waited in an adjoining room for more than an hour. The Surgeon General's behavior constrained us from speculating on the meeting we were excluded from. He seemed oddly disinterested in the proceedings and when Roderick asked him a question the man replied mechanically, in a voice devoid of any inflection. Perhaps sensing our concern, he offered fatigue as an explanation," Lloyd said.

It was getting quite late, near midnight, as a distant clock chimed eleven times. Nadene was sagging in her chair and she was evidencing symptoms of the hour with drooping eyelids. Lloyd noticed her lethargy and feeling compelled by her draining energy and interest decided to quickly summarize his reminiscences.

"Eventually we were invited back to the conference room," Lloyd hastily remarked, "and the President thanked us for waiting. He seemed to ignore the Surgeon General, casting a disparaging look in his direction, before turning to me. He wanted to know the side effects of Triad-Amine, a question that surprised me. I told the President that it was too early to know but based on the limited data available at the time there seemed to be no serious adverse events. He seemed noticeably relieved as if a weight were lifted from his shoulders."

Nadene perked up as Lloyd neared the finale, "I remember timorously asking the President why he needed this information."

With cold eyes and a stern expression, the President had replied, "We are losing the war. Too many soldiers are deserting and many eligibles for induction are fleeing. We have doctors issuing fraudulent medical exemptions and news media undermining the war. I listened carefully to your presentation and after discussing it with my closest advisors I am convinced that Triad-Amine can turn the tide and help us win the war. It seems that Triad-Amine extinguishes the fear response in humans and all the related maladaptive behaviors, from a military perspective, mind you, that enfeebles service members. I can see Triad-Amine reducing fear-induced desertions, misuse of mind-numbing alcohol and other illicit drugs, and military malfeasance. I believe that the Triad-Amine-induced dissociative state disconnecting the user from bodily sensations and its amnestic effect can eliminate the dread of combat death. Service members devoid of emotionality would be perfect warriors."

Lloyd concluded his narration. The rest of the story was well-known and given the late hour repetition was unnecessary. As might be imagined, the Camp David meeting was never publicized, and the President ordered the participants not to disclose the details. A few days after meeting with the President the Surgeon General contacted Roderick, who in turn relayed a message to Lloyd directing the man to cease all future research with Triad-Amine. The project would continue, Lloyd was assured, by a special agency the President would create. Lloyd was miffed by the Presidential rebuff and adding insult to injury, neither Roderick nor Lloyd received any further feedback as events unfolded in the coming weeks.

Nadene fell asleep after her husband's narration. Nadene awakened just as Lloyd finished, and bleary-eyed apologized for her somnolence. She stumbled off the couch and unsteadily made her way to their bedroom without a word fell asleep on the bed.

Lloyd had a fitful night's sleep in contrast to his wife's restful slumber. Towards the morning a vivid dream kept the man asleep. As the theater of his mind played the scenes, he was in a hospital room with a partially drawn curtain obscuring his view. He could just barely discern what appeared to be a bassinet. A woman with a distorted, bloated face emerged from the room and with an evil grin said, "Be seeing you." And then like a puff of smoke she faded away. Lloyd walked towards the room and drawing the curtain awakened in a cold sweat. For a moment the man hovered between his fantasy and reality, uncertain of the boundary. Nadene's quiet breathing restored Lloyd's lucidity.

Lloyd fumbled for the clock. It was a few minutes past 6 am. With a gasp he jumped out of bed, displeased with sleeping an hour past the usual time. Nadene awakened as he left the bed, and noting the time, quickly set about making breakfast. Her hurried preparations placed a cold bowl of cereal and a hot cup of coffee on the dining room table. She called for Lloyd who hurriedly appeared and gulped the meal down. After kissing Nadene, he dashed out the door.

Nadene could not help but notice that her husband seemed troubled, not by his tardiness, but by something else. Perhaps, she thought, "I can ask him about this tonight."

Like her husband, Nadene compressed her morning routine. She dared not be late for the Foresight Educational Symposium for Adults and incur the wrath of Jonas. She was also curious how Jonas would consolidate sessions four and five.

All the front seats were occupied when Nadene arrived. Jonas seemed to smirk as she surveyed the area, and with few options, the woman reluctantly walked to the back of the room. With everyone in attendance Jonas' shrill voice pierced the air.

He began by reminding the group, "There are two sessions after today's abridgment of sessions four and five. Sessions six and seven are the most important. If anyone misses these two sessions without a bona fide excuse I am required to report the absence to the Home Guard. At a minimum, you would have to repeat the entire series. You could also be subject to fines. In preparation for session six, I would encourage everyone to carefully review their handouts. Session seven is by far the most important. Everyone will be separated into small groups for discussions. I will assign the individuals to each group and assign the topic. I hope that everyone will submit their decisions at the end of the small group discussions. If not, you have one week to consider the options."

With that warning, Jonas turned to the session's topic. It was a boring rendition, perhaps novel for many in the room but Nadene knew the complete story. Not once did Jonas mention her husband's contributions nor General Roderick. He credited the entire research discovery of the behavioral triad and the chemical substance to the Surgeon General. The most galling statement even attributed the name Triad-Amine to the man's genius. Of course, Nadene rationalized, Jonas did not know about the President's meeting with her husband.

After a ponderous factually inaccurate dissertation on Triad-Amine Jonas pivoted to its exploitation. Again, the President's role was publicly suspected but never proven. In any event, military commanders started clamoring for Triad-Amine's widespread use. It was never known what propelled the tidal wave of interest, but the force was sufficient to drown dissenting voices, sweeping all resistance aside.

The Department of Defense launched a Triad-Amine Research, Advancement, and Distribution section referred to in policy papers and public disclosures by its acronym TRAD. With exceptional speed, TRAD's tentacles seized large swaths of manufacturing, logistical, and investigational resources.

Jonas emphasized the government's salutary coordination that supported the success of TRAD, "Bringing Triad-Amine from concept to creation and then implementation was a marvelous demonstration of your government's prowess."

It seemed like the man's head swelled with pride, or so Nadene imagined. She thought the dark side of Triad-Amine would not be part of Jonas' presentation. But that was to be expected, she sighed since Foresight owed its existence to Triad-Amine.

Jonas did address two of the controversies, "TRAD leadership debated how to educate service members in terms of whether Triad-Amine use would be voluntary or mandatory. Military commanders wanted compulsory use by all combat deployed service members. Its use by personnel in support positions could be voluntary. That argument prevailed."

The other matter debated by TRAD leadership focused on refusals. What should be done if combat deployed service members adamantly rejected Triad-Amine? TRAD leadership took a hard line and with hastily passed legislation made refusal a criminal offense. A service member's avowed refusal to take Triad-Amine was a strict liability offense, eliminating any excuses and holding the naysayer fully culpable for their refusal.

Punishment was harsh; imprisonment without parole for the duration of the war or ten years, whichever was greater, and a dishonorable discharge and forfeiture of any future federal employment.

Triad-Amine was still experimental when TRAD delivered the drug to military units. There were many unknowns at the time such as Triad-Amine's adverse events and its length of action. Based on preliminary research, TRAD informed service members that the behavioral effects from one dose of the drug lasted several weeks. TRAD reassured skeptical service members that the drug was safe and vowed that ongoing studies would identify any problems.

TRAD quickly delivered Triad-Amine to frontline combat units. Each service member received a glass vial containing a single dose of Triad-Amine and while in formation, and under the watchful gaze of military leaders, they ingested the drug.

Commanders uniformly obtained service members' approval to take Triad-Amine while in formation, breaching long-established privacy policies. Military authorities abandoned medical confidentiality for two reasons, one explicit and the other implicit. The explicit rationale was based on the urgent need to defeat the enemy, with slogans such as "swallow your pride and help turn the tide" resonating across the battlefields. Implicitly, military leaders leveraged the power of group peer pressure.

Rumors of Triad-Amine refusals surfaced but the extent of dissents was never publicly revealed. Military leaders were instructed to remove service members who dared protest while they were in a military formation and then conduct an interrogation. According to Jonas, only a tiny number "cold-heartedly" abandoned America.

Triad-Amine reached its peak blood level within twelve hours of consumption. The first signs of the drug's effect were the characteristic features; the vacant stare, negligible blinking, a dull, empty, expressionless face, and a less tangible emotional detachment.

Any pre-existing anxiety disappeared as did any concern for combat injury or death. Military leaders tested the premise repeatedly and when satisfied that Triad-Amine had vanquished fear, reported the results to higher echelons. To be clear,

Triad-Amine did not ablate the fear response but, like alcohol intoxication, users simply did not care.

The Department of Defense closely monitored Triad-Amine's rollout. Their initial objective was achieving a fifty percent saturation among combat troops, at which point the Triad-Amine laced service members would begin a massive counterattack. The remaining service members would constitute the reserve element once they too were "Triad-Amized", a colloquial term adopted throughout the ranks.

Triad-Amine's swift and secret disbursement was a TRAD success story. The enemy's intelligence collected bits and pieces about the drug but never enough to solve the puzzle. They could only guess that an attack was imminent.

Jonas rose to the session's apogee, "The Department of Defense and TRAD achieved a remarkable coup. The enemy was completely surprised by the ferocious assault mounted by our forces in the Mississippi combat theater. We launched a ground and air attack that shook the earth. Reverberations from the massive explosions were felt across the nation."

With an uncharacteristic zeal, Jonas continued, "Within three days we routed the enemy. We captured thousands and thousands of prisoners of war. When debriefed, the prisoners-of-war, without exception, were astonished by the America service members' newfound fighting vigor."

News commentators celebrated the astonishing battlefield reversal. The enemy's military forces were in tatters and the unrelenting American campaign threatened their complete annihilation. It was the enemy's unconditional surrender that finally ended the bloodshed.

Jonas ended his presentation with a triumphant cheer, "Triad-Amine won the war!"

His concluding remarks echoed a sentiment broadcast across the nation. It was, Nadene thought, a serious miscalculation awarding heroic status to the drug. Doing so, trivialized the sacrifices of all service members, particularly those in the pre-Triad-Amine era. It also set the stage for the future exploitation of the drug, opening a dark and sinister chapter in American politics that led to the creation of Foresight.

On the way home, Nadene could not stop worrying. What was once an abstract concept was morphing into reality. Ever since receiving the Central Government's letter directing their attendance at the Foresight Education Symposium, she had consciously repressed the matter and through daily distractions managed to keep her fear at bay. With the sixth Foresight session looming her defenses crumbled.

Nadene fumbled for the door key, dropping her purse as she did so. She scrambled to retrieve the contents scattered across the floor and with a sigh opened the door. It was dark inside. She remembered closing the curtains earlier to keep the scorching sun out. The silence was everywhere which deafened the woman.

Proceeding mechanically, she opened the curtains which brightened the room but not her mood. A boisterous blow at the door echoed on the walls, breaking Nadene's brooding. She listlessly ambled to address the disturbance and opening the door was greeted by the babysitter along with an exuberant cry as Clio and Alexander recognized their mother.

A wave of worry washed over Nadene as she returned the greetings with exclamations of joy and cooing compassion. For a moment, she reveled in the distraction, but Foresight inevitably intruded. Reflexively, she clutched her children in a tender embrace but there was no escaping the government's claws. Decisions were required.

Lloyd came home early, noticed Nadene's pensive mood, but he needed no explanation. While his wife entertained Clio and Alexander, he changed clothes and then went to the kitchen, determined to relieve his wife of the tedious chore of making dinner. Rummaging through the pantry he settled on spaghetti, a reliable staple for a quick meal.

While her husband was preparing dinner, she made similar arrangements for Clio and Alexander. With the children's portions nearby and the adult's plates full of steaming pasta, the family satisfied their appetite. Nadene was especially attentive to the children.

After dinner, Nadene broached the untouchable subject, "The Foresight session tomorrow will preview the Central Government's argument advocating that all children receive Triad-Amine XR."

"I know," Lloyd quietly agreed.

"It's depressing when I look at the other people in our class. They scribble notes, are super attentive, and when I am leaving after Jonas' lecture, I see most everyone lingering in the room, trying to ask questions but the man never answers," she concluded.

She paused and looking at Clio and Alexander noted their wilting behavior, a sure sign they would soon be fast asleep. Nadene carried both to their cribs and firmly tucked them in for the night. It was only then that she felt the oppressive burden of her weariness.

She returned to the family room sofa and idly thumbed through a book but while her eyes scanned the pages her mind was preoccupied with Foresight. Lloyd sat next to his wife and noticing her abstraction suggested they watch a television show. She numbly agreed.

Lloyd reached for the remote control and the screen flickered to life. A solemn voice announced, "Citizens with last names ending with the letter M will be receiving their invitations from the Central Government's Foresight Committee this week." It seemed a cruel reminder of their plight and before the government announcer finished, Nadene grabbed the remote control and silenced the intruder.

Nadene gave faint thought to skipping the sixth session, but she rightly conceded that would only postpone the inevitable. Donning a black dress as a means of symbolic protest she snagged a front-row seat, much to the visible consternation of Jonas. With her arms crossed and a fixed stare, her body posture shouted defiance, but Jonas was not cowed.

"Welcome to the sixth session," Jonas ebulliently proclaimed. "Today we will review the many benefits of Triad-Amine so you can make the properly informed decision for your children tomorrow. The Central Government would prefer you decide after the last session but generously permits an additional week. Parents choosing the Central Government's preferred option of administering Triad-Amine XR to your children must do so before their second birthday."

Nadene shifted uncomfortably in her chair and self-consciously interpreted his gaze in her direction as a sneering rebuke. She stiffened and regained her composure barely listening to the man.

"Triad-Amine XR is the next generation of the drug. The XR or extended releases preparation ensures a lifelong benefit," Jonas explained and then continued with a rhetorical question "What are the benefits of Triad-Amine?"

"None," Nadene thought.

"Triad-Amine won a war," Jonas repeated and then answered his question, "and its unique attributes are responsible. Just imagine the gift you give your child. A life not dominated by fear. No more painful memories. Harnessed emotional vicissitudes. Reason over feelings."

Jonas paused for effect, letting his consequential words weigh on the audience. "The Central Government's investigations sponsored by TRAD prove without a doubt that individuals opting for Triad-Amine XR experience virtually no anxiety or depression. The result has been a dramatic drop in substance use disorders and mental illness. Suicide is unknown among those taking Triad-Amine."

The man laughed by adding, "Of course, the drug companies are unhappy with the precipitous decline in prescriptions for mood-altering medications."

Nadene suffered through the remainder of the presentation. A compilation of videos showcased the wonders of Triad-Amine. Among the most disturbing were parent interviews, conspicuously cuddling their infants, expressing gratitude for the Central Government's promise of a blissful, carefree life for their offspring.

Jonas turned the projector off after the videos and exhorted the group, "Review your notes and handouts. Tomorrow I will assign you to small groups. Anticipate four to six people in a group."

Uncharacteristically, Jonas wished everyone a good night and pleasantly smiled. To Nadene, it was like an indifferent restaurant server suddenly becoming amiable as they presented the check; in a thinly disguised effort to ensure a handsome tip.

"But why did Jonas affect geniality," she wondered, but in her eagerness to leave the room she gave no further thought to the riddle. On the way home, she purchased two sandwiches and a large bag of chips, looking forward to a quiet evening with her family.

Lloyd again left work early. Nadene and the children were awaiting his arrival and after completing dinner Lloyd asked Nadene, “Are you ready for the last session tomorrow?”

“Yes,” she said, “and I do expect subtle pressure to submit our decision when the session concludes.”

As it turned out, the pressure was not subtle, and the first inkling of trouble occurred shortly after Nadene arrived for the seventh and final session of the Foresight Education Program for Adults. Triumphantly, strutting like a victorious field commander, Jonas announced, “The Central Government thanks you for your attention and attendance and now eagerly awaits your family’s decision. I’m sure you recognize the value of Triad-Amine XR for your children’s future role in society.”

From the audience smiling faces beamed at the man seemingly confirming Jonas’ prediction of the parent’s choices but even so, the Central Government-mandated session number seven and so Jonas proceeded, “I will now assign everyone to a small group.”

Taking a prepared list from his pocket Jonas methodically populated each small group with four members, except for one. Staring at Nadene the man drawled, “We have an odd number of participants for this round of Foresight Education Program for Adults. The last small group will consist of Nadene Lane, Mona Jayne, and Curt Jayne.”

Nadene was surprised at the selection but then instantly recalled that Jonas witnessed their previous contretemps. She guessed that Jonas hoped for more fireworks by throwing them together.

Shuffling chairs noisily filled the room as group members formed their little circles. Curt and Mona did not move. Nadene dragged her chair over and set next to Mona. With everyone in position, Jonas provided directions, “Session seven allocate 90 minutes for small group discussions. During this time, be open and honest. Share your thoughts about Triad-Amine XR for your children. Perhaps you still have reservations. Voice them. Get feedback from your group. Since many of you have already decided to give your children Triad-Amine XR you can complete the authorization, give it to me, and then you are finished and can leave."

Following Jonas' remarks, Nadene rested her gaze on Mona and Curt. Mona looked small and pale, and her hands trembled slightly as she stared at the floor. Curt sat erect with his head thrown high and his legs furiously bouncing up and down while scornfully studying Mona. Dripping with contempt, he demanded, "Mona, we need to wrap this up and get out of here. As you well know, I firmly believe we need to administer Triad-Amine XR. It is the right thing to do."

Surprisingly, Mona's eyes blazed with defiant anger, and looking straight at the man, "Right for who?"

Embarrassed by his wife's response, Curt angrily retorted, "Right for our children! Are you a doubter? Do you think it is in the best interests of a child's social development to question the Central Government?"

The cowed woman struggled for a comeback, "I know you have the interests of our children in mind but I'm not sure that Triad-Amine is the right way."

Curt, visibly vexed by his wife's intransigence, pivoted towards Nadene and shouted, "You're the one responsible for this. You've filled her head with nonsense – and your husband a member of the Home Guard!"

Nadene leaned forward, straightened her dress, and mustering her composure looked straight at the man, "Mona can think for herself. I thought the purpose of today's session was to openly discuss Triad-Amine."

Her calm demeanor and rational appeal momentarily disarmed Curt but the eyes and ears of the other attendees forced the man to remain quiet. His ruby red cheeks and distorted mouth exposed the rage bubbling below the surface.

"There's nothing more to talk about," Curt declared, "since we have decided to proceed with Triad-Amine."

Mona wilted but felt powerless to disagree. Curt brusquely signed the Parents Triad-Amine Authorization and shoved the form in front of his wife who meekly attached her signature. He then summarily stood up, motioned for Mona to follow, and without a word, they left the room.

Nadene was relieved at Curt's departure, but she felt sorry for Mona. Jonas smirked at her seeming discomfiture, but she needled the man for the last time by rising and leaving with nary a word.

Friday night was always special. Lloyd made a large bowl of buttered popcorn and Nadene added chips and dip, ramen noodles, and an assortment of cookies. They would then settle in for two movies. This evening was no different. They both consciously avoided discussing Foresight, saving that for the weekend.

The next morning Nadene prepared a light breakfast and after attending to Alexander and Clio broached the Foresight dilemma with Lloyd. She briefly mentioned Curt's disagreeable outburst and Mona's timidity.

"We have a whole week to decide," she said.

"We decided a long time ago," Lloyd affirmed, "not to have Clio and Alexander subjected to Triad-Amine XR. Of course, our decision will have consequences. As a senior officer with the Home Guard, I can expect more than just murmurs asserting my disloyalty."

"According to the official position of the Central Government there cannot be any repercussions, retaliation, or other subterfuge based on parent's choices," Nadene determinedly pointed out.

"True in words but not in actions," Lloyd cynically countered.

A boisterous cry from Clio changed the subject. Nadene hastened to her crib and spotting the distress, changed the diaper. The contented child soon fell asleep. For a few minutes, Nadene lingered, thinking about both children, and imagining what their future life would be like. Never for a moment did she doubt her decision, but she inwardly worried about the Central Government's professed deference to free choice.

Lloyd joined her and placing his arms around his wife commented, "You are a wonderful, courageous woman!"

Monday came too soon. Lloyd took the day off, joining Nadene, and together they drove the short distance to the local Foresight precinct. When they arrived they confidently made their way to an open window and handed a signed “Parents Non-Authorization Form” to a surprised clerk.